Yu Hua

TO LIVE

Yu Hua was born in 1960 in Zhejiang, China. He finished high school during the Cultural Revolution and worked as a dentist for five years before beginning to write in 1983. He has published three novels, six collections of stories, and three collections of essays. His work has been translated into French, German, Italian, Dutch, Spanish, Japanese and Korean. In 2002 Yu Hua became the first Chinese writer to win the prestigious James Joyce Foundation Award. *To Live* was awarded Italy's Premio Grinzane Cavour in 1998 and was named one of the last decade's ten most influential books in China. Yu Hua lives in Beijing.

Michael Berry is an assistant professor of contemporary Chinese cultural studies at the University of California, Santa Barbara. He is the author of a forthcoming collection of interviews with Chinese filmmakers and the translator of Ye Zhaoyan's *Nanjing 1937: A Love Story* and Chang Ta-chun's *Wild Kids: Two Novels About Growing Up*.

TO

LIVE

TO
LIVE

A   N O V E L

YU
HUA

Translated and with an Afterword by

MICHAEL BERRY

ANCHOR BOOKS

A Division of Random House, Inc.

New York

AN ANCHOR BOOKS ORIGINAL, AUGUST 2003

Library of Congress Cataloging-in-Publication Data
Yu, Hua, 1960–
[Huo zhe. English]
To live : a novel / Yu Hua ; translated from the Chinese by Michael Berry.
p.   cm.
ISBN 1-4000-3186-9 (pbk.)
I. Berry, Michael.   II. Title.
PL2928.H78H8613   2003
895.1'352—dc21
2003043688

Book design by Jo Anne Metsch

www.anchorbooks.com

Printed in the United States of America
10   9   8   7   6   5   4   3

TO
LIVE

When I was ten years younger than I am now, I had the carefree job of going to the countryside to collect popular folk songs. That year, for the entire summer, I was like a sparrow soaring recklessly. I would wander amid the village houses and the open country, which was full of cicadas and flooded with sunlight. I had a special affection for that bitter tea that farmers brew. There would always be a bucket of just that kind of tea under a tree by the ridge between the fields, and without a second thought I would ladle out enough to fill my tea-stained bowl. Once I'd filled it to the brim, I'd start bullshitting with some of the male workers. The girls would whisper among themselves and then stifle their chuckles as I'd swagger off. I once spent a whole afternoon talking with an old man who kept a melon patch. I ate more melons that day than I ever had in my life. When I stood up to leave, I suddenly realized that I had as much difficulty walking as a pregnant woman. Later that day, I sat on the porch with a woman who had already become a grandmother. As she weaved a pair of straw sandals she sang "Ten Month Pregnancy" for me. What I loved most was sitting before the peasants' houses just as dusk fell. As the sun's rays came down through the delicate branches, I would watch the peasants pour well water onto the ground, cooling the hot dust and sand. Holding the fan they passed over to me, I would try the pickled vegetables, which always tasted like salt. I would watch the girls and talk with the men.

I wore a wide-brimmed straw hat on my head and a pair of slippers on my feet. A towel hung down from my belt behind me; I made it look like a tail patting me on the butt as I walked. All day my mouth was wide open as I yawned, strolling aimlessly through the narrow trails that wove between the fields. My slippers made a funny sound, "ba da ba da," as the dust along the trail went flying upward. It was as if a truck had sped by.

I'd wander all over the place, not even remembering which villages I'd been to and which I hadn't. As I'd approach the next country village, I'd often hear the children yelling, "Hey, that guy who always yawns is back!"

And so the people in the village knew that the man who told dirty stories and sang sad songs had come back again. Actually I learned all those dirty stories and sad songs from them. I knew everything that interested them, and naturally this was also what interested me. I once came across an old man with a bloody nose and a swollen face sitting atop the ridge crying. His sadness filled his entire body. When he saw me coming he looked up, and his weeping grew louder. I asked him who beat him like this, and, scraping the mud off his pants with his fingernail, he told me with anger that it was that ungrateful son of his. When I asked him why, he kept beating around the bush but wouldn't explain. I immediately surmised that the old man must have been putting the moves on his daughter-in-law. Then on another occasion, I was hurrying on my way at night when the glow of my flashlight fell upon a pair of naked bodies beside a pond. One was pressing against the other. When I shined my light on them, except for a hand scratching a thigh, the two bodies lay absolutely still. I quickly turned off my light and got out of there. One afternoon during the height of the farming season, hoping to get a drink of water, I walked into a house whose doors had been left wide open. A man wearing shorts and looking quite flustered stopped me and led me outside to a well. He eagerly hoisted up a bucket of water for me from the well, then like a rat scurried back into his house. These were all common occurrences, almost as common as the folk songs I heard. When I gazed at the green earth that surrounded me, I came closer to understanding why the crops here grew so vigorously.

That summer I almost fell in love. I met an enchanting young girl, and even today her dark complexion glitters and radiates before my eyes. When I saw her, her pants were cuffed up high as she sat on the grass beside the river. Watching over a flock of large, plump ducks, she held a bamboo pole to prod them and keep them together. This timid sixteen- or seventeen-year-old girl spent a scorching afternoon with me. Every time she smiled she would lower her head in embarrassment. I noticed how she secretly rolled her pants back down and hid her bare feet in the thick grass. That afternoon I spoke endlessly and irresponsibly of my plans to take her away to see the world. She was both frightened and pleased. At the time I was in quite high spirits and very sincere about what I said. During that short time with her, I was overcome by a bliss that extended throughout my body and soul—never once did I stop to think about tomorrow. Only later when her three brothers, each of whom was built like an ox, approached, did I start to get scared. I felt the best thing for me to do would be to get out of there—the faster the better—that is, unless I wanted to end up really marrying their little sister.

It was just as summer arrived that I met an old man named Fugui. That afternoon I made my way over to a tall tree with lush foliage to get some relief from the blistering sun. The cotton in the fields had already been harvested. A few women wearing scarves were collecting the cotton stalks—every now and then their asses would wiggle as they removed the mud from the stalk roots. I took off my straw hat and, reaching for the towel behind me, wiped the sweat from my face. Next to me there was a pond, which had turned golden under the radiance of the sun. As I sat against the tree trunk facing the pond, I suddenly felt like I needed a nap. I lay down on the grass under the shade of the tree. Covering my face with my straw hat and using my backpack as a pillow, I closed my eyes.

This "me" of ten years before lay down amid the leaves and long grass and slept for two whole hours. During this time a few ants crawled up my leg, but even in my deep sleep my finger accurately flicked them off. I felt as if I had come to a shore, and the echoing shouts of an old man poling a bamboo raft seemed to reach my ears from far away. I awakened from my dream, and the voice calling out was actually crisp and clear. After I turned around I saw an old man in one of the nearby fields patiently trying to coax an old ox into working.

The ox, probably already exhausted from plowing the field, stubbornly lowered his head and refused to move. The bare-chested old man leaned on the plough behind his beast, seemingly frustrated by the ox's attitude. I heard his bright voice say to the ox, "Oxen plough the fields, dogs watch over the house, monks beg for alms, chickens call at the break of day and women do the weaving. Have you ever heard of an ox that didn't plough the land? This is a truth that has been with us since ancient times. Come on, let's go."

The weary old ox, after hearing the old man's lesson, raised his head as if admitting his mistake. Pulling the plow, he began to move forward.

I noticed the old man's back was just as black as the ox's. Even though the pair had already entered the twilight of their lives, they still managed to noisily plough the rugged land, the earth breaking up like a wave crashing on the shore. Afterward I heard the old man's hoarse yet moving voice sing an old folk song. First he sang a long introductory melody, then came two lines of verse:

> The emperor beckons me; he wants me to marry his daughter.
> The road to the capital is long and distant; I don't want her.

Because the journey is long, he is unwilling to be the emperor's son-in-law. The way the old man seemed to relish his own clever-ness made me burst out laughing. The ox seemed to be slowing up, so the old man once again began to urge him on, "Erxi, Youqing, come on, let's not be lazy. Jiazhen and Fengxia are doing a good job. Hell, even Kugen does okay."

Just how many different names can one ox have? My curiosity got the better of me, and I walked over to the edge of the field. As I approached the old man I asked him, "How many names does this ox have?"

The old man, using the plow to support himself, straightened up. After looking me over he asked, "You a city boy?"

"Uh huh," I nodded.

The old man seemed pleased with himself. "I could tell right away."

"Just how many names does this ox have?" I repeated.

"He's got only one," the old man replied. "He's called Fugui."

"But just now you called him a whole bunch of names."

"Oh . . ." The old man smiled and gestured cryptically for me to move closer. As I neared him it seemed as if he wanted to say something but stopped. When he saw the ox raise its head, he gave him a reprimand, "No eavesdropping! Lower your head!"

The ox did lower his head, and then the old man whispered to me, "I'm afraid he'll discover he's the only one working the field, so I call out some other names to fool him. If he hears that there are other oxen around working the fields, he'll work harder and won't feel so depressed."

Seeing the old man's dark face smiling in the sunlight was quite moving. The wrinkles on his face moved about happily. They were caked with mud, just like the small dirt trails that ran through the fields.

Afterward the old man and I sat down under that lush tree. And on that bright afternoon, he began to tell me about himself.

⌐⌐

Forty years ago my dad would often stroll back and forth across this land. He would be wearing a black silk outfit and would always have his hands clasped behind his back. Just as he went out, he'd tell my mother, "I'm going out to take a walk around the property."

The moment the workers saw Dad strolling around his land they would hold their hoes with both hands and respectfully call out, "Master."

When my dad went into the city, all the city people would call him "sir." My dad was of very high social status, but every time he squatted down to take a shit he was just like a poor man. He never liked relieving himself in the house on the chamber pot next to the bed. Just like the animals, he liked shitting out in the open. Every day as dusk would near, dad would let out a belch— the sound was almost exactly the same as that croaking sound that frogs make. Then he would step outside and slowly walk toward the manure vat.

When he got there he'd be annoyed that the side of the vat was dirty. He'd raise his leg and climb up, squatting on top. My dad was old and his shit was getting older with him; it was harder and harder to force out. Our whole family would hear his grunting and groaning coming all the way from the vat.

For decades my dad always shit like this. When he got to be over sixty he was still able to climb up there and squat for a long time. His legs had as much strength as the talons of an eagle. My dad liked to watch the sky gradually change color until the darkness enveloped his farmland. When my daughter, Fengxia, was three or four she would often run out to the edge of the village to watch grandpa taking a shit. Dad was really old by then. When he squatted up on the manure vat his legs would tremble a bit, and Fengxia would ask him, "Grandpa, why are you shaking?"

"It's just the wind blowing," Dad would reply.

At the time our family circumstances had yet to take a turn for the worse. Our family had over one hundred *mu*° of land. The land from here all the way to the factory's chimney over there was owned by my family. Near and far, my father and I were known as the old and young rich masters. When we walked, the sound our shoes made was like the sound of coins clanking against each other. My wife, Jiazhen, was the daughter of the owner of the rice store in the city. She was also born into a rich family. A wealthy woman marries a wealthy man—it's like piling all the money up. The sound of money pouring down on top of money—it's been forty years since I've heard that sound.

I'm the prodigal son of the Xu family—or, as my dad would say, I'm a bastard. I studied for a few years at an old-style private school. When the schoolteacher, wearing the traditional long gown, called on me to read a paragraph aloud, it was my happiest moment. I stood up, holding my string-bound edition of "The Thousand Word Essay," and announced to my teacher, "Listen good now! Daddy's going to read to you!"

The next time he saw my father, my teacher, who was really getting on in years, told him, "I guarantee you that when that son of yours grows up, he'll be nothing but trouble."

Ever since I was little I've been hopeless, as my father would say. My teacher used to say I was a rotten piece of wood that could not be carved. Now that I think about it, they were both right. But at the time that's not how I saw things. I thought, I've

° Chinese unit of area equivalent to ½ acre or 0.0667 hectares.

got money, I'm the only flame the Xu family still has burning. If I'm extinguished, the Xu family will be finished.

When I was in private school I never walked anywhere—our family had a hired worker who would carry me on his back. When school got out he would already be waiting there, respectfully bent over. After I climbed on, I'd hit him on the head and say, "Changgen, let's go!"

Our worker Changgen would start to run. I'd be on top, bobbing about like a sparrow on the branches of a tree. Then I'd say, "Fly!"

Changgen would take longer strides and jump as if he could fly.

When I got older I started to build up a taste for going into town. Sometimes I wouldn't come home for ten or fifteen days. I wore a white silk shirt, and my hair was smooth and shiny. Standing in front of the mirror and seeing my head of black, flowing hair, I knew that I looked like a rich man.

I loved to go up to the whorehouse to listen to those loose women moaning and groaning all night long. Listening to those sounds was just like scratching a good itch. Once the day comes that a man starts to go whoring, gambling can't be too far behind. Whoring and gambling are just like a pair of arms or legs: inseparable. Later I began to like gambling even more—whoring was just to loosen up a bit. Whoring is like drinking a lot of water and needing to relieve oneself, or, said bluntly, it's like taking a piss. But gambling is completely different. Gambling made me both happy and tense. And it was especially that sense of tension that brought me an almost indescribable feeling of comfort. I was like a monk caught up in his daily routine of ringing the bell, completely listless. Every morning I'd wake up with my only worry being how I should spend the day. My father would sigh in despair, reprimanding me for failing to bring honor to our ancestors. I would think that bringing honor to our ancestors wasn't my job alone. I would say to myself, why should I give up my days of fun to worry about boring stuff like honoring the ancestors? Moreover, when my dad was young he'd been just like me. Our family used to have over two hundred *mu* of land, but once my father got his hands on it he managed to lose over half. I said to my father, "Don't worry, my son will honor the ancestors."

We should leave something good for the next generation anyway. My mom laughed when she heard this, and later she secretly told me that Dad had once said the same thing to my grandfather. I thought, you see, he forces what he doesn't want to do onto me. Why should I listen to him? At the time, my daughter, Fengxia, was just four years old, and Jiazhen was pregnant with our son, Youqing. Because she was six months pregnant, Jiazhen was naturally no treat for the eyes. When she walked it looked like she had a pair of steamed buns stuffed down her pants. Her legs didn't go forward when she walked, but side to side. I remember being so annoyed by her appearance that I even said to her, "Look at you. As soon as the wind blows your stomach doubles in size."

Jiazhen would never contradict me. But after hearing me insult her, she couldn't have been very happy and quietly retorted, "The wind didn't blow *that* hard."

Actually, after I started gambling I really did want to honor my ancestors. I wanted to win back that one hundred *mu* of land my dad lost. When my dad asked me what I was doing playing around in the city, I said to him, "I don't play around anymore. I'm doing business."

He asked, "What kind of business?"

As soon as he heard he lost his temper. When he was young he had said the same thing to my grandfather. When he found out I was gambling he took off his cloth shoes to hit me. I dodged to the left and ducked to the right. I thought after he hit me a few times it would be over. I was surprised to find that my father, normally only active when coughing, became increasingly violent as he flailed me. I wasn't a fly that was going to remain still while he tried to swat me. I restrained his hand and shouted, "Dad, what the fuck is wrong with you? If it weren't for the fact that you're the one who brought me into this world, I'd beat the hell out of you! Fucking relax!"

I held back his right hand, but Dad used his left hand to take off his right shoe. He was still bent on hitting me. I held on to his left hand so he couldn't get close enough to strike. He was so angry that he trembled for a long while before crying out, "Bastard!"

"Go to hell!" I told him.

I pushed him with both hands, and he fell down into the corner against the wall.

When I was young, I ate, drank, whored and gambled—I took part in every disreputable thing there was. The House of Qing was the whorehouse I used to go to. There was a fat prostitute there who really won my affection. When she walked, her fat butt was just like the two lanterns that hung outside, shaking from side to side. When she lay in bed she would wobble around. When I was pressed on top of her it felt like being asleep on a boat, rocking back and forth as I floated down a river. I would often have her carry me piggyback to go shopping—riding on her back was just like riding on the back of a horse.

Mr. Chen, my father-in-law, who was the owner of the rice store, always stood behind the counter wearing a black silk shirt. Whenever we were passing by his shop, I would pull that prostitute's hair to tell her to stop. Then I would take off my hat and pay my respects to my father-in-law. "How have you been feeling lately?"

As I asked, my father-in-law's face would look like a preserved egg. Me, I'd just giggle and continue on my way. Later my dad told me that on a few occasions my father-in-law was so angry with me it made him physically sick.

"Give me a break," I told my dad. "You're my father, and my behavior's never even made *you* sick. Just because he's got health problems, what right does he have to blame me?"

Mr. Chen was afraid of me, and I knew it. When I passed his shop riding on that whore's back, my father-in-law would be startled into retreat—like a rat scurrying back into his little hole. He didn't want to see me, but as a son-in-law passing a father-in-law's store, you should always have some manners. So I would call out, wishing my father-in-law well as he scurried away.

The wildest time was just after the Japanese surrender, when the Nationalist troops entered the city to recover their lost territory. That was truly an exciting day—both sides of the city streets were flooded with people holding small colored flags. Nationalist flags of a white sun against a blue sky jutted out at a slant from all the shops. My father-in-law even had a portrait of Chiang Kai-shek as large as two doors hanging before his store; the three hired hands at the rice shop stood under Chiang's right-hand pocket.

I spent that whole night gambling at the House of Qing. I felt muddleheaded, as if a heavy bag of rice had been placed on my shoulders. It had been over half a month since I'd been home, and my clothes reeked of a sour stench. I dragged that fat prostitute out of bed and had her carry me home. I also hired a rickshaw coolie to follow us so he could take the prostitute back to the House of Qing once I got home.

As the prostitute carried me toward the city gate she wouldn't stop yapping, blabbering on about how not even the god of thunder strikes people while they are asleep, and yet just as she had gotten to sleep I had the nerve to wake her up. She kept complaining about how coldhearted I was. I slipped a silver coin down her shirt and that shut her up. As we got close to the city gate I saw crowds on either side of the road, and my spirit suddenly soared.

My father-in-law was the head of the city's chamber of commerce. From far away I saw him standing in the center of the street, yelling, "Everybody get ready. Stand up straight, and as soon as the Nationalist army arrives everybody must clap and cheer."

Someone noticed me and jokingly yelled, "They're coming! They're coming!"

My father-in-law thought the army had arrived and scuttled off to one side. My legs were wrapped around that whore as if I were riding a horse. I said to her, "Run! Run!"

With crowds bawling with laughter on both sides of the street, the prostitute, huffing and puffing, went into a light jog.

"At night you screw me and during the day you ride me!" She cursed me as we went. "You coldhearted bastard! You're going to be the death of me!"

Over and over, I grinned and nodded in respect to the swarms of people roaring with laughter. When we came before my father-in-law I pulled the prostitute's hair. "Stop! Stop!"

"Ow!" the prostitute yelped as she came to a halt.

In a blaring voice I said to my father-in-law, "My esteemed father-in-law, your son-in-law wishes you a good morning."

That time I really did a good job of making my father-in-law lose face. At the time he just stood there stupefied, his lips trembling. After what seemed like an eternity he finally said in a hoarse voice, "My dear ancestors! Get out of here."

The voice that emerged from his lips didn't seem like it belonged to him.

My wife, Jiazhen, of course knew about my "colorful" romps in the city. Jiazhen was a good woman. For me to have had the good fortune to marry such a virtuous person in this life must have been repayment for having been a barking dog in the last. Jiazhen was always submissive toward me. While I was out screwing around she'd be at home worrying about me. But she would never say anything, just like my mother.

My escapades in the city were actually a bit too much. Jiazhen, of course, was a wreck. She was so disturbed that she had trouble keeping herself together. One day I came home from town and, just as I sat down at the dinner table, I noticed a strange smile on her face as she brought out four different dishes. She poured me a glass of wine and sat down next to me while I ate and drank. Her beaming expression seemed a bit strange. I couldn't imagine what good fortune had befallen her. I thought as hard as I could, but couldn't figure out what the special occasion was. I asked her, but she wouldn't say. She just gazed at me with a strange, elated smile on her face.

Those four dishes were all vegetable dishes. Jiazhen had prepared each one differently, but as I got to the bottom, I started to find pieces of pork hidden in each dish. At first I didn't really pay attention to this, but as I ate the last dish, I discovered that there was again a piece of meat on the bottom. At first I was stumped but then I began to laugh out loud. I understood what Jiazhen was up to. She was trying to teach me that although women all look different on the outside, when you get down to it they are all the same.

"I understand this little principle," I told Jiazhen.

But even though I knew what she meant, that didn't change the fact that when I saw a woman who looked a little different on the outside, I couldn't help thinking that she really was different. It was actually a hopeless situation.

Jiazhen would never let me know when she was upset with me—that was just the kind of person she was. But in her round-about way she still would try to get me in the end. I, on the other hand, wouldn't put up with either soft or hard tactics; neither my father's cloth shoes nor Jiazhen's cooking could stop me. I still loved going into town, and I still loved visiting the whorehouse. It was really my mom who understood a bit of what makes men tick. She said to Jiazhen, "Men are nothing but a bunch of gluttonous cats."

When Mom said this she not only exonerated me, but also exposed some inside information about my dad. Dad was sitting nearby, and as soon as he heard this his eyes squinted like two little peepholes and he began to giggle. When Dad was younger he couldn't contain himself when it came to the ladies. It wasn't until he was too old to screw around that he began to behave himself.

The House of Qing was also where I usually gambled. I'd often play mah-jongg, nine card and dice. Every time I gambled I lost, and the more I lost, the more I wanted to win back that hundred *mu* of land my father lost when he was young. In the beginning I would pay up right there, and if I didn't have money I'd just steal jewelry from Jiazhen and my mom. I even stole my daughter Fengxia's gold necklace. Afterward I just set up an account on credit. The creditors all knew about my family's wealth, so they let my debts ride. Once I started playing on credit I stopped keeping track of how much I lost, and the creditors didn't remind me. But every day they were secretly scheming away my family's one hundred *mu*.

It wasn't until after Liberation that I finally found out the winning party had everything set up. No wonder I always lost and never won—they had been secretly digging a hole for me. At the time there was a Mr. Shen at the House of Qing. He was about sixty years old, and his eyes were as cunning and bright as a cat's. He wore a long blue gown and would usually sit in the corner with his back straight. His eyes would be closed as if he were dozing off. Only after the action at the gambling table started to get exciting would Mr. Shen begin to cough and casually walk over, selecting a good spot from which to watch. He would never have to stand for long before someone would get up and offer him his place. "Mr. Shen, have a seat."

Mr. Shen would lift his long gown as he sat down and address the other three gamblers: "Please proceed."

No one in the House of Qing ever saw Mr. Shen lose. The blue veins in his hands would be practically popping out as he shuffled the deck of cards. All you could hear was the fluttering sound of wind as the deck became long and short, disappearing and reappearing in his hands. It made my eyes tired just watching.

Once when Mr. Shen was drunk he said to me, "Gambling relies entirely upon a good set of eyes and a quick pair of hands. You've got to train your eyes to open wide as a melon and your hands to be as slippery as an eel."

After the Japanese surrender, Long Er came. He spoke with a mixed accent, and just by listening to him you could tell he was a rather complicated person. He was a man who had been to many places and seen the world. He didn't wear a long gown; instead he wore clothes made from pure white silk. Two other men came with Long Er to help him carry a large wicker chest.

The games between Mr. Shen and Long Er that year were really amazing. The gambling room at the House of Qing was flooded with people as Mr. Shen gambled with Long Er and his men. Behind Long Er stood a waiter with a dry towel on a serving tray. From time to time Long Er would grab the towel to wipe his hands. We all thought it interesting that he didn't use a wet towel to wipe his hands, but a dry one; he would wipe his hands as if he had just finished a meal. In the beginning Long Er would always lose. Although it didn't seem to bother him, the two men who came with him could barely take it. One of them would curse under his breath while the other would take deep sighs. Mr. Shen always won, but the expression on his face was not that of a winner. Mr. Shen knitted his brow as if he had lost a bundle. He was getting on in years, and after gambling half the night he would start to breathe heavily, and the sweat on his forehead would drip down. His head hung down, but his eyes bore into Long Er's hands like nails.

"This round decides everything," Mr. Shen said.

Long Er took the towel from the tray, and as he wiped his hands one last time he said, "All right."

They piled all of their money on the table. The money took up practically all the space, leaving just a small open area in the center. Each of them got five cards. After Long Er showed four of his cards, his two men instantly lost hope and, pushing the cards aside, said, "It's over, we've lost again."

But Long Er quickly said, "We haven't lost, we've won."

As he spoke, Long Er showed his last card—it was the ace of spades. When the two workers saw, they began to laugh. Actually, Mr. Shen's last card was also an ace of spades—he had three aces and two kings. Long Er had three queens and two jacks. When Long Er showed his ace of spades, Mr. Shen seemed to be in shock for a while, then he finally put his cards away and said, "I lost."

Both Long Er's and Mr. Shen's ace of spades had come from their pockets. One pack of cards can only have a single ace of spades, so when Long Er showed his first, Mr. Shen knew he had no choice but to admit defeat. That was the first time we ever saw Mr. Shen lose. Leaning on the table to stand up, Mr. Shen clasped his hands and bowed to Long Er and his men before turning to leave. As he approached the door he smiled and said, "I'm getting old."

From then on no one saw Mr. Shen again. I heard someone say that he rode away on a rickshaw the next morning at the crack of dawn.

After Mr. Shen left, Long Er quickly took his place as the top gambler in town. Long Er was different from Mr. Shen. While Mr. Shen would never lose, Long Er would lose when the stakes were low, but never when the stakes were high. I used to gamble with Long Er at the House of Qing. Sometimes I lost and sometimes I won, but because of this I never really felt like I was losing. Actually, when I won it was always small change, but when I lost it was a fortune. I was left in the dark, all the while thinking that I was just about to bring honor back to my ancestors.

Jiazhen came looking for me on what would be my last night of gambling. When she arrived it was almost dusk—Jiazhen told me that later; at the time I had no idea if it was night or day. Jiazhen, who was seven or eight months pregnant with our son, Youqing, came to the House of Qing. When she found me she kneeled down before me in silence; at first I didn't even see her. I was doing exceptionally well that day. We were playing dice, and, eight or nine times out of ten, the numbers were coming up in my favor. Sitting across from me was Long Er. As soon as he saw the numbers he'd giggle, "Well my friend, it looks like I've lost again."

After Long Er beat Mr. Shen by pulling a fast one, no one in the House of Qing, including me, dared bet on cards with Long Er. Long Er and I would always play dice, but even at dice Long Er was an expert. He almost always won and rarely lost. But that day I had him in the palm of my hand—he kept losing to me. With narrow eyes and a cigarette dangling from his lips, he acted as if everything was all right. He would snicker whenever he lost, but as his thin arms pushed the money over to my side of the table, he couldn't have appeared more begrudging. I thought, Long Er, you should suffer at least once. People are all the same: When they're taking the money from someone else's pocket, their faces light up and it's all smiles, but as soon as it's their turn to lose they all cry like they're in mourning. I was ecstatic until I felt someone tugging on my clothes. I looked down and saw my wife. Seeing Jiazhen kneeling there made me mad. I thought, my son hasn't even been born yet, and here she is kneeling. This really was too much. I said to Jiazhen, "Get up! Get up! Stand the fuck up!"

Jiazhen really listened—she stood right up. I said, "What the hell did you come here for? Hurry up and go home."

When I finished with what I had to say, I just ignored her and watched Long Er raise the dice above his head, shaking them a few times as if he were praying to the Buddha. As soon as he threw them down, his face lost all color.

"Rubbing too many women's asses must bring bad luck," he said.

As soon as I realized I had won again, I said, "Long Er, you'd better go wash your hands."

Long Er laughed as he said, "After you wipe your mouth clean, we'll see."

Jiazhen tugged on my clothes. As soon as I looked I realized she was kneeling again. She quietly pleaded, "Come home with me."

Go home with a woman? If Jiazhen wasn't intentionally trying to make a fool out of me, I didn't know what she was doing. All at once my temper flared. I looked at Long Er and the others—they were all laughing at me. I screamed at Jiazhen, "Take your ass home!"

But Jiazhen persisted. "You come with me."

I slapped her twice, and her head swayed back and forth like a toy rattle. After having been hit, she still kneeled there, saying, "I won't get up until you agree to come home with me."

It hurts to think about it now. When I was young I was a real asshole. A great woman like that, and I hit and kicked her. But no matter how hard I hit her, she just kneeled there and wouldn't get up. In the end I would grow tired of hitting her. Her hair was a mess, and tears were running down her face. I took a handful of the money I had just won and gave it to two of the guys who were standing there watching. I had them carry Jiazhen away. As they left I told them, "The farther the better!"

As Jiazhen was carried out, her hands firmly clasped her protruding belly, which held my son. She didn't scream or yell. She was carried out to the main street, where the two men left her. Leaning against the wall to support herself, she struggled to get to her feet. By then it was completely dark out. She slowly made her way home. Years later, when I looked back on that incident, I asked Jiazhen whether she hated me back then. She shook her head, "No."

Wiping the tears from her face, my wife passed the entrance to her father's rice shop. She stood there a long time watching the silhouette of her father's face reflected on the wall by the kerosene lamp. She knew that he was checking the accounts. After standing there for a while, lost in her tears, she left.

That night Jiazhen walked over ten *li*° in the dark to get home. All alone, and more than seven months pregnant with Youqing, she walked that wet, bumpy road home, with dogs barking after her the whole way.

A few years before, Jiazhen had been a student. At the time there was a night school in town. Jiazhen, carrying a kerosene lamp and wearing a moon white cheongsam, was going to class with a few of her girlfriends. I saw her while I was turning a corner; she walked over with a swing in her step. The sound of her high-heeled shoes tapping the stone pavement was like the sound of falling rain. Jiazhen was really beautiful back then, and my eyes froze on her. Her hair was neatly combed behind her

° Chinese unit of length equivalent to ½ kilometer or ⅓ mile.

ears, and when she walked her cheongsam would crease at the waist. I thought to myself, I want her to be my wife.

After Jiazhen and her friends passed by giggling, I asked a cobbler sitting on the ground nearby, "Whose daughter is that?"

"That's the rice dealer Chen Ji's daughter," the cobbler said.

As soon as I got home I told my mom, "Quick, find a matchmaker. I want to marry the daughter of the rice shop owner, Mr. Chen."

The night after Jiazhen was carried off, my luck started to go sour. I lost a whole bunch of games in a row. Before my eyes, the pile of money I had accumulated disappeared like the water you wash your feet in. Long Er couldn't stop giggling—his face was almost disfigured from his excessive laughing. My losing streak lasted until sunrise. I gambled until my head was dizzy, my vision blurry and I burped up smelly gas from my stomach. Finally I bet the biggest stakes I had ever risked in my life. I wet my hands with my saliva thinking that the fruits of a thousand springs were resting on this throw. Just as I was about to throw the dice, Long Er stretched out his hand to stop me. "Slow down."

Long Er waved to one of the waiters, saying, "Give Master Xu a hot towel."

It was then that the people watching went back to sleep. Aside from Long Er's two right-hand men, the only people paying attention were the people at the gambling table. Later I learned that Long Er had bought off that waiter. The waiter handed me a hot towel, and, as I wiped my face, Long Er secretly switched the dice to a pair he had tampered with. I didn't notice a thing. After wiping my face I threw the towel down on the tray. Then I picked up the dice and shook them with all my might. After throwing them I thought, not bad, a pretty big number.

When it was Long Er's turn, he let everything ride on number seven. He cupped his hands, then tightly clasped them together, yelling, "Seven."

One of the dice had a hole dug out of it and was filled with mercury. When Long Er's hands met and the dice came together, the mercury in the fixed die fell to the bottom. He tossed the die and, after rolling over a few times, it stopped on seven.

As soon as I saw that it was a seven, my head began to pound. This time I lost bad. But when I thought again I figured, it's okay, I can play on credit, and then I'll have a chance at winning everything back like I always did. Feeling a bit relieved I said to Long Er, "Put it down in the book."

Long Er waved for me to sit down and said, "I can't let you play on credit anymore. You've already lost your family's 100 *mu* of land. If I extend your credit, what will you use to pay me back?"

When I heard Long Er's words I violently cut off my yawn before it was finished.

"That's impossible," I stuttered. "It can't be."

Long Er and two other creditors took out the account book and systematically went through it with me. Then Long Er patted me on the head, saying, "Young master, take a good look. The signatures are all written in your hand."

I suddenly realized that six months ago I had begun to owe them, and in the past six months I had gambled away all the property my ancestors had left. After going through half the books I said to Long Er, "Don't bother counting."

I stood back up and, like a diseased chicken, walked out of the House of Qing. By then it was already light out. I stood in the middle of the street, not knowing where to go. Someone I knew carrying a basket of bean curd brightly called out to me, "Good morning, Mr. Xu!"

His voice nearly scared the hell out of me, and I blankly stared back at him. His eyes squinted as he smiled, and he said, "Look at you! You look like shit!"

He thought I'd worn myself out with those women. He didn't realize that I was bankrupt, as poor as a hired worker. I forced a smile as I watched him saunter away. I figured it was a bad idea to stand there, so I started to walk.

I made my way over to my father-in-law's rice shop, where two workers were replacing a door panel. When they saw me they started to laugh—they thought I was going to yell out "good morning" to my father-in-law again. But where would I have had the courage or strength for that? I drew my head back and, staying close to another house, quickly passed by. I heard my father-in-law inside coughing followed by the "puh" sound of him spitting on the floor.

And so just like that, muddleheaded and confused, I walked to the edge of town. For a while I even forgot I had lost my family's fortune. My mind had become empty, like a hornet's nest that has been stirred up. When I got outside of town I saw a small trail extending out toward me, and once again I was scared. I wondered what I should do next. I took a few steps down the trail, but my feet wouldn't move. In all directions there was not a soul in sight. I simply wanted to hang myself with my belt and be done with it. Lost in thought I dragged myself forward, but when I passed an elm tree it took only one look for me to realize that I had not the slightest inclination to take off my belt. I didn't really want to die, I just wanted to find a way to punish myself. I figured there was no way that damned debt would hang with me, so I said to myself, "Forget it, don't kill yourself."

This debt was to be paid by my dad. As soon as I thought of Dad, my heart went numb. This time he would probably beat me to death. As I walked I kept trying to think of a way out, but no matter what, everything seemed to lead to a dead end. I had no choice but to head home. Being beaten to death by my dad was better than hanging from a tree like some stray dog.

I didn't realize it, but during that short walk home I had lost a whole lot of weight and my eyes had grown dull and colorless. When my mom saw me she screamed out in surprise. Staring at me in disbelief, she asked, "Are you Fugui?"

Looking at my mom, I forced a smile and nodded my head. Shocked, she uttered something else, but I was no longer paying attention to her. I pushed the door open and went into my room. Jiazhen, in the middle of combing her hair, was also taken aback when she saw me. She gazed at me with her mouth gaping. As soon as I thought of how I had beaten her when she came to persuade me to go home the night before, I fell to the ground and, kneeling before her, muttered, "Jiazhen, I'm finished."

After speaking those words I began to cry out loud. Jiazhen rushed over to help me up, but being pregnant with Youqing, how could she support me? She called my mom over, and the two of them pulled me onto the bed. As I lay on the bed, bubbles of saliva dripped from my mouth. I looked like a corpse. They were scared to death and began patting me on the shoulder and rocking my head. I pushed them away and said, "I've lost everything we have."

My mother appeared dumbstruck; she stared at me with a look of intensity and asked, "What did you say?"

"I've lost everything," I repeated.

The look on my face convinced her. My mother sat down on the floor and, wiping her tears, said, "If the upper beam is not straight, the lower ones will go aslant."

Even then my mother still loved me. She didn't blame me, she blamed my father.

Jiazhen also cried. She patted me on the shoulder and tried to console me. "As long as you don't gamble anymore, everything will be all right."

I had nothing left. Even if I had wanted to gamble, I wouldn't have had any money to stake a bet. I heard Dad in the next room shooting off his foul mouth. He still didn't know that he was penniless—he was simply annoyed at being disturbed by the two women crying. As soon as she heard my father's voice, Mom stopped crying. She stood up and walked out, with Jiazhen following her. I knew that they were going into my father's room, and after a while I heard my dad begin screaming, "Bastard!"

It was just then that my daughter, Fengxia, pushed the door open and came in. She closed the door and in a shrill voice said, "Dad, hurry up and hide! Grandpa's going to beat you."

I just stared at her without moving a muscle. She then came over and tried pulling me away by the hand; when I wouldn't budge she began to cry. Seeing Fengxia cry was like having a knife pierce my heart. Even at such a young age, Fengxia was trying to protect her dad. Just looking at her made me feel like I deserved to be cut to pieces.

I heard my father angrily approaching, shouting, "You bastard! I'm going to dismember you, castrate you! I'm going to chop you into little pieces, you fucking bastard!"

Okay Dad, come on in and chop me to pieces, I thought to myself. But as soon as Dad approached the door he fell on the ground, knocking himself unconscious. I heard Mom and Jiazhen shouting as they picked him up and brought him to his bed. After a while I heard the woodwind-like sound of my father weeping.

Once my father took to his bed, he lay there for three days. The first day he cried like a sad bird, and after the sobbing stopped he began to sigh. All the sounds carried to my room. I heard the echoes of his grieving voice, "Retribution, it's retribution."

On the third day, my father received guests. While the sound of his coughing filled the room, his voice was so low it could barely be heard. That night my mother came over to tell me that Dad wanted to see me. I got up from bed thinking, if this isn't the end, I don't know what is. I figured that after resting in bed for three days, Dad must have the strength to beat me half-dead, if not annihilate me. I told myself that no matter how bad he beat me, I wouldn't hit back. As I approached Dad's room I had no energy. My body grew weak, and it felt as if my legs didn't belong to me. After entering his room, I stood behind my mother, stealing a glance at Dad as he lay in bed. He opened his eyes and looked at me. His white beard moved as he said to my mom, "Leave us."

My mom walked past me to leave. As soon as she left I felt empty inside. At first I thought, he might leap right out of bed and attack me. But he just lay there not moving. The blanket covering his chest slid off the bed and onto the floor.

"Fugui . . ."

Dad patted the side of the bed, saying, "Sit down."

My heart raced as I sat down next to him. As he stroked my hand I realized that his was as cold as ice. It was a chill that went straight to my heart. In a low voice, he said, "Fugui, a gambling debt is still a debt. Since ancient times there's never been anything that says you shouldn't pay your debts. The hundred *mu* of land and the house—I'm giving them up. Tomorrow they'll bring the copper cash. I'm too old to carry the load. You'll have to carry the money to repay the debt yourself."

Dad let out a long sigh as he finished. I was moved to tears. I knew he wasn't going to beat me, but the words he spoke were as painful as death itself. It was as if my head had been severed by a blunt knife yet failed to fall off. Dad patted my hand. "Go to bed."

The next morning, just as I got up, I saw four men come into our courtyard. In front was a rich man wearing silk. He looked at the three poorly dressed porters walking behind him and, waving his hand, said, "Put it down."

Putting their load down, the three porters used their shirts to wipe the sweat off their faces. The rich man looked me in the eye but instead of addressing me called out for my father. "Master Xu, the merchandise you wanted has arrived."

Carrying the title deed for the house and property, Dad coughed repeatedly as he staggered out. He handed the deeds over and bowed slightly as he said, "Sorry to have troubled you."

Pointing to the three chests of copper cash, the man said to my father, "It's all there, you can count it if you'd like."

My dad was completely without the qualities of a rich man. He just said respectfully, "That's all right, there's no need. Come in and have a cup of tea."

"No, thanks," the man said.

Then he looked at me and asked my dad, "Is this the young master of the house?"

Dad nodded as he looked at me and snickered, saying, "Before you deliver the merchandise, pick some pumpkin leaves to put on top. Don't let anyone steal it."

It was on that day that I carried the copper money over ten *li* into town to repay the debt. Mom and Jiazhen picked the pumpkin leaves we used to cover the top of the chest. When Fengxia saw them picking leaves, she picked out the two biggest to put on top. As I prepared to leave, Fengxia, not knowing I was going to repay the debt, gazed at my face and asked, "Dad, will it be a long time before you come home again?"

My eyes watered up, and I almost dropped a tear as I heard her words. Without delaying another moment I lifted the load and walked toward the city. When I got to town, Long Er, seeing me carrying the load, affectionately called out, "Young master Xu, come on over."

I placed the load down before him. Pushing away the pumpkin leaves, he knit his brow and said, "Aren't you making things hard on yourself? Exchanging some of this for silver dollars would save you a lot of trouble."

By the time I brought him the last load of copper coins, he'd stopped addressing me as young master. He nodded as he said, "Fugui, just put it down here."

Another creditor who was a bit friendlier patted me on the shoulder and said, "Fugui, let's have a drink."

After hearing this Long Er swiftly added, "Yes, yes, have a drink. It's my treat."

I shook my head, thinking I'd better go home. After just one day my silk clothes were ruined and my shoulders were oozing with blood. Alone, I walked home. I cried as I walked, I walked as I cried. Carrying the money that day had exhausted me to the point that every joint in my body felt dislocated. I wondered how many people had died of exhaustion for my ancestors to make this money. It was then that I figured out why my father had insisted on copper coins and not silver: he wanted me to understand this truth. He wanted me to know that money does not come easily. Thinking about it this way, I could no longer walk. I squatted down beside the road and cried until the muscles in my stomach began to twitch. It was then that our family worker Changgen, the same servant who used to carry me to private school, came over carrying a beat-up bag. He had worked for our family for decades, but now he, too, had to leave. My grandfather had taken him in at a young age after Changgen lost his parents. In the years that followed he never married. Just like me his eyes were flooded with tears, and the flesh of his bare feet was split open. Seeing me bent over beside the road, he called out, "Young master."

I screamed at him, "Don't call me young master, I'm an animal!"

He shook his head. "An emperor begging for food is still an emperor. You may have no money, but you're still young master."

Hearing his words, more tears rolled down my face, which I had just wiped dry. He squatted down beside me and, burying his face in his hands, broke down in tears. After weeping together in silence I finally said to him, "Changgen, it's getting dark. You'd better go home."

Changgen stood there for a while and then, step by step, began to walk away. I heard his droning voice echo, "What home do I have left?"

I had hurt Changgen, too. Seeing him walk off in solitude, my heart felt wave after wave of pain. Only after Changgen had walked so far that I could no longer see him did I finally stand up and walk toward home. By the time I arrived, night had already fallen. Our family worker and maid had both already left. Mom and Jiazhen were in the kitchen, one making a fire while the other was preparing dinner. My dad was still lying in bed. Only Fengxia was as happy as before—she still didn't know that from now on we would suffer bitterness and poverty. Bouncing and vivacious, she came over, pounced onto my legs and asked, "Why do they say I'm not a 'miss' anymore?"

I caressed her small face but failed to utter a single word. At least she didn't continue asking. She used her fingernails to scrape the caked-on mud off my pants and said happily, "I'm washing your pants for you!"

When it was time to eat, my mother approached the door to Dad's room to ask, "Should I bring your food in?"

"I'll come out to eat," Dad replied.

Holding the kerosene lamp with three fingers, Dad emerged from his room. The glow from the lamp danced upon his face, leaving it half illuminated and half cloaked in darkness. His back slumped over as he coughed incessantly. After sitting down he asked me, "Did you settle the debt?"

"It's settled."

"That's good, that's good," Dad quietly repeated.

After seeing my shoulders he continued, "And your shoulders were rubbed raw?"

I didn't make a sound but secretly looked at my mom and Jiazhen. Their eyes were brimming with tears as they looked at my shoulders. Dad, after slowly swallowing a few mouthfuls of rice, put his chopsticks down on the table and pushed his bowl away. After a while he continued, "A long time ago, our Xu family ancestors raised but a single chicken. When that chicken grew up it turned into a goose, the goose in turn grew into a lamb, and the lamb became an ox. This is how our family became rich."

Dad's voice turned into a whisper. He stopped for a moment, then continued, "When it came into my hands, the Xu family ox became a lamb, and the lamb turned back into a goose. When it came down to you, that goose became a chicken, and now we are left without even a chicken."

When Dad finished his sentence he began to cackle. He laughed and laughed until his laughter turned to tears. He extended two fingers and pointed them toward me. "The Xu family has begotten two prodigal sons."

Less than two days later Long Er came. His appearance had completely changed. Opening his mouth wide to let out a sinister laugh, he revealed two new gold teeth. He had bought our house and land at a low mortgage rate and had come to check out his new property. Long Er kicked the foot of the wall, then pushed his ear up against the wall and patted it with his hand, saying, "Sturdy. Sturdy."

Long Er then went outside to take a walk around the property. When he came back he bowed to my father with his hands folded in front, saying, "Looking at these bright green fields, I can rest at ease."

As soon as Long Er came we had to move out of the family house, which had been passed down for generations, and into a small thatched hut. The day we moved, my father strolled in and out of the different rooms with his hands clasped behind his back. Finally, he said to my mother, "And I thought I would die in this house."

My dad brushed the dust off his silk clothes and, extending his neck, crossed the threshold. Just like before, Dad clasped his hands behind his back and leisurely made his way to the manure vat. The sky was just beginning to grow dark, and only a few farmers were still working in the field. They all knew my father was no longer the owner, yet they held on to their hoes, calling out, "Master."

My dad smiled slightly and, waving his hand, said, "No need to call me that."

The land my father now strolled on was no longer his. His legs trembled as he walked to the edge of the property. He stopped in front of the manure vat and looked around in all directions. Then he undid his pants and squatted down.

That day as dusk settled, my dad didn't make a sound while he took his shit. His squinting eyes stared far off, and gradually the narrow trail leading to town became blurry. A worker standing beside him was bending over to reap some vegetables. By the time the farmer stood back up, my father could no longer see that small trail.

Dad fell from atop the manure vat. The worker, hearing a noise, quickly turned around to see my father lying on the ground. His head didn't move as it rested against the manure vat. Holding a sickle, the worker rushed over to my father, asking him, "Master, are you okay?"

My dad's eyelids fluttered. Staring at the worker, he asked in a raspy voice, "Who are you?"

The worker bent over and said, "Master, it's me, Wang Xi."

After thinking for a while, Dad said, "Oh, Wang Xi. Wang Xi, there's a stone beneath me that's hurting my back."

Wang Xi turned my father over to find a rock the size of a man's fist. He tossed it aside. Lying there, my dad quietly uttered, "That's much better."

"Should I help you up?" Wang Xi asked.

Dad shook his head. Sighing, he replied, "No need."

And then my father asked him, "Have you ever seen me fall before?"

Wang Xi shook his head. "No, master."

My dad seemed a bit happy, and he asked again, "So, it's the first time?"

"Yes, master," said Wang Xi.

My dad chuckled for a moment before closing his eyes. His neck went crooked as his head slid from against the manure vat onto the ground.

That day we had just moved into our thatched hut. My mother and I were inside cleaning. Fengxia happily helped us straighten up. She still didn't know that from now on we were going to suffer. Jiazhen was walking from the pond with a bundle of clothes in both arms when Wang Xi ran up to her, saying, "Madame, the master's had an accident. I'm afraid he's not going to make it."

From the hut we heard Jiazhen screaming, "Mom! Fugui, Mom . . ."

Before she could say any more, Jiazhen began to cry. I immediately figured that something must have happened to Dad. I ran out of the hut to see Jiazhen standing there with the whole bucket-load of clothes on the ground before her. When Jiazhen saw me she called out, "Fugui, your father . . ."

My head began to buzz and, as fast as I could, I ran to the other side of the family plot. When I got to the manure vat, Dad had already stopped breathing. I pushed him and yelled, but he didn't respond. I didn't know what to do. I stood up and turned around to see Mom running toward me on her bound little feet, crying and screaming. Jiazhen was right behind with Fengxia in her arms.

After Dad died my whole body felt utterly drained, as if I had contracted some disease. All day I sat on the floor of our thatched hut. All I could do was heave deep sighs and let the tears run down my face. Fengxia would often sit on the floor and keep me company. As she played with my hands she asked, "Did Grandpa fall down?"

When she saw me nod she continued, "Was it the wind that blew him over?"

My mom and Jiazhen didn't dare cry too loudly. They were afraid I wouldn't be able to take it and would end up the same way as my father. Sometimes I would clumsily bump into something, and the two of them would be taken aback. Only after they saw I didn't collapse on the ground like Dad would they ease up and ask, "Are you all right?"

Those days my mother would often say to me, "As long as you are happy, being poor is nothing to be ashamed of."

She was trying to comfort me. She still thought it was poverty that was causing my suffering, but actually, in my heart, all I was thinking about was my father. In one sense Dad died by my hand, and now my mom, Jiazhen and even Fengxia had to stay with me and suffer.

Ten days after my dad passed away, my father-in-law came. He held his long gown with his right hand, and his face was ghostly pale as he made his way out to the country. Following him was a carriage covered with flowers and draped in red silk, with more than ten young men crowded around on either side beating bells and gongs. When the country folk noticed, they all rushed to look. They thought it was someone's wedding but couldn't figure out why they hadn't heard any such news. Then someone asked my father-in-law, "Whose family has met with such good fortune?"

Keeping a straight face, my father-in-law said loudly, "*My* family!"

At the time I was at my father's grave. I heard the ringing of the bells and the gongs and saw my father-in-law rushing furiously to our thatched hut. He turned around and motioned to the sedan bearers to place the carriage on the ground and to stop the ringing of the bells and gongs. I knew he wanted to take Jiazhen away. My heart raced and pounded, but I didn't know what to do.

Hearing the noise, my mom and Jiazhen went outside.

"Dad!" Jiazhen exclaimed.

Looking at Jiazhen, my father-in-law asked my mother, "And the animal?"

My mother kept a smiling face and asked, "Do you mean Fugui?"

"Who else?"

My father-in-law turned around and saw me. He took two steps toward me and shouted, "Beast! Come here!"

I stood there without moving—how could I dare move? My father-in-law waved his fist at me, shouting, "Come over here, you animal! Why don't you come over here and wish me 'good morning'? Listen to me, you bastard. Do you remember what it was like when you married Jiazhen? Well that's what it is going to be like today when I take her away. Look, this is a wedding carriage, these are bells and gongs. I'm going to make today even more memorable than the day you married her!"

After shouting, my father-in-law turned around and said to Jiazhen, "Hurry up and go inside to get your things ready."

Jiazhen stood there without moving and called out, "Daddy."

My father-in-law stamped his foot in fury. "Hurry up!"

Seeing me standing in the distance, Jiazhen turned around and went inside. It was then that my mother's tears started up and she said to my father-in-law, "Please, allow Jiazhen to stay."

He looked at my mother and waved his hand, then he turned around and yelled to me, "Animal, from now on you'll have nothing to do with Jiazhen! The Chen family will never again have any dealings with you Xus!"

My mother bent over to plead with him. "I beg of you, for the sake of Fugui's father, let Jiazhen stay."

My father-in-law rushed at my mother, barking, "He even drove his own father to the grave!"

After shouting, even my father-in-law himself thought he was a bit out of line. Softening his voice a bit, he said, "Don't blame me for being cruel. It's all because of that animal's wild behavior that things have gotten to this stage."

After he finished, he turned toward me again and yelled, "I'm leaving Fengxia for your family. The child in Jiazhen's stomach will belong to the Chen family!"

My mother stood to one side crying. Wiping away her tears, she said, "How am I supposed to make this up to the Xu family ancestors?"

Carrying a bag, Jiazhen emerged from the hut.

"Get in the carriage," my father-in-law ordered.

Jiazhen turned her head to look at me. When she got to the carriage she turned around to look at me once more, and then to look at my mother before getting into the sedan. It was then that Fengxia came running from out of nowhere. As soon as she saw her mother in the wedding carriage, she wanted to go along. She was halfway in when Jiazhen's hand pushed her out.

My father-in-law waved his hand to the sedan-chair carriers, and the carriage was lifted up. Inside, Jiazhen began to wail with grief.

"Sound the drums!" my father-in-law ordered.

More than ten young men began beating and banging on drums and gongs with all their might, drowning out the sound of Jiazhen's crying. As the carriage took to the road, my father-in-law, holding his long gown, walked just as quickly as the carriage bearers. My mom with her twisted little bound feet followed pathetically behind; only when she reached the edge of the village did she stop.

And then Fengxia ran over to me. Opening her eyes wide she said, "Dad, Mom went away in a sedan chair."

Seeing how excited Fengxia was, I could barely take it. I said to her, "Fengxia, come here."

Fengxia walked over beside me. Caressing her face I said, "Fengxia, don't you ever forget I'm your daddy."

Upon hearing this, Fengxia was all smiles and replied, "And don't you forget I'm Fengxia."

When Fugui's story got to this point, I couldn't help but let out a giggle. This scoundrel of forty years ago was today sitting bare-chested on the grass, the sunlight filtering through gaps between the tree leaves and into his squinting eyes. His legs were covered with mud, and patches of white hair sprouted from his shaven head. Sweat trickled down over the wrinkles on his chest. At that moment his old ox was in the golden water of the pond, with only its head and back exposed. I saw the water slapping against the ox's long black back, just as water crashes on the shore.

This old man was the first person I had bumped into after beginning my life of carefree travel. I was young and without troubles or worries. Every new face filled me with excitement and joy, and I was deeply attracted by anything I didn't know. It was just at this time in my life that I came upon Fugui. Never before had anyone so completely confided in me the way he did

*when he vividly recounted his story. For as long as I was willing
to listen, he was willing to talk.*

My chance meeting with Fugui filled my later days of collecting folk songs with happiness and anticipation. I imagined that
this rich, flourishing land was full of people like Fugui. And in
later years I did meet a lot of old men like him. They wore their
pants just like he did, with the crotch area drooping down near
their knees. The wrinkles on their faces were filled with sunlight
and dirt. When they smiled at me, I noticed only a handful of
teeth left in their empty mouths. Although they would often cry,
it was not because they were unusually sad. Sometimes they
would cry even when they were happy and perfectly at peace.
Their hands were as coarse as a dirt road. Raising their hands to
wipe away the tears from their eyes was as common a gesture as
flicking a piece of straw off one's clothes.

But I never again met anyone as unforgettable as Fugui. Never
did I meet anyone who was not only so clear about his life experiences, but also able to recount them so brilliantly. He was the
kind of person who could see his entire past. He could clearly see
himself walking as a young man, and he could even see himself
growing old. It's very rare to meet this kind of old man in the
country. Perhaps the difficulties and hardships of life destroy the
others' memories. They often face the past with a kind of numbness. Not knowing what to do, they simply dismiss the past with
an awkward smile. They lack interest in their own experiences.
Just like gossip or hearsay, they remember only fragments—
which often are not even related to their own experience. One or
two sentences is enough to express everything they stand for. I

often hear the younger generation mocking them: "Once they hit old age, they start living like dogs."

But Fugui was completely different. He liked thinking about the past. He liked talking about his life. It seemed that in this way he could relive his life again and again. His story grabbed me in the same way the talons of an eagle clutch the branches of a tree.

After Jiazhen left, my mother would often sit off to one side, secretly wiping her tears. At first I tried to think of something to say to comfort her, but as soon as I saw her expression, the words just wouldn't come out. In the end, she was the one who often tried to cheer me up. "Jiazhen doesn't belong to anyone but you. No one can take her away."

Hearing this I could only swallow a sigh. What could I say? A strong and healthy family had been smashed apart like a clay jar. When night came, I would often lie in bed unable to sleep. I carried inside of me hatred for so many things, but when it came down to it I hated myself most. At night I worried too much, and during the day my head ached. All day I had no energy to harvest the crops. Thank god there was Fengxia. Fengxia would often pull me by the hand and ask, "Dad, a table has four corners. If you chop off one corner, how many are left?"

I didn't know where Fengxia had heard this, but when I said three corners, Fengxia would smile ear to ear and laugh uncontrollably. She would say, "Wrong! There are five corners left."

Listening to Fengxia, I wanted to laugh but couldn't. I thought of our original four-person family. When Jiazhen left it was like cutting off a corner, not to mention the child she was carrying. I told Fengxia, "Wait until your mom gets back and there'll be five corners."

After we sold everything of value in the house, my mother would take Fengxia out to dig up wild vegetables. Carrying a basket on her arm, Mom would be off, unable with her twisted little feet to walk as fast as Fengxia. Her hair was completely gray, yet she had to learn to do hard physical labor for the first time in her life. Mom would hold Fengxia by the hand and watch her every step. My mother's careful manner almost brought me to tears.

I knew that I could never again live the kind of life I once had. I had to support Mom and Fengxia. I talked to Mom about borrowing some money from some friends and relatives in town to open a small shop. After hearing my idea, Mom didn't utter a sound; she didn't want to leave. When people get old they're like that, unwilling to move. I said to Mom, "The house and land all belong to Long Er now. Setting up our home here is just the same as anywhere else."

After hearing this, Mom was silent for a long time before saying, "Your father's grave is still here."

That one sentence made me stop thinking of any new ideas. After going through all of my options, I decided my only choice was to approach Long Er.

Long Er had become the landlord here. Holding a teapot in his right hand, he would stroll the fields in his silk shirt. He was

so cocky, always laughing, exposing his two big gold teeth. I originally thought he was quite cordial to people, but sometimes
he'd open his mouth to yell at the more offensive farmers. Slowly
I realized he only wanted people to notice his gold teeth.

Long Er was still fairly courteous to me whenever I saw him.
He would often laugh and say, "Fugui, come inside for some
tea."

I never went to Long Er's home because I was afraid I would
get emotional. I had lived in that house since I was born,
and now it belonged to Long Er's family. How was I supposed to
feel?

But actually when your life has been reduced to the level that
mine had, you really don't care about all that much. The old saying "Poverty lowers the ambition of man" seemed to apply to me.
That day when I went to see Long Er, he was sitting in the old-
fashioned wooden armchair in the parlor. His two legs were
propped up on a stool as he held a teapot in one hand and waved
a fan with the other. When he saw me come in, he grinned.
Chuckling, he said, "It's Fugui! Get a stool for yourself and have
a seat."

Long Er was slumped back in the wooden chair, motionless; I
didn't really expect him to offer me any tea. After I sat down, he
asked, "So Fugui, you're here to borrow money, is that it?"

Before I could say no, he continued, "According to reason I
really should lend a little bit to you. But as the saying goes, 'You
can save someone in times of emergency, but not from poverty.'
Me, I only save people from emergencies, not from poverty."

I nodded my head, explaining, "I would like to rent a few *mu* of land."

Long Er smiled slyly and asked, "How many do you want to rent?"

"Five *mu*."

"Five?" Long Er's eyebrows shot up, and he asked, "Can your body handle that?"

"With a little practice I'll be fine," I answered.

He thought about it and said, "Because we've known each other for a long time, I'll give you five *mu* of good land."

Long Er must have had a heart after all, because he really did give me five *mu* of good, fertile land. All by myself, I planted that five *mu* of land, though I almost died of exhaustion in the process. Never before had I done farmwork, so I learned from watching the other farmers. There's no need to mention how slow I was. As long as it was still light outside, I was out in the field. And even when it got dark, if there was moonlight I'd still be out there working. The crops have to be planted at the proper time. If you miss the right time to sow the seeds, then you will miss the entire season. When that happens, not only will you be unable to raise a family, but even paying back Long Er's rent grain would have been an impossibility. As the saying goes, "Slow birds need an early start." Well, I was the slow bird who never finished.

My mother really loved me, so she would work with me in the fields. But she was getting old, and her feet made work difficult. Once she bent over it would take her a long time to stand up again. When she would sit down in the field, I'd say to her, "Mom, hurry up and get back inside."

But Mom would shake her head and say, "Four hands are better than two."

"If you get sick, then I'll have to take care of you. And then there won't be any hands!" I retorted.

Hearing this, she slowly walked back to the ridge between the fields to sit with Fengxia. Every day, Fengxia would sit on the ridge and keep me company. She would pick a whole bunch of flowers and put them in a pile next to her legs. As she picked each one she would ask what kind of flower it was. How was I supposed to know what kinds of flowers they were? I would say, "Go ask Grandma."

My mom, sitting on the ridge, would often call out to me when she saw me working with the hoe, "Careful not to cut your foot!"

When I used the sickle she would be even more worried. She would constantly repeat, "Fugui, don't cut your hand!"

Even with my mom on one side reminding me, it wasn't much use. There was too much to do, so I had to work fast. As soon as I would pick up the pace I would inevitably slice my foot or cut my hand, and as soon as my hand or foot would start to bleed, my mother would become frantic. On her twisted little feet, she'd run over and press a clump of mud on the wound to stop the bleeding. And then she would scold me for not being more careful. Once her mouth got going, it went on forever. But I couldn't talk back or she'd start to cry.

My mom would often say the mud of the earth is the best

thing for people's health. Not only could it grow crops, but it could cure diseases, too. In all the years since then, whenever I've injured myself, I've always pressed a clump of wet mud against the wound. My mom was right: you shouldn't scoff at those clumps of mud, as they're a cure for all kinds of sicknesses.

When you're working to the point of exhaustion every day, you don't have time to worry about other things. After renting the land from Long Er, I would fall into a deep sleep each night the moment my head hit the pillow. There was no way I had time to think about anything else. Looking back now, those days were both difficult and exhausting, but my heart was at peace. I thought that the Xu family was once again like a little chicken. If I kept working as I had, within a few years that chicken would become a goose. And one day the Xu family would once again be rich.

I stopped wearing silk clothes after losing the house to Long Er. I wore an outfit my mother had made for me from coarse cloth. When I first began to wear those clothes they felt really uncomfortable, especially the way they rubbed against my skin, but as time went by they became more comfortable. One day Wang Xi died. Wang Xi had been one of our tenants. He was two years older than I was, and before he died he told his son to give me his old silk shirt. He never forgot that I used to be the young master. He wanted me to have the wonderful feeling of wearing silk clothes once more before I died. Me, I felt bad because Wang Xi's heart was really in the right place, but as soon as I put on that silk shirt, I took it right off. That slimy, uncomfortable feeling was unbearable. It felt like I was wearing clothes made of snot.

Then, three months after Long Er had rented the land, Changgen, our family's old worker, showed up. I was working in the field, and Mom and Fengxia were sitting on the ridge. Changgen walked over, wearing torn clothes and leaning on an old, withered tree branch. He was still carrying the same bag and, in his other hand, clasped an empty alms bowl. He'd become a beggar. Fengxia saw him first. She stood up and called, "Changgen! Changgen!"

When my mother saw that it was Changgen, who had grown up in our home, she hurried to greet him. Changgen, wiping away his tears, said, "Madame Xu, I missed the young master and Fengxia. I just came back to see them."

Changgen walked out to the field. When he saw me wearing those coarse clothes covered in mud, he began to cry like a wounded bird, asking, "Young master, how could you have ended up like this?"

After I lost our family property, Changgen was the one who suffered most. Changgen had worked for our family all his life, and, according to custom, when he got old it was supposed to be our family that took care of him. But once our family was reduced to poverty, he had no choice but to leave. All he could do was beg to get by.

Seeing Changgen come back broke my heart. When I was little he would carry me all around on his back. And when I got older I never paid much attention to him. I never dreamed he would return to see us.

"Are you doing all right?" I asked Changgen.

Wiping away his tears, he replied, "Okay."

I asked, "You still haven't found a family to give you work?"

Changgen shook his head. "At my age, whose family would want to hire me?" Hearing this, I wanted to cry. But Changgen still didn't feel his life was difficult—he was crying for me.

"Young master, how can you take this kind of suffering?" he asked.

That night Changgen stayed over in our thatched hut. My mother and I decided to let Changgen stay with us. Although from now on life would be even harder, I told my mom, "Even if it's difficult, we've got to let him stay. If each of us eats just two mouthfuls less of rice we'll be able to support him."

My mom nodded. "Changgen has such a good heart."

The next morning I told Changgen, "Changgen, you've come back at the perfect time. I was just short a helper. From now on you'll stay here."

After hearing my words, Changgen looked at me and laughed. He laughed and laughed until tears began to fall.

"Young master, I don't have the energy to help you any-more," Changgen quietly uttered. "Your good intentions are enough."

With those final words, Changgen left. No matter how hard we tried we couldn't stop him. He said, "Let me go. I'll be back to visit you some other time."

After Changgen left, he came back once more. He brought a

piece of red silk for Fengxia to tie her hair up with. He had found it somewhere, and after cleaning it off he tied it to his waist and brought it all the way here especially for Fengxia. I never saw Changgen again after that.

Since I rented Long Er's land, I was his tenant. I couldn't call him Long Er like I used to; I had to call him Master Long. In the beginning, when Long Er heard me address him like that, he would wave his hands and say, "Fugui, there's no reason for the two of us to be so formal."

But as time went by he got used to it. When I was out in the field he would often come by to chat with me. Once when I was cutting the rice and Fengxia was behind me picking up the fallen ears, Long Er swaggered over. He said to me, "Fugui, I've given up. From now on I'm not going to gamble. No one's a winner at the gambling house. I'm quitting while I'm ahead so as to avoid ending up like you someday."

I bowed to Long Er and said respectfully, "Yes, Master Long."

Long Er pointed to Fengxia and asked, "This is your little brat?"

I bowed again, saying, "Yes, Master Long."

I saw Fengxia standing there with the rice ears in her hand, looking stupefied as she stared at Long Er. I quickly said to her, "Fengxia, hurry up and pay your respects to Master Long."

Fengxia followed my example and bowed to Long Er, saying, "Yes, Master Long."

I would often think of Jiazhen and the child in her belly. Two months after Jiazhen left, a messenger came with an oral message. He said Jiazhen had given birth to a boy. My father-in-law had named him Youqing. My mother quietly asked the messenger, "What's Youqing's last name?"

"Xu," the man replied.

I was out in the field when the message came. My mother rushed out, running on her twisted little feet to tell me. Before she was finished I wiped away my tears. As soon as I heard Jiazhen had borne me a son, I threw down my hoe and began running toward town. I took about ten steps and then stopped. I was afraid that if I went into town to see Jiazhen and our son, my father-in-law wouldn't let me past the door. I said to my mother, "Ma, hurry up and get your things together so you can go visit Jiazhen and the rest of them."

My mom kept saying she wanted to go into town to see her grandson, but after a couple of days she still hadn't gone anywhere. I was in no position to press her. According to custom, if Jiazhen was taken away by her family, then it was her family's responsibility to see her back home. My mom told me, "Youqing's surname is Xu. Jiazhen will be coming home soon."

She added, "Jiazhen's body is weak. It's better for her to stay in town for a while so she has a chance to recover."

When Youqing was six months old, Jiazhen came home. When she returned she didn't ride in a carriage—she walked over ten *li* carrying Youqing in a bag on her back. With his eyes closed and his little head bumping against his mother's shoulders, Youqing came home to meet his dad.

Jiazhen returned wearing a crimson cheongsam and carrying a white bag under her arm. She was beautiful when she came home. Both sides of the road along the way were golden with blooming rapeflowers, and honeybees made a buzzing sound as they flew around. Jiazhen approached our thatched hut and, without pausing, walked up to the door. She stood in the doorway smiling at my mother.

My mother was sitting down weaving a pair of straw sandals. She raised her head to see a beautiful woman standing in the doorway. Jiazhen's body blocked the sunlight, making her silhouette glow. My mother didn't recognize Jiazhen, nor did she see Youqing behind her. My mother asked her, "Who are you? Whom are you looking for?"

After hearing this, Jiazhen's face lit up. She said, "It's me, Jiazhen."

At the time, Fengxia and I were in the field. Fengxia sat on the ridge watching me work. I heard a voice call me. The voice sounded like my mother's, but then again it didn't really sound like hers. I asked Fengxia, "Who's yelling?"

Fengxia turned around to look. She said, "It's Grandma."

I stood up and saw Mom bending over outside the hut, calling me with all her strength. Next to her was Jiazhen in that crimson cheongsam, holding Youqing. As soon as Fengxia saw it was her mother, she made off toward her. I stood there in the paddy field, staring at the way my mother was bending over to call me. She was straining herself, her two hands resting on her knees to prevent the top part of her body from falling over. Fengxia ran too fast, faltering and wobbling over the ridge before finally pouncing on Jiazhen's leg. Holding Youqing, Jiazhen squatted down to hug Fengxia. It was only then that I finally walked up the ridge. Mom was still calling me, and the closer I got to them the more muddleheaded I became. I walked all the way over to Jiazhen and smiled at her. Jiazhen stood up and gazed at me for a moment. I was such a poor sight that Jiazhen lowered her head and gently began to sob.

Her eyes filling with tears of joy, Mom said to me, "I told you Jiazhen is your woman, and no one can take her away."

As soon as Jiazhen came back, our family was complete. Now I had a helper when I worked, and for the first time I began to love and care for my wife. Actually Jiazhen was the one who pointed out to me that I was treating her differently; I myself didn't even realize it.

"Why don't you go up to the ridge for a rest?" I asked her.

Jiazhen was born to an upper-class family in town, and her skin was soft and delicate. My heart broke watching her doing this heavy labor. When Jiazhen heard me telling her to take a rest, she was so happy that she smiled and said, "I'm not tired."

My mother often said, as long as a person is happy at work, then poverty is nothing to be ashamed of. Jiazhen took off her cheongsam and put on the same coarse cloth clothes that I had been wearing. All day she smiled, even though she was so tired that she could barely catch her breath.

Fengxia was a good kid. When we'd moved from our brick house to this thatched hut she stayed as happy as always, and when we had to eat coarse grain she never once went outside to spit it out. When her little brother came home she was even happier. From then on she didn't keep me company in the field—all she wanted to do was hold her baby brother. Poor Youqing—his sister had the opportunity to have four or five good years, but he only stayed in town for six months. Then he came to suffer with me. I feel it's my son I've let down the most.

Life went on like this for a year before my mother got sick. In the beginning she was just dizzy—Mom said everything was fuzzy and blurry when she looked at us. I really didn't think anything of it. I thought, She's getting old, of course her vision isn't as clear as it used to be. Then one day, while Mom was making a fire, her head suddenly fell to one side, resting against the wall as if she was asleep. When Jiazhen and I returned from the field she was still leaning like that. Jiazhen called out to her, but Mom didn't answer. When Jiazhen reached out her hand to shake her, Mom slid down the wall. Jiazhen cried out to me in fear. When I rushed into the kitchen, Mom woke up and stared at us for a while. We tried talking to her, but she didn't answer. Then after a while she smelled something burning and realized that the rice was burnt. It was only then that she finally opened her mouth and said, "Heavens, how could I have fallen asleep?"

In a panic, Mom started to get up but fell right back down. I rushed to carry her to her bed. Over and over again, Mom kept saying that she had fallen asleep, as if she was afraid that we wouldn't believe her. Jiazhen pulled me aside and said, "Go into town and get a doctor."

Getting a doctor takes money, so I stood there without moving. From beneath her mattress, Jiazhen handed me two silver coins wrapped in a handkerchief. Seeing those silver coins made my heart ache—that money was what Jiazhen had brought back from town; all she had left were those two coins. But mother's health made me worry more, so I took those two silver *yuan*.

Jiazhen carefully refolded the handkerchief and put it back under the mattress. She then handed me a set of clean clothes to change into. I said to Jiazhen, "I'm going."

Jiazhen didn't say anything, but saw me to the door. I walked a few steps and turned to see her again. She was fixing her hair as she nodded to me. This was the first time I had left Jiazhen since she had returned home. My clothes were ragged yet clean, and I headed toward the city wearing the new straw sandals that my mother had woven for me. Fengxia sat on the ground near the door, holding Youqing. Noticing how clean and tidy my clothes were, she asked, "Dad, aren't you going down to the field to work?"

I walked fast, and within half an hour I arrived in town—it had been over a year since I'd been there. As I entered the town I felt a kind of emptiness inside. I was afraid I'd bump into an old acquaintance. Who knew what they would say seeing me wearing these raggedy clothes? I was most afraid of seeing my father-in-law. I didn't dare walk down the street the rice shop was on—I preferred to take a detour through some side alleys to avoid running into him. There was only a handful of doctors in town, and I knew every one of them. I also knew which doctors were straightlaced and which made their money by questionable means. I thought for a while and figured it was probably best to get Dr. Lin, who had set up shop next to the silk store. This old man was a friend of my father-in-law's. To save Jiazhen a little face he would probably give me a discount.

As I passed the estate of the county magistrate, I saw a child in silk tiptoeing to the door, trying to grab hold of the copper door-knocker. The child was about the same age as Fengxia, and I suspected he was the magistrate's son. I walked up to him and said, "I'll help you knock."

The child nodded happily, and I grabbed hold of the knocker, banging it a couple of times. Someone inside responded, "Come in."

It was then that the small child said, "Let's run!"

It still didn't hit me what had happened. The child managed to stay out of sight by keeping close to the wall before slipping away. As soon as the door opened a man dressed in servant's clothes appeared. Taking one look at the clothes I was wearing, he just pushed me away without saying a word. I never expected he would do that, and with that one shove I lost my balance and fell down the steps. I picked myself up, and while initially I just wanted to forget it and be on my way, the servant followed me down the stairs to kick me, adding, "You dare come begging without taking a good look at what kind of place this is!"

All at once my temper flared, and I cursed him. "I'd rather gnaw at the rotten bones in your ancestors' graves than beg from you!"

He jumped on me and began hitting me. I took a blow to the head, but not without kicking him. There we were wrestling in the middle of the street. This guy was sly, and seeing that he couldn't beat me he tried kicking me in the groin. Me, I kicked him in the butt a few times. Neither one of us really knew how to fight, so we just wrestled around for a while until a voice from behind yelled, "What a pathetic sight! Two animals grappling about—it's pathetic as all hell!"

We stopped fighting and turned around to see a brigade of
Nationalist troops in yellow uniforms standing behind us. There
were about ten cannons the size of doors being pulled by horses.
The man who had just yelled had a pistol on his belt; he was an
official. The servant really knew how to kiss up. As soon as he saw
the official he immediately nodded and bowed. "Senior officer,
greetings senior officer."

The official waved his hands at us, saying, "Two stupid mules
that don't even know how to fight. Come on and pull this cannon
for me."

As soon as I heard this, the hair on my head stood on end—he
was going to conscript us. The servant was also nervous. He
walked forward and said, "Senior officer, I'm from the house of
the county magistrate."

The official said, "The son of the county magistrate should be
even more willing to serve his country."

"No, no." The servant was so scared he began to stutter. "I'm
not the magistrate's son. Beat me to death and I still wouldn't
dare claim to be his son. Platoon leader, I'm the county magistrate's servant."

"Fuck you!" the official cursed. "I'm the company commander!"

"Yes, yes, company commander, I'm the county magistrate's
servant."

No matter what the servant said it was not only no use, but
it started to annoy the company commander. The commander
stretched out his hand and gave him a wicked slap across the

face. "Stop with the fucking bullshit and go pull the cannon!" he ordered. He looked at me: "You, too!"

I had no choice, so I grabbed hold of one of the horses' reins and went with them. I thought, when the time comes I'll find an opportunity to escape. The servant was still up front pleading with the commander. After walking a ways, the commander surprisingly granted his wish.

"Okay, okay, you can leave," he said. "Little bastard's annoying the hell out of me!"

The servant was so happy, I thought he was going to kneel down and kowtow to the commander. But he didn't kneel, he just kept wringing his hands as he stood before the commander. The company commander said, "What the hell are you waiting for? Get the hell out of here!"

The servant said, "Yes, yes, I'm just leaving."

As the servant finished he turned around and left. The commander took his pistol from his holster, and, straightening his arm and closing one eye, took aim at the servant. The servant had taken over ten steps when he turned around to take a look. What he saw shocked him, and he stood there without moving. Like a sparrow in the night he let the commander take his aim. It was then that the commander said to him, "Get going! Walk!"

The servant thumped to the ground. Kneeling, he called out through his tears, "Company commander, company commander, commander."

The commander fired a shot at him. It didn't hit him, but a ricocheting rock cut his hand. His hand started to bleed. The commander waved his gun at the servant saying, "Stand up, stand up."

He stood up, and the company commander said, "Get out of here, go!"

He cried repentantly, stammering as he spoke, "Commander, I'll pull the cannon."

The commander extended his arm again and for a second time took aim, saying, "You'd better start running!"

And then, as if the servant suddenly understood, he turned around and began to run like hell. Just as the commander fired off a second shot, the servant ran into an alley. Looking at his gun, the commander cursed, "Fuck, I closed the wrong eye."

The company commander turned around and, seeing me standing behind him, approached me with his gun held out. He pressed the barrel of the pistol against my chest and said, "You can leave, too."

My legs began to tremble uncontrollably. I figured even if he closed both eyes this time, he'd still send me to heaven with a single bullet. I pleaded, "I'll pull the cannon, I'll pull the cannon."

With my right hand I grabbed the reins; with my left I firmly grasped the two silver coins in my pocket that Jiazhen had given me. As we left the city I saw some thatched huts in the fields that looked like mine. I lowered my head and began to cry.

I went north with this cannon battalion, and the more we walked the farther away we got. A month later we arrived in Anhui province. The first couple of days all I wanted to do was run away, and at the time I was not the only one with desertion in mind. Every couple days, one or two familiar faces would be missing from the battalion. I wondered if they really had run away, so I asked a veteran soldier called Old Quan.

"Nobody gets away," explained Old Quan.

Old Quan asked me if I heard those shots fired at night while we were asleep, and I said I'd heard them. He told me, "Those are your deserters. Even the lucky ones who aren't shot end up being caught by other units."

As Old Quan spoke, my heart froze. Old Quan told me he was conscripted during the War of Resistance. When his troop set out for Jiangxi he deserted, but within a few days he was conscripted again by the troop going to Fujian. By then he had been in the army six years and had yet to fight the Japanese. All he'd fought were communist guerrilla detachments. During his period of conscription, Old Quan had run away seven times, and each time another unit had captured him. The last time he tried to escape he had made it within a hundred *li* of his home, and then he ran into this cannon battalion. Old Quan said he didn't want to run away anymore.

"I'm sick of running," he said.

After we crossed the Yangtze River we wore cotton-padded jackets. And as soon as we passed the Yangtze, my dream of deserting also died. The farther I got from home, the less courage I had to attempt escape. In our company we had about a dozen fifteen- or sixteen-year-old boys. Among these soldiers was a kid named Chunsheng, from Jiangsu province. He would always ask me if there was really fighting to the north, and I'd say there was, but actually I didn't know. I thought, if you're a soldier then fighting should be inevitable. I was closest with Chunsheng. He would always be next to me, pulling my arm, asking, "Do you think we'll be killed?"

"I don't know," I'd reply.

As he asked me this my heart would feel wave after wave of pain. After we crossed the Yangtze, we began to hear the sound of cannons and guns. In the beginning it would echo from far away, but after walking two more days the gunfire grew louder and louder. It was then that we arrived at a small village. There weren't any animals in that village, let alone people—there wasn't a living being anywhere in sight. The company commander ordered us to set up the cannons, and I knew that this time we were really going into battle. Someone walked over and asked the commander, "Commander, where are we?"

The commander said, "You're asking me? Well, how the fuck am I supposed to know? Who the fuck am I supposed to ask?"

The company commander didn't know where we were, and the peasants had all run away. I looked around in all directions. Other than some bare trees and a few thatched huts, there was nothing. Two days later there were more and more common soldiers in yellow uniforms. They came unit by unit from all directions, and some of the battalions set up camp right beside us. After another two days we still had yet to fire a single cannon when our company commander told us, "We've been surrounded."

We weren't the only company to be surrounded—there were somewhere around a hundred thousand Nationalist troops that were surrounded within a twenty *li* square area. Everyone in

sight was wearing these yellow uniforms; it looked like a temple
fair. Old Quan was really something. He sat on a dirt mound outside a tunnel, smoking and watching the yellow-skinned common soldiers go back and forth. From time to time he'd say hello
to one of them—he really knew a lot of people. Old Quan had
been all over, having drifted through seven different units. He
laughed, told dirty jokes to some old friends and exchanged gossip on some other soldiers. It seemed as if everyone they asked
about was either dead or someone had just seen them within the
last few days. Old Quan told Chunsheng and me that back in the
day all those guys had tried to run away with him. Just as Old
Quan was speaking, someone called over in our direction, "Old
Quan, you're still not dead?"

Old Quan bumped into another old friend. Quan laughed.
"You little bastard, when did they catch you?"

Before that guy could reply, someone else called Old Quan,
who turned his head to look and jumped up to yell, "Hey, where's
Old Liang?"

The guy laughed and yelled back, "Dead."

Dejected, Old Quan sat back down, cursing, "Fuck, he still
owes me a silver piece."

"You see?" Old Quan proudly continued, telling Chunsheng
and me, "Nobody succeeds in deserting."

In the beginning the Liberation Army just surrounded us, but
they didn't attack right off, so we weren't really afraid. The company commander wasn't afraid, either. He said that Generalissimo Chiang Kai-shek would send in tanks to save us. Later, even
when the rifle and cannon shots in front of us got louder and

louder, we weren't scared, just bored. The company commander still hadn't ordered us to start firing the cannons. One veteran soldier thought that sitting idle while our brothers-in-arms were on the front lines shedding their blood and sacrificing their lives was no kind of plan, so he asked the commander, "Shouldn't we fire a few shots from the cannons?"

At the time the commander was in a tunnel gambling. He furiously snapped back, "Fire the cannons? In which direction should we fire them?"

The company commander had a point: What if our cannons hit our Nationalist brothers-in-arms? The Nationalist troops in front would instantly turn around and teach us a lesson. This wasn't a game. The commander ordered us to stay in the tunnels. We could do whatever the hell we wanted, as long as we didn't fire the cannons.

After being surrounded for a while our supplies of food and ammunition were close to empty. Whenever a plane appeared overhead, the Nationalist troops below crowded together like a colony of ants. No one wanted the trunks of ammunition that were thrown out of the plane; everyone piled onto the bags of rice. As soon as the plane left, the soldiers who got their hands on some rice would carry it off to their tunnels. Two men would carry one bag while others beside them would fire shots into the air to protect the carriers. Only then would the crowds start to break up, and everyone would return to their tunnels.

Before long, groups of Nationalist troops surged out of their tunnels toward the houses and leafless trees. Men were climbing on the roofs of thatched houses near and far, tearing down huts and cutting down trees. This was almost like going into battle, and the cacophony that followed almost drowned out the sounds of the gunshots in the forward position. In less than half a day, all the houses and trees were gone. All that was left on the desolate land were soldiers walking around with house beams and tree branches on their shoulders, while others carried planks and stools. After returning to their tunnels they began to cook rice. The smoke rose up, twisting and turning in the sky.

At the time, what we had most of were bullets. No matter where you'd lie down they would press up against you until it hurt. After all of the houses and trees around us had been torn and cut down, soldiers flooded the land, cutting dead grass with their bayonets. The scene was just like the busy season when farmers harvest rice. There were even a few soldiers who, covered in sweat, dug at the roots of some trees. And then there were some who started to dig up graves, using the weathered coffin boards as fuel for fire. As they dug up the coffins they'd just throw the bones of the deceased to one side, not even bothering to rebury them. When you're in the kind of situation we were in, bones of the deceased are nothing to be afraid of. If you had to sleep pressed up against them you wouldn't even have a nightmare. There was less and less firewood to cook the rice with, while there was more and more rice. No one fought over the rice anymore. In fact, Old Quan, Chunsheng and I carried a few bags of rice back to our tunnel to use as a bed to sleep on, so we could avoid the discomfort of bullets pressing against us.

It had gotten to the point when all possible sources of cooking fuel were exhausted, yet the Generalissimo still hadn't come to save us. It was a good thing that the planes stopped air-dropping rice and began sending down flatbread. As soon as the packages of flatbread hit the ground, our brothers dived recklessly on top like animals trying to get their share. The way they piled on top of one another, layer after layer, was exactly how my mom used to weave the soles of my shoes. The way they screamed was no different from a pack of wild wolves.

"Let's split up and snatch some," suggested Old Quan.

Splitting up was our only chance of getting our hands on some flatbread. We crawled out of the tunnel, and I chose a direction. There were shots being fired close by, and there would often be stray bullets whizzing past me. One time I was making a run for it when the guy next to me suddenly just fell down. I thought he had passed out from hunger, but when I turned around I saw that half of his head was missing. It scared me so bad that my legs went soft and I almost collapsed. Getting your hands on some flatbread was even harder than it had been to get rice. It was said that the Nationalists were losing more men by the day, but as soon as that plane would appear in the sky, everyone suddenly popped out of the ground, and the barren earth appeared instantly to have grown row after row of grass that moved with the plane. As soon as the flatbread was air-dropped, the soldiers on the ground split up, each person rushing to the parachute he had his eye on. The bread packages weren't sturdy, either, so as soon as they hit the ground they broke apart. Dozens if not a hundred men would all rush to the same spot. Some of the soldiers collided, knocking each other unconscious before they even got close to the drop point. I tried to get some, but aside from a few measly bread cakes, all I ended up with was a sore body—it was as if someone had tied me up and whipped me with a belt. When I got back to the tunnel, Old Quan was already sitting there. His face was all black-and-blue, yet he hadn't even ended up with as many bread cakes as I had. Old Quan, who had been in the army eight years, still had a good heart. He put his bread on top of mine and said, "Wait until Chunsheng gets back, and we'll eat together." We kneeled down in the tunnel with our heads sticking out, watching for Chunsheng.

After a while we saw Chunsheng running with his back arched, and he was carrying a pile of rubber shoes. The kid was so happy his face was bright red. He tumbled into the tunnel and, pointing at the rubber shoes that covered the ground, asked us, "Did I get a lot or what?"

Old Quan flashed me a confused look and asked Chunsheng, "Can we eat them?"

Chunsheng said, "We can use them to cook rice."

We thought about it and immediately realized that Chunsheng was on to something. Seeing there wasn't a single mark on Chunsheng's face, Old Quan said to me, "This little bastard has got one up on both of us."

From then on we didn't fight over flatbread; we followed Chunsheng's method. When everyone was piled up on one another fighting over bread, we took off their shoes. Some didn't flinch, while others would kick wildly. We carried a steel helmet with us and would viciously hit those naughty feet with it. The feet that took our beatings would twitch a few times and then become stiff, as if they had been frozen. We carried the rubber shoes back to our cave to start a fire. At least we had rice, and this way we could avoid getting our asses whipped. As we cooked our rice we watched those barefoot guys half-walking, half-hopping around in the middle of winter. We couldn't stop laughing.

The sounds of the guns and cannons came closer and closer, and it didn't seem to matter if it was night or day. We stayed in our tunnel and slowly grew accustomed to the noises outside. Often a bomb would explode nearby. All of the cannons in our company were destroyed; we never got the chance to fire even a single shot, and already they had become a pile of worthless steel. We became increasingly bored. After a few more days, Chunsheng wasn't even scared anymore—being scared was no use. The gun and cannon shots got closer and closer, but we always thought they were still far away. The worst was that it was growing colder by the day. At night we could only sleep a few minutes at a time before we would wake up freezing. The cannon explosions outside would shake the ground and leave us with our ears ringing.

No matter what anyone said, Chunsheng was still a child. On one occasion he was sleeping like a baby when a bomb exploded nearby, jolting him awake. After jumping out of his makeshift bed, he went outside and stood on top of our tunnel, yelling angrily in the direction of the explosions, "Quiet the fuck down! You're so noisy I can't get any sleep!"

As I rushed to pull him back in, bullets were already flying back and forth above our tunnel.

The Nationalist front was getting smaller by the day. Unless we were starving, in which case we would sneak out to look for something to eat, we didn't dare climb out of our cave. Every day thousands of wounded were carried away. Our unit was stationed in the lower area of the front, so it became a haven for the wounded. During those days we spent holed up in our tunnel, Old Quan, Chunsheng and I would stick our heads out to watch the wounded soldiers being carried over on stretchers, their arms missing and legs broken. Before too much time could pass, another long string of stretchers would come by. The guys carrying the stretchers would arch their backs and, running over to an empty space on the ground near us, yell, "One, two, three." When they got to three they'd turn the stretchers over as if they were dumping out garbage, then throw the wounded on the ground and leave them. The wounded were in so much pain they screamed out in agony—string after string of their screams and cries reached us. Old Quan eyed those men carrying the stretchers, and as they walked away he cursed them. "Animals!"

There were more and more wounded soldiers. As long as there were explosions on the front, there were more stretchers headed our way. Yelling, "One, two, three," they'd drop the wounded on the ground. At first the injured lay in different piles, but before long the piles all ran together. They continued screaming out in agony. As long as I live I'll never forget the sound of those tortured screams. As Chunsheng and I watched we felt wave after wave of bitter cold drive into our hearts—even Old Quan knit his brow in anger. I wondered how we were supposed to fight this battle.

As soon as night fell it began to snow. For a long time there were no more gunshots. We only heard the cries of the thousands of wounded men left for dead outside the cave. Their screams seemed like a combination of crying and laughter. That sound of unbearable pain—I never again in my life heard such a terrifying sound. The snow was like a floodwater rushing down over us, one large flake after another. In the darkness we couldn't even make out the falling snowflakes—there was only the feeling of our bodies becoming damp and cold. The soft snowflakes would melt slowly in our hands, but before long another thick layer would accumulate.

Hungry and cold, the three of us huddled up together to sleep. By then the planes rarely came, so it was very difficult to find things to eat. Any hope of the Generalissimo coming to save us was dead; from that point on no one knew if we would survive. Chunsheng pushed me and asked, "Fugui, are you asleep?"

"No," I whispered.

He then nudged Old Quan, who didn't respond. Sniveling, Chunsheng said to me, "This time we're not going to make it."

As I heard this I could feel my tears welling up inside. It was only then that Old Quan opened his mouth. Stretching his arms he said, "Don't talk about this depressing stuff."

He sat up and said, "I've been in dozens of battles since I was a kid, and each time I say to myself: I've got to live. Bullets have brushed by every part of my body, but they've never hurt me. Chunsheng, as long as you believe you won't die, you'll make it."

After that no one said a word, but we were each lost in our own thoughts. All I thought about was my family. I imagined

Fengxia sitting by the door holding Youqing, and I pictured my mom and Jiazhen. I thought and thought about them until I was all blocked up inside and couldn't breathe. It felt as if someone were holding my nose and covering my mouth.

After midnight, the cries of the wounded outside the tunnel gradually faded. I thought that most of them had fallen asleep. There were only a few left still moaning in pain. Those sounds, one phrase at a time fading in and out, sounded like someone talking: You ask a question, he answers. The dreary voices didn't seem to come from the living. And then after a while there was only one voice left crying. That voice was so soft it seemed like a mosquito buzzing back and forth around my face. After I listened for a while it didn't seem to be groaning, but rather singing a short melody. All around it was so silent that not a sound could be heard, only that voice, eternally twisting and turning. I listened until tears fell from my eyes. After the tears melted the snow on my face, they trickled down my neck, making it feel like a cold wind had blown in.

When the sun came up there was not a sound. We stuck out our heads to look; the thousands of wounded troops who had been calling out the night before were all dead. They lay there in disarray, not moving a muscle, covered by a light blanket of snow. Those of us hiding in the tunnels who were still alive stared blankly at them for what seemed like an eternity. No one said a word. Even a veteran like Old Quan, who had seen god-knows-how-many corpses, stared dumbfounded for a long time. Finally he sighed and, shaking his head, said to us, "It's terrible."

As Old Quan spoke he climbed out of the tunnel and walked

over to the field of the dead. Bending as he turned over this one and picked up that one, Old Quan walked among the dead. Every now and again he'd squat down to wipe someone's face with the snow. It was then that the firing resumed, sending a series of bullets flying our way. Chunsheng and I immediately snapped out of our daze and called out to Old Quan, "Get back here, quick!"

Old Quan didn't answer us—he just kept looking around. After a while he finally stood up, turned around to look our way and began walking toward us. As he approached he held up four fingers to Chunsheng and me. Shaking his head he said, "I know four of them."

As soon as he finished, Old Quan's eyes suddenly opened wide and his legs froze. Then he fell kneeling on the ground. We didn't know what had happened—but then we saw a string of bullets shooting by. We screamed with everything we had, "Old Quan, hurry!"

It was only after calling a few times and seeing that Old Quan still hadn't moved that I realized it was over. Old Quan had been hit. I quickly climbed out of the tunnel and ran toward him. When I got to him I saw that his back was soaked in blood. My vision went blank, and I cried out in tears to Chunsheng. After Chunsheng ran over, the two of us carried Old Quan back to the tunnel. On the way back, bullets whizzed by, brushing past us.

We laid Old Quan down, and I used my hand to stop the pool of blood on his back. His back was wet and hot, and the blood, still flowing, oozed out from the cracks between my fingers. Old Quan's eyes blinked slowly as if he wanted to see us for a moment, and then his lips quivered. His voice sounded hoarse as he asked us, "What's the name of this place?"

Chunsheng and I raised our heads to look around. How were we supposed to know what this place was? We could only go back to looking at Old Quan. He closed his eyes tightly for a while before slowly opening them. As they opened they got larger and larger, and his mouth was crooked as if he was forcing a smile. We heard his raspy voice say, "I don't even know the name of the place where I'll die."

Not long after finishing that sentence, Old Quan died. As he took his last breath, Old Quan's head tilted to one side. Chunsheng and I both knew that he was gone; we stared at each other for a long time. Chunsheng cried first, and as soon as he began to weep, I, too, could no longer hold back my tears.

Later we saw the company commander, who had changed into civilian clothes. With paper banknotes tied to his waist and carrying a bag, he was heading west. We knew he wanted to escape with his life. With the banknotes stuffed under his clothes, he walked with a rolling gait, making him look like a fat old woman. A young soldier called out to him, "Commander, isn't the Generalissimo Chiang Kai-shek going to save us?"

The commander turned around and said, "You idiot, at a time like this not even your own mother would save you! Why don't you save yourself?" Another soldier took a shot at him but missed. As soon as he heard the sound of bullets coming at him, the commander started to run like mad, and his former air of authority completely disappeared. A whole bunch of guys extended their guns to shoot him, and the commander cried out as he jumped back and forth in the snow, running farther away.

The sounds of cannon and gunfire were right under our noses. We could see the shadows of the soldiers shooting on the front, and through the veil of gunpowder smoke we could see the bodies, one after another, sway and fall to the ground. I estimated that I wouldn't make it past noon—sometime before then it should be my turn to die. After making it through a month amid the gun blasts and bomb explosions, I wasn't really afraid of death. I just felt that dying in the dark like this was really an injustice. Not even my mother or Jiazhen would know where I had died.

I looked at Chunsheng, and he looked back at me with a long face, his hand still on Old Quan's body. We had eaten uncooked rice for a few days until Chunsheng's face became swollen. He stuck out his tongue to lick his lips and said to me, "I want some flatbread."

It had gotten to the point where life or death wasn't important anymore. As long as we could taste some flatbread before we died we'd be satisfied. Chunsheng stood up, and I didn't bother to tell him to watch out for bullets. He looked around for a while and said, "Perhaps there's some flatbread outside. I'm going to go look."

As Chunsheng crawled out of the tunnel I didn't stop him. No matter what, we were both going to be dead before noon anyway, and if he could really get his hands on some flatbread before then, well, good for him. He looked exhausted as he crossed over the field of corpses. After taking a few steps, he turned around to say to me, "Don't go anywhere. I'll be back as soon as I get my hands on some flatbread."

With his hands at his sides and his head lowered, he entered the cloud of thick smoke in front of him. The air was dense, filled with the burning scent of gunpowder. The smoke-filled air made my throat itch, and small grains of charred ash got caught in my eyes.

Before noon all those still alive in the tunnels had been taken prisoner. When the Liberation Army, guns in hand, came charging forward, an old soldier told us to put our hands up. His anxious face turned blue as he ordered us not to touch the guns on our waists. He was just as scared as we were. One communist soldier, not much older than Chunsheng, pointed the dark barrel of his pistol at me. My heart stopped and I thought, this time I'm really dead. But he didn't shoot. He just shouted an order at me. As soon as I heard him command me to crawl out, my heart started beating wildly, and my wish to live returned. I crawled out of the cave and he said to me, "Put your hands down."

Immediately I relaxed my hands, as well as my anxious heart. All by himself, the soldier marched us twenty-odd prisoners south. Before getting too far we met up with an even larger group of captives. All around us thick smoke twisted and turned as it rose toward the heavens, moving as if it were heading toward the same place in the sky. The ground was bumpy and rough, littered with dead bodies and the blasted remains of firearms and shells. A military truck blackened by flames still made a rustling sound. After we walked for a while, twenty Liberation soldiers came toward us from the north, carrying large white steamed buns. The buns were still hot, and just looking at them made my mouth water. The official escorting us said, "Line yourselves up!"

I had never imagined they would feed us. How wonderful it would have been if only Chunsheng had been there. I gazed off into the distance, not knowing if he was dead or alive. We huddled up close together in more than twenty different lines. Each of us got two steamed buns, and I had never before heard the sound of so many people eating at the same time. It was even louder than the sound of a couple hundred pigs devouring their feed. Everyone ate too fast, and a few even started coughing their guts out, each one seeming to cough louder than the next. The guy beside me coughed louder than anyone—he coughed so hard that he was in tears and had to hold his waist. Even more people got the buns stuck in their throats. They lifted their heads and stared up at the sky without moving.

The next morning we were all summoned over to an empty field. We sat in neat rows on the ground in front of two tables. A guy who looked like a top official spoke to us. First he gave us a barrel of stuff about liberating all of China and then he said, "Whoever is willing to join the Liberation Army, stay where you are, if you want to go home, stand up and go pick up your travel allowances."

As soon as I heard I could go home, my heart began to race violently. But when I saw the pistol on that official's waist I began to get scared—it seemed too good to be true. Most people stayed where they were without moving, but a few actually did get up to leave. They walked up to the table and picked up their travel allowances. The official kept staring at them. After they got their travel money they picked up a travel certificate and went on their way. In my heart I was convinced that that official was going to take out his gun and shoot them, just like our company commander had done. But as they walked into the distance the official still didn't take out his gun. I started to get nervous, realizing that the Liberation Army was really willing to let us go home. After fighting this battle, I knew what this thing called war was. I promised myself never to fight again. I wanted to go home. I stood up and walked over to the official. I dropped to my knees and began to wail like a baby. I had originally planned on telling him that I wanted to go home, but when the words got to my lips they changed. I called out over and over, "Company commander, commander, commander . . ."

Nothing else would come out. The official helped me up and asked me what I wanted to say. But I just kept calling him company commander; I kept crying. One of the Liberation troops standing beside me corrected me, "He's the regimental commander."

As soon as he said this I was scared to death. I thought, I'm fucked. But I heard the roaring laughter of the prisoners sitting on the ground, and I saw the regimental commander laughing as he asked me, "What was it that you wanted to say?"

It was only then that I finally relaxed and said to the commander, "I want to go home."

The Liberation Army let me go home, and they even paid my travel expenses. Heading south I rushed the whole way home. When I got hungry I just used some of the travel money the Liberation Army had given me to buy something to eat. When I was tired, I just looked for a plot of flat ground and went to sleep. I couldn't bear how much I missed home. Just thinking about being able to reunite in this life with my mom, Jiazhen and my two kids filled me with laughter and tears. Overcome by homesickness, I ran south.

As I got to the Yangtze River, I realized that the south had yet to be liberated. The Liberation Army was just getting ready to cross the river. I couldn't pass and was delayed there a couple of months. I had to go all over looking for work to do so I wouldn't starve to death. I knew the Liberation Army needed boat rowers, and back when I had money I had learned how to row a boat just for the fun of it. On a number of occasions I almost joined the Liberation Army to help it row across the Yangtze. I figured that since they had been so good to me, I ought to do something to repay their kindness. But I was really terrified of war and afraid I'd never see my family again. For the sake of Jiazhen and my family I said to myself, I won't repay them, I'll just remember that the Liberation Army was good to me.

Keeping behind the Liberation Army as it fought its way south, I made it home. Altogether I'd been gone almost two years. When I left it was mid-autumn; when I came back it was the beginning of autumn. Covered in mud, I walked the road home. When I got to my village I found it hadn't changed a bit. As soon as I saw it, I began to rush forward. I saw my family's old brick house, and then I saw our thatched hut. As soon as I laid eyes on the thatched hut I couldn't help but break into a run.

Not far from the edge of the village I saw a girl around seven or eight with a boy around three cutting grass. The second I saw that girl in her raggedy clothes I recognized her—she was my Fengxia. Fengxia held Youqing's hand as he stumbled along. I called out to them, "Fengxia, Youqing!"

Fengxia didn't hear me, but Youqing turned around to see me. Fengxia kept pulling him as his head turned around crookedly to look at me. I yelled again, "Fengxia, Youqing!"

This time Youqing pulled his sister to a stop and Fengxia turned around to see me. I ran over to them and, kneeling down, asked Fengxia, "Fengxia, do you still remember me?"

Fengxia opened her eyes wide and looked me over. Her lips moved but she didn't say anything. I said to Fengxia, "I'm your daddy."

Fengxia smiled, and her mouth opened wide, but she still didn't make a sound. At that moment I sensed that something wasn't quite right, but I didn't think much of it. I knew that Fengxia recognized me. When she smiled at me I saw she had lost all her teeth. As I reached out my hand to touch her face, her eyes lit up and she brought her face closer to my hand. Then I turned to Youqing. He of course didn't recognize me. Youqing was so scared that he cuddled up close to his sister. I tried to pull him, but he ran away. I said to him, "Son, I'm your dad."

Youqing hid behind his sister. Tugging on her, he said, "Let's go."

It was then that a woman started running toward us, crying out my name. I recognized that it was Jiazhen, stumbling as she ran. When she got to me she called out, "Fugui!"

She then fell to the ground and began to bawl. I said to Jiazhen, "Why are you crying? What's there to cry about?"

Yet, before I could finish my sentence, I had also started to weep.

I was finally home and, seeing that Jiazhen and the kids were doing well, I felt at peace.

Hugging, we all walked back to the hut. As soon as we got close, I started calling out, "Mom, Mom."

I called out to her as I ran into the hut, but after one look I saw she wasn't there. My vision went blurry for a moment, and I turned around and asked Jiazhen, "Where's Mom?"

Jiazhen didn't say a word. She just looked at me, her eyes glistening with tears. I knew where Mom had gone. I stood in the doorway with my head lowered, and the tears began to fall.

Mom had died just over two months after I'd left. Jiazhen told me that before Mom died she kept telling Jiazhen over and over, "I'm sure that Fugui didn't go gambling."

Heaven knows how many times Jiazhen went into town to see what she could find out about me, but in the end not a soul told her I was forced into the army. And my poor mom—even though she had tried to console Jiazhen, when she died she didn't even know where I was. Fengxia also had had it hard. A year before, after running a high fever, she had lost her voice. She hadn't been able to speak since. Jiazhen cried as she told me this. Fengxia, sitting across from us, knew we were talking about her. Fengxia smiled softly at me; seeing her smile was like a needle piercing my heart. Youqing also recognized me as his dad, but he was still a little bit afraid of me. As soon as I'd pick him up, he'd instantly struggle to go see Jiazhen and Fengxia. But no matter what, I was back home. The first night, no matter how hard I tried, I just couldn't get to sleep. I was squeezed together between Jiazhen and the two kids, listening to the sound of the wind blowing the straw on the roof and gazing at the glittering moonlight beaming in through the crack between the door and its frame. I felt both fulfillment and warmth. After a while I caressed Jiazhen and the children. I said to myself over and over again, "I'm home."

After I got home, the village began land reform, and I was given five *mu* of land, the same five *mu* that I had originally rented from Long Er. Long Er was really in deep trouble—he was labeled a landlord, and after not even four years of putting on airs, Liberation came and he was finished. The Communist Party confiscated his land and divided it among his tenants. But Long Er would rather die than admit he was finished. He tried to intimidate some of his tenants, and when they wouldn't give in to his threats, he even tried to beat them. Long Er screwed himself. The people's government had him arrested, calling him a despotic landlord. Even after being taken to the city prison, Long Er still showed no understanding of the times. He was as stubborn as a mule. In the end he was executed.

The day they executed Long Er, I went to watch. Only at the last minute before he died did Long Er start to break down. Someone said that as he was dragged out of town on his way to the execution ground, tears and drool ran down his face and he said to a friend, "Even in my dreams I never imagined I'd be executed!"

Long Er really was extremely foolish. He thought that they'd lock him up for a few days and that would be that. Never for a second did he believe they'd execute him. It was during the afternoon in a neighboring village that they shot Long Er. They began by digging a hole. A crowd of people from all the neighboring villages came to watch. When Long Er came by he was all tied up—they practically had to drag him. His mouth was half-open as he huffed and heaved, trying to catch his breath. Long Er glanced at me as he passed by. I didn't think he had recognized me, but after a few steps he forced his head around. Sniveling, he yelled, "Fugui, I'm dying for you!"

After hearing him yell that, I was flustered. I thought it would perhaps be best if I left and did not see how he died. I squeezed my way out of the crowd and walked away in the opposite direction. After taking about ten steps I heard the "bang" sound of a gunshot and thought, Long Er is really done for. I never imagined that it would be followed by a second "bang," and then three more—all together there were five shots. I wondered if they were executing someone else. On the way back I asked someone from my village, "How many people did they execute?"

"Just Long Er," he replied.

Long Er really got dealt a bad hand. He took five shots—I'm afraid all five of his lives, if he had that many, were wiped out.

After Long Er was executed, cold chills ran up and down my neck the whole way home. The more I thought about it, the more I realized just how close I had come to being in Long Er's shoes. If it hadn't been for my father and me, the two prodigal sons, I would have been the one to be executed. I rubbed my face and arms—they were all okay. I thought, I should have died but didn't. I escaped with my life from the battlefield, and when I came home Long Er took my place as the fall guy. The graves of my ancestors must have been in the right place.

"This time," I said to myself, "I've got to keep on living."

When I got home, Jiazhen was stitching the soles of my shoes. She took one look at how pale my face was and got scared nearly to death. She thought I was sick. But when I told her what I had been thinking, her face turned white, too, and then blue.

"That was really close," she whispered.

Later, I didn't take it so much to heart. I figured there was no reason to scare myself like this; it was all fate. As the saying goes, "If you escape a calamity with your life, there is bound to be good fortune to follow." I figured the second half would just get better and better. I told this to Jiazhen. She broke a strand of thread with her teeth and looked at me.

"I don't want any kind of good fortune," she said. "I'll be happy if I'm able to sew you a new pair of shoes each year."

I understood what Jiazhen meant: My wife just wished that from now on we would never again be apart. Seeing how much older her face looked, my heart began to ache. Jiazhen was right. As long as our family could be together every day, who really cared about good fortune?

Fugui's narration stopped here. I realized we were both sitting right in the sun. The changing path of the sunlight had caused the shadow of the tree to gradually leave us and turn in another direction. Fugui's body shook a bit before he could stand up. As he patted his knees he said to me, "My whole body keeps getting stiffer and stiffer. Only one part keeps getting softer."

After hearing that, I couldn't help but laugh out loud. I looked down at his drooping pants and saw some blades of grass there. He also laughed, happy that I got his joke. Then he turned around and called out to his ox, "Fugui."

The ox had emerged from the water and was eating the grass beside the pond. He stood under a pair of willow trees. The willow branches extending over his back had lost their perpendicular quality and appeared disorderly and crooked. Brushing against the ox's back, a few leaves floated slowly to the ground. The old man called out again, "Fugui."

The ox's rump looked like a big rock as he slowly moved back into the water, and then his head reappeared, breaking through the willow branches. His two round eyes leisurely turned to look at us, and the old man told him, "Jiazhen and the rest of them have already started working. You've rested enough. I know you haven't eaten your fill, but who told you to stay in the water so long?"

Fugui led the ox to the irrigated field, and while he was hooking up the plow he said to me, "When oxen get old, they're just like old men. When they are hungry they've got to rest for a while so they have energy to eat."

I sat back down under the shade of the tree. Putting my backpack behind me, I leaned up against the tree and used my straw hat as a fan. Long flaps of skin on the ox's stomach were sagging; as he moved the plow, his stomach was like a big water balloon, with the water sloshing around inside. I noticed Fugui's pants hanging down, which looked just like the skin on the ox's stomach.

That day I sat in the shade of the tree until dusk fell. I didn't leave because Fugui's story wasn't finished.

⊡

Those years after I returned home were difficult, but I guess you could say they went smoothly. Fengxia and Youqing got bigger by the day, and me, I got older and older. I didn't really notice, and neither did Jiazhen. I just felt like I didn't have as much energy as I used to. Then one day when I was carrying a load of vegetables into town, a friend called out to me as I passed the old silk shop, "Fugui, your hair's turned all gray."

It had only been six months since I'd last seen him. As soon as he said that I began to feel really old. When I got home I looked Jiazhen up and down. She didn't know what was going on. She lowered her head to look herself over, and looked behind her, and finally asked, "What are you looking at?"

I laughed as I told her, "Your hair's gray, too."

That year Fengxia turned seventeen, and she began to look like a woman. If she hadn't been deaf and mute, people would have already been knocking on our door with marriage proposals. All the people in the village said Fengxia had grown up into a pretty young woman; she looked almost the same as Jiazhen had when she was young. Youqing was twelve years old and was going to elementary school in town.

Some years earlier, Jiazhen and I had hesitated about whether or not we should send Youqing to school—we simply didn't have the money. At the time Fengxia was only twelve or thirteen, and although she could help Jiazhen and me with some work in the field and around the house, she was still dependent on us. Jiazhen and I discussed whether we should just give her to someone else and be done with it. That way we could save some extra money for Youqing to go to school. Even though Fengxia was deaf and mute, she was smart. As soon as Jiazhen and I started discussing giving her away, Fengxia would come over and stare at us. Her two eyes would blink and our hearts would want to break, and we wouldn't bring it up again for a couple of days.

But seeing Youqing getting closer and closer to school age, I knew I couldn't put it off any longer. I had some of the people in the village ask around to see if anyone was willing to raise a twelve-year-old girl. I told Jiazhen, "If a good family wants her, Fengxia will have an even better life than she has now."

Jiazhen nodded, but her tears still fell. A mother's heart is always a bit soft. I tried to convince Jiazhen to be a little more open-minded. Fate had dealt Fengxia a cruel hand, and I was afraid that in this life she was going to suffer the worst. But Youqing shouldn't suffer all his life—only if we let him go to school would he have a good future. We couldn't allow the kids to be set back by poverty. At least one of them should be able to have a better life one day.

The people in the village who had asked around about Fengxia came back saying she was a little too old; had she been a year younger there would have been a lot of families interested. Hearing that, we pretty much gave up on that idea. We never expected that a month later two different families would send messages saying they wanted our Fengxia. One family wanted her for their daughter, the other wanted her to look after an old couple. Jiazhen and I both thought that the family without a daughter was better. If they took Fengxia as their daughter they would love her and care for her more than the elderly couple would. We sent a verbal message for them to come take a look. The couple came, and after seeing Fengxia they really liked her, but as soon as they learned she couldn't speak they changed their minds. The husband said, "She looks good, but . . ."

Without finishing they politely left. Jiazhen and I had no choice but to let the other family take Fengxia. The other family didn't care whether or not Fengxia could speak, just as long as she would work hard.

The day they came to take Fengxia away I was carrying my hoe, getting ready to go out to the field, and she immediately grabbed a basket and sickle to go with me. For years, whenever I went out to work in the field, Fengxia would always be by my side cutting grass; I had grown accustomed to having her with me. That day, when I saw her following me, I pushed her away so she would go back. She looked at me with her wide eyes. I put down my hoe and pulled her back to the hut. I took the basket and sickle out of her hands and threw them in the corner. She was still looking at me with her large eyes, not knowing that we had given her away. When Jiazhen gave her a crimson outfit to change into, she no longer looked at me, but just lowered her head and let Jiazhen help her change clothes. That outfit was made from the material of Jiazhen's old cheongsam. As Jiazhen buttoned her up, Fengxia's tears fell one by one onto her leg. Fengxia knew she was going to leave. I took my hoe and walked out. When I got to the door I said to Jiazhen, "I'm going out to the field. When they come to get Fengxia, you just let her go. Don't come looking for me."

When I got to the field, I took my hoe in hand and tried to get to work, but I just couldn't get my energy up. Looking around and not seeing Fengxia there cutting the grass made me feel empty inside. Realizing that I would no longer have Fengxia there next to me as I worked the field, I could hardly stand it. I felt like all my energy had drained away. It was then that I saw Fengxia standing on the ridge, with a fifty-year-old man beside her holding her hand. Fengxia's tears flowed down her face; she cried so hard that her body began to shake. Fengxia's tears were silent. From time to time she'd raise her hand to wipe her eyes, and I knew she was doing it so she could see her daddy clearly. The man smiled to me and said, "Don't worry, I'll take good care of her."

Finishing his sentence, he tugged Fengxia away, and she left with him. As Fengxia's hand was being pulled away, she kept her body twisted in my direction, so she could keep looking at me. Fengxia walked farther and farther away until I could no longer see her eyes, and after a while I couldn't even see her arms, which she kept raising to wipe the tears from her eyes. By then I couldn't take it—with my head cocked to one side, the tears began to fall. When Jiazhen came by I blamed her. "I told you not to let them come over. I told you not to let them come see me."

Jiazhen said, "It wasn't me. Fengxia wanted to see you."

After Fengxia left, Youqing stopped listening to us. When Fengxia was taken away, Youqing just watched, not knowing what was going on. Only after Fengxia had gotten far away did Youqing scratch his head and slowly make his way home. I saw him looking over at me a few times, but he didn't come over to ask what was going on. When he was still in Jiazhen's stomach I had hit him, so he was scared of me.

Without Fengxia at the table during lunchtime, Youqing took two bites and refused to eat any more. His eyes moved back and forth from Jiazhen to me. Jiazhen said to him, "Hurry up and eat."

He shook his little head, asking his mom, "And Sis?"

As soon as Jiazhen heard him she lowered her head and said, "You hurry up and eat."

This little fellow put his chopsticks right down and loudly demanded that his mother tell him. "When is Sis coming back?"

I was already a mess with Fengxia leaving. When I saw Youqing going on like this, I hit the table and said, "Fengxia's not coming back."

Youqing was so scared his body shook. Then, seeing that I hadn't really lost my temper, he twisted his mouth, lowered his head and said, "I want Sis."

Jiazhen told him we had given Fengxia away to somebody else to save money so he could go to school. Hearing that Fengxia had been given away, Youqing opened his mouth and began wailing. He screamed through his tears, "I'm not going to school, I want Sis!"

I just ignored him, thinking, if he wants to cry then let him cry. I didn't expect him to start up again: "I'm not going to school!"

His whining was starting to make me crazy. I yelled at him, "What the hell are you crying about?"

Youqing was terrified, and his body recoiled. When he saw me lower my head and go back to eating, he got up from his stool and walked over to the corner. Suddenly he screamed out again, "I want Sis!"

This time there would be no getting around a beating. I grabbed the broom from behind the door, walked over to him and said, "Turn around."

Youqing looked at Jiazhen and obediently turned around with his two hands resting against the wall. I said, "Take off your pants."

Youqing turned his head to look at Jiazhen, then after undoing his pants he turned around again to look at her. Seeing that his mom didn't come to stop me, he got scared. As I raised the broom he timidly pleaded, "Daddy, please don't hit me."

His words made my heart go soft. Youqing hadn't really done anything wrong. Fengxia had taken care of him since he was little. He and his sister had always been close, and it was only natural for him to miss her. I patted him on the head and said, "Hurry up and eat."

Two months later, it came time for Youqing to go to school.

The day Fengxia was taken away she wore a set of nice clothes, but when Youqing went to school he still had nothing but rags. As his mother, Jiazhen couldn't help but feel terribly upset. She squatted down before him and tried to fix his clothes, pulling them here and patting them there.

"He doesn't have a single nice outfit," she said to me.

Who would have guessed that Youqing would now start up again? "I'm not going to school."

Two months had already passed, and I thought he'd forgotten what had happened with Fengxia. But when the day came for him to go to school, he started up all over again. This time I didn't lose my temper. I just patiently explained to him that we had given Fengxia away so he could have an opportunity to go to school, and only if he studied hard could he make it up to his sister. Youqing stubbornly stood up and raised his head.

"I'm not going!" he insisted.

"Is your ass getting itchy?" I asked him.

He turned right around and stomped inside. After entering the room, he yelled, "Even if you beat me to death I won't go!"

I thought, this kid must really want a beating. And so, broom in hand, I followed him in. Jiazhen stopped me.

"Not too hard, just scare him a little bit," she whispered. "Don't really beat him."

When I walked in, Youqing was already lying on the bed with his pants pulled down to his thighs, exposing his little bottom. He was waiting for me to do it. But seeing him like that, I couldn't bring myself to hit him. I thought I'd try to persuade him with words first. "There's still time if you change your mind and agree to go."

He sharply cried out, "I want Sis!"

I aimed at his butt and hit him once, but he just clasped his head and said, "It doesn't hurt!"

I hit him again, but he still said, "It doesn't hurt!"

Youqing was forcing me to lay into him. He was really pissing me off. I hit him with all my strength, and this time he couldn't take it. He started wailing like a baby, but I didn't care—I hit him again with all my strength. But Youqing was, after all, still a kid, and before long he really couldn't take it. He begged me, "Daddy, please don't hit me. I'll go to school."

Youqing was always a good kid. When he came home from his first day of school, he trembled as soon as he saw me. I thought he was still scared because I had hit him that morning. I tried getting him to warm up to me by asking how he liked school, but he just lowered his head and softly grunted. While we were eating he looked utterly terrified whenever he raised his face to look at me, which made me feel terrible. I regretted that I had hit him so hard that morning. When we were almost finished eating, Youqing called out to me, "Dad."

After a pause, Youqing continued, "My teacher wanted me to tell you that he criticized me today. He said that I can't sit still and that I'm not studious."

As soon as I heard that, my temper flared. We had given Fengxia away and he still didn't study hard. I slammed my bowl down on the table, and he started to cry. Through his tears he said, "Dad, please don't hit me. It was because my butt hurt that I couldn't sit still."

I quickly pulled down his pants to look. His bottom was all black-and-blue from my hitting him that morning. How could anyone be expected to sit still with a bruised bottom like that? Seeing my son trembling made my heart break and my eyes well up.

A few months after Fengxia was taken away, she came running back. She returned in the middle of the night. Jiazhen and I were both in bed when we heard someone knocking on the door. First she knocked very lightly, but after a while she knocked a couple more times. I wondered who it could be so late. I crawled out of bed, and when I opened the door I saw Fengxia standing there. In my surprise I forgot that she was deaf and quickly said, "Fengxia, hurry up and come in."

As soon as Jiazhen heard me she jumped right out of bed and ran over to the door without even putting on her shoes. The second I pulled Fengxia inside, Jiazhen, in tears, embraced her. I gave her a little push so she wouldn't go on like that.

Fengxia's hair and clothes were soaked from the dew. We brought her over to the bed so she could sit down. She pulled my sleeve with one hand and Jiazhen's clothes with the other. Her body trembled, as she was choked with tears. Jiazhen wanted to fetch a fresh towel to dry Fengxia's hair, but Fengxia wouldn't loosen her grip on Jiazhen's clothes. Jiazhen had to settle for caressing her daughter's hair with her hands. Only after a long time did Fengxia finally stop crying and relax her grip on us. We took our hands back and looked her over. We wanted to see whether that family had worked her like an animal. After looking her over carefully we couldn't really tell; she'd already had those thick calluses on her hands before she left. Only after I looked again at her face and saw there were no marks or scars did I feel a bit at ease.

After Fengxia's hair was dry, Jiazhen helped her out of her clothes and let her go sleep with Youqing. When Fengxia lay down she looked at her sleeping brother for a while and secretly smiled; only then did she close her eyes and go to sleep. When Youqing turned over he put his hand on Fengxia's mouth and it looked as if he was slapping his sister in the face. After Fengxia fell asleep she looked like a motionless little cat, quiet and good.

When Youqing woke up in the morning and saw his sister, he frantically rubbed his eyes and took a second look to see if it was really Fengxia. Before he even put on his clothes he leaped out of bed and yelled, "Sis! Sis!"

Youqing had the giggles all morning long. Jiazhen told him to hurry up and eat; he still had to get to school. As soon as he heard this he stopped smiling; he stole a glance at me and quietly asked Jiazhen, "Is it okay if I don't go today?"

"No way," I said.

He didn't dare say anything else, but as he put on his backpack to go out the door he stamped his foot a few times in anger. Then, fearing I'd lose my temper, he quickly scurried off. After Youqing left, I had Jiazhen prepare a set of clean clothes to send Fengxia back in. When I turned around there was Fengxia holding a basket and sickle, waiting for me by the door. Seeing the pleading look in Fengxia's eyes, I didn't have the heart to send her back. I turned to Jiazhen, and it seemed as if her eyes were pleading with me also.

"Let's let Fengxia stay another day," I said to her.

After dinner I took Fengxia back. She didn't cry; she just sadly gazed at her mother and then her little brother. Then, holding on to my sleeve, she walked back with me. Youqing was behind us crying and making a scene, but since Fengxia couldn't hear anyway, I just ignored him.

That trip was really difficult. I wouldn't let myself look at Fengxia; I just kept walking forward. We walked until it got dark, with the wind blowing against my face and down my neck. Fengxia continued holding on to my sleeve with both hands and didn't make a sound. After nightfall, she stumbled on some rocks and fell over. I squatted down to rub her feet, and she placed her two hands around my neck. Her hands were so cold—they were almost lifeless. I carried Fengxia the last part of the way. We got to town, and, seeing we were getting close to that family's house, I stopped under a streetlight, put Fengxia down and looked her over again. Fengxia was a good kid, and even then she didn't cry. She just opened her eyes up wide and looked at me. I extended my arm to caress her face, and she also caressed mine. As soon as I felt her touch my face, I was no longer willing to see her off to that family. I picked Fengxia up and carried her back home, her tiny arms holding on to my neck. Part of the way home she suddenly hugged me with all her strength. She knew I was taking her home.

Seeing us arrive home, Jiazhen looked shocked. I said, "I'm

not sending Fengxia back, even if it means our whole family has to starve to death."

A gentle smile appeared on Jiazhen's face—she smiled and smiled until tears began to appear.

When Youqing was about ten years old and had been going to school for two years, our life finally seemed to be going a bit better. Fengxia would work with us in the field, and she was at the point where she could carry her own weight. We were raising two lambs, and Youqing was in charge of cutting grass to feed them. Every morning, as the first glimmer of dawn shone through, Jiazhen would wake up Youqing. He would throw his sickle in a basket and make his way out of the house to go cut grass, carrying the basket with one hand and rubbing his sleepy eyes with the other. He looked pathetic, being at just that age when kids never want to get up. But what could we do? If Youqing didn't go cut grass, our two lambs would starve. By the time Youqing got back from carrying his basket of grass, he would almost be late for class. Stuffing a bowlful of rice down his throat, he would still be swallowing as he ran off to school. When he came back in the afternoon, he had to cut more grass, and only after he fed the lambs would he himself eat. Of course he would be late again for his afternoon classes. Youqing was then only ten years old, yet every day he had to run over fifty *li* to school and back.

Running around like that, it was only natural that Youqing would wear out his shoes. Jiazhen, having been born into a well-to-do family in town, felt that a student like Youqing mustn't go barefoot to school, so she made him a pair of cloth shoes. I myself felt that as long as you studied hard at school it really didn't matter much if you had shoes or not. After he had worn his new shoes for only two months, I saw Jiazhen knitting a pair of soles. I asked whom she was making them for, and she said Youqing.

The work in the field already exhausted Jiazhen to the point where she had no energy, and now Youqing was going to push her over the edge. I picked up Youqing's two-month-old pair of shoes to have a look. What kind of shoes were these? The soles were worn so thin that they were almost unwearable, and the laces and front part of one shoe had completely fallen off. When Youqing came back carrying his basket full of grass, I threw the shoes over to him and pulled him by his ear to show him, "Have you been wearing these, or gnawing on them?"

Youqing rubbed his sore ear, grimacing with pain. He wanted to cry but didn't dare.

"If you keep wearing them like that, I'll cut off your feet!" I warned him.

But I was wrong. Our family's two lambs relied entirely upon Youqing to feed them. Doing such hard work at home took away from Youqing's time, so he always had to run to school. When he got out in the afternoon, he wanted to get home early to cut grass, so he ran. And I haven't even mentioned Youqing's job of fertilizing the fields with the lamb manure. Who knew how many pairs of shoes we could buy for Youqing with the money we got every year from selling the lambs' wool. After I yelled at him, Youqing would go barefoot to school, putting on his shoes only after he got there. One time it snowed but he still ran to school barefoot in the snow. As his father, I could hardly bear it. I told him to stop. "What's that in your hand?"

He stood in the snow, staring blankly at the pair of shoes in his hands, not knowing what to say. I said, "Those are shoes, not gloves. Put them on."

Only then did he finally put them on. Drawing back his head, he waited for what I had to say next. I waved my hand at him. "Get going."

Youqing turned around and started running toward town. But I saw him stop before he had gotten too far and take his shoes back off. This kid was really impossible.

In 1958 the people's communes were established. Our five *mu* of land all went to the commune, leaving us only a small plot of land in front of our hut. The village head was no longer called the village head—he was now called the team leader. Every morning the team leader would stand under the elm tree near the village entrance and blow a whistle. Tools in hand, all the men and women in the village would assemble at the village entrance as if they were in the military. The team leader would establish the daily tasks, and we'd all disperse and get to work. Everyone in the village thought it was fresh and new, lining up and then going down to the fields to work. Some of the people would laugh at each other and crack jokes about the others. When Jiazhen, Fengxia and I lined up we were in pretty good order, but some of the other groups looked just terrible. These families included both the young and the old, and one group even had an old lady with bound feet. Seeing those groups, the team leader would say,

"Look at this bunch! No matter if I look at you horizontally or vertically, you still look horrible!"

Naturally, Jiazhen was reluctant to see our five *mu* of land be returned to the people's commune. For the past ten years our family had completely depended upon this five *mu* to survive, and then, in the blink of an eye, this land became the public's. Jiazhen would often say, "If they reallocate the land later, I want our same five *mu* back."

Who could have known that before long even cooking pots would have to be turned over to the people's commune? They said it was to smelt iron. One day the team leader went door-to-door smashing pots and pans. When he got to our house he laughed and said, "Fugui, are you going to hand it over yourself, or do we have to go in and smash it?"

Since everyone's pots were to be broken anyway, I figured there was no real way out, so I said, "I'll get it, I'll get it."

I carried our pot out and placed it on the ground. Two young men raised their hoes and smashed it. All it took was four or five blows to smash a good pot to pieces. Jiazhen stood by watching, so upset she even shed a few tears. She said to the team leader, "Now that our pot is broken, how are we supposed to eat?"

"You'll eat in the dining hall," the team leader said, waving his arms. "The village is setting up a communal dining hall. Smash your pots and nobody will have to worry about cooking at home anymore. You'll save a lot of energy and at the same time we'll all be on our way toward communism. If you're hungry, just pick yourself up and head on over to the dining hall. We've got fish and meat—so much you'll choke to death!"

The village set up a dining hall and our supplies of rice, salt, firewood—everything—were all confiscated by the village. The biggest shame was our pair of lambs. Youqing had raised them to be plump and strong, but even they had to be given up. That afternoon, as we carried our rice and salt over to the dining hall, Youqing, his head drooping, led our two lambs toward the drying ground. Deep down he was filled with reluctance. He had fed and cared for them with his own two hands. Every day he ran all the way to school and then all the way home, all for our lambs. He brought the lambs down to the drying field, where everyone in the village turned their oxen and sheep over to the village stockman, Wang Xi. Although the others were also reluctant to give their animals away, after handing them over to Wang Xi they all turned around and went home. Only Youqing remained—he stood there biting his lip without moving. Finally he asked Wang Xi in a pathetic voice, "Is it okay if I come back to visit them every day to give them a hug?"

As soon as the village dining hall opened up, mealtime each day became quite a show. Every family sent two women to pick up the food. They had to get in a long line just like the steamed breadline I was in while a prisoner of the communists. The sound of all those women yammering away was like the twittering sound of a flock of sparrows that flies in when it's time to dry out the rice husks. The team leader was right: having a dining hall really did save a lot of effort. If you were hungry, all you had to do was line up and you'd have plenty to eat and drink. The portions were unlimited; you could eat as much as you wanted, and every day there was meat. The first couple of days the team leader, with his bowl in hand, happily went laughing from door to door, asking everybody, "So, did it save you a lot of energy? Do you think the people's commune is a good idea or what?"

Everybody in the village was happy. They all said it was a great idea and the team leader responded, "These days our lives are more comfortable than that of a carefree loafer!"

Jiazhen was happy, too. Every time she and Fengxia came back carrying our food, she'd say, "There's meat again!"

Jiazhen would put the food on the table before going out to call Youqing. After calling out to him a couple of times, we'd see him appear, running along the ridge carrying a basket full of grass. He was actually going to bring our two lambs some grass. The village's three oxen and twenty-some lambs were all kept in the same livestock shed. As soon as those animals were taken by the people's commune, it was their bad luck. They were often underfed and hungry. As soon as Youqing entered the shed he'd be surrounded. Youqing would call out to his lambs, "Hey! Hello! Where are you guys?"

When his two lambs would emerge from the herd, Youqing would put the grass on the ground in front of them. At the same time he had to push away the other animals. Only after his lambs were done eating would Youqing, breathing heavily and sweating, run home. Almost late for school, he would chug down his rice as if he were drinking water, pick up his book bag and be off.

Seeing him still running back and forth like this, I felt angry inside but didn't say anything. I was afraid that if I said something other people would say that I was politically backward. But one time I just couldn't take it. I told Youqing, "If other people take a shit why the hell should you go wipe their asses?"

Youqing didn't understand what I meant, and after looking at me for a while he began to giggle. That pissed me off so bad I almost slapped him upside the head.

"Those lambs belong to the commune now," I said. "What the hell do you have to do with them?"

Youqing would bring grass to them three times a day, and just as it was getting dark he would go and give his two lambs a hug. The guy in charge of the animals, Wang Xi, seeing how much Youqing cared for his lambs, said to him, "Youqing, why don't you bring them home with you tonight? Just bring them back first thing tomorrow morning."

Youqing knew I wouldn't let him, so he shook his head and said to Wang Xi, "My dad will yell at me. I'll just cuddle with them."

As time went by there were fewer and fewer lambs left in the shed, because every few days they'd slaughter another one. In the end, Youqing was the only one who would still bring grass to the lambs. When Wang Xi saw me, he said, "Youqing's the only one who still thinks about them every day. The others only think about them when they're hungry."

Two days after the village dining hall opened, the team leader sent two young men into the city to buy a cauldron for smelting iron. The team leader pointed to the heap of smashed pots and iron sheets that were piled up in the drying field and said, "We ought to hurry up and start smelting that stuff. It's worthless just sitting there."

After the two young men, carrying a straw rope and a shoulder pole, went into the city, the team leader accompanied the town *fengshui*° expert on a leisurely stroll around the village. He wanted to find an ideal spot with perfect *fengshui* to smelt iron. The *fengshui* expert in his long gown walked back and forth with his squinting smile. As he approached each family's house, the family members inside must all have been holding their breath. All it would take would be one nod from this hunchbacked old man and that family's house would be gone.

The team leader accompanied the *fengshui* expert all the way to our front door. I stood outside the door with my heart caught up in an uncertain panic. The team leader said, "Fugui, this is Mr. Wang. He's come by to have a look."

"Good, that's great," I said, nodding my head.

With both hands clasped behind his back, the *fengshui* expert looked around in all directions and he said, "This is a great spot, the *fengshui* here is good."

As soon as I heard that I felt dizzy and thought I was really done for. It was a good thing that at that moment Jiazhen came out. When Jiazhen saw it was the same Mr. Wang she used to know, she called out to him.

° *Fengshui,* also known as geomancy, is the Chinese art of determining the geographic location of a house, tomb, office, etc., that will have the greatest positive influence on the fortune of the individual, family or company that uses it.

"Well, if it isn't Jiazhen," replied Mr. Wang.

Jiazhen smiled. "Come in for some tea."

Mr. Wang waved his hands saying, "Some other time, some other time."

Jiazhen said, "My dad said you've been up to your neck in work lately."

"Yes, I've been really busy," Mr. Wang said, nodding his head. "The people who want me to come check out their *fengshui* are all lining up!"

Saying that, Mr. Wang looked at me and asked Jiazhen, "Who is this?"

Jiazhen said, "This is Fugui."

As Mr. Wang smiled, his eyes squinted to the point that all you could see was a single thin crack. He nodded and said, "I know, I've heard about him."

Seeing the expression on Mr. Wang's face, I knew he was thinking back to me gambling away all my family's property. I just smiled at Mr. Wang, and he put his two fists together in a cordial gesture, saying, "We'll talk again some other time."

Finishing, he turned around and said to the team leader, "Let's go somewhere else and look."

Only after the team leader and the *fengshui* expert left did I truly let out a sigh of relief. My thatched hut escaped unharmed, but Old Sun was really up shit's creek. The *fengshui* expert took a fancy to his house. The team leader requested that Old Sun and his family vacate the house, but Old Sun squatted down in the corner, crying like a baby. He didn't want to move. The team leader said to him, "What are you crying about? The people's commune will build you a new house."

Old Sun's two hands clasped his head, and he continued to cry, but he didn't say a word. By the time dusk fell, the team leader figured there was no other way, so he got a few of the young guys in the village to pull Old Sun out of his house and move everything outside. After they pulled Old Sun outside, he grabbed on to a tree, and no matter what he wouldn't let go. The two young guys pulling him looked at the team leader and said, "Team leader, we can't move him."

The team leader, turning to look, said, "Okay, you two come over here and start the fire."

Matches in hand, the two young guys got up on a stool and lit a match against the straw on the roof. But the straw was already mildewed, and it had just rained the day before, so it was almost impossible for them to get a fire going. The team leader said, "Fuck, I don't believe that the fire of the people's commune can't even burn down a raggedy old house like this."

The team leader rolled up his sleeves, getting ready to do it himself, when someone said, "Add some oil. Just a little bit will do."

After thinking, the team leader said, "Of course! Why didn't I think of that? Quick, go down to the dining hall and get some oil."

I used to think that I was the only wastrel—I never imagined that the team leader was one, too. I stood less than a hundred feet away, watching the team leader and the rest of them take perfectly good oil and pour it over the straw. The oil was being taken right out of our mouths and now, in their hands, was going up in smoke and flames. They poured the oil we were meant to cook with on the straw roof, and the flames whisked upward, dancing in the sky, while the smoke rolled back and forth across the roof. Old Sun was still hugging the tree, his eyes fixed on his burning house. Poor Old Sun—only after his house was burned to ash and the surrounding ground was blackened by the flames did he finally wipe away his tears and stagger away. The people in the village heard him say, "My pot's been smashed, my house has been burned, it looks like I should probably die, too."

That night Jiazhen and I could barely sleep. If Jiazhen hadn't known that *fengshui* expert, Mr. Wang, who knew where our family would have wound up? The more we thought about it the more we became convinced that it all came down to fate. It was just a shame about Old Sun—Jiazhen kept thinking that we had pushed this catastrophe on him. I also thought so, but that's not what I said.

"Actually, it was the catastrophe that found him," I said. "You can't really say we pushed it on him."

The iron smelting area was evacuated, and the cauldron they had purchased in town arrived. They had also bought a petrol drum. A whole bunch of the villagers had never seen a petrol tank before, and they all thought it was a really curious object. They asked what kind of gadget it was. I had seen them before during the war so I told them, "It's a petrol drum. It's the rice bowl a car uses to eat."

The team leader kicked this automotive rice bowl and said, "It's too small!"

The guy who bought it said, "They didn't have any bigger ones. I guess we'll just have to smelt one cauldron at a time."

The team leader was the kind of guy who liked to hear reasonable ideas. It didn't matter who came up with them. Just as long as they sounded reasonable, he'd believe them. He said, "That makes sense. After all, taking one bite never made anyone fat. We'll just smelt one cauldron at a time."

Seeing so many people surrounding the petrol drum, Youqing, with his basket full of grass, temporarily postponed his trip to the livestock shed to come over and see what was going on. His head rubbed and bumped against my waist as he emerged from the crowd. I thought, who could this be? But as soon as I looked down I saw that it was my son. Youqing yelled out to the team leader, "When you smelt iron, you've got to add water."

Everybody laughed when they heard this, and the team leader said, "Add water? This little guy is thinking about cooking meat."

When Youqing heard this he started to giggle and said, "Otherwise before the iron is smelted you'll burn a hole through the bottom of the cauldron."

Who could have known that upon hearing this the team leader would raise his eyebrows, turn to me and say, "Fugui, you've got a little scientist in your family. What this kid said is exactly right."

With the team leader complimenting my son, I was naturally happy, even though it was actually a lousy idea. First they set the petrol tank up where Old Sun's house had stood. They threw in all those broken pots, iron sheets and other stuff, and then they added water, covering the vat with a wooden cover. This was how we went about smelting iron. As soon as the water inside began to boil, the wooden cover would shake, dancing up and down as the steam rushed out. In the end, smelting iron really wasn't that much different from cooking meat.

Every day the team leader would go over a few times to check it out. Each time he removed the wooden lid, the water and steam rushing out would scare him so bad he'd jump back a couple steps and yell out, "It's hot as hell!"

Waiting until the smoke died down a bit, he would stick a pole down in the vat, poking around to see if the iron had begun to soften. After he was finished poking, he'd curse, "Fuck, it's still hard as a rock!"

During the time the village was smelting iron, Jiazhen got sick. She got a kind of sickness that made her feel exhausted. At first I thought it was just a symptom of old age that she should start to feel like this. One day I was carrying the goat manure out to fertilize the field, which at the time was dotted with bamboo poles that stuck out of the ground. Originally there were little red paper flags hanging from the ends of these poles, but after a few rains the red flags were gone. All that was left were the bamboo poles with some bits of dangling red paper. Jiazhen also carried the goat manure. She walked and walked, and then her legs suddenly went soft and she had to sit down. The farmers all snickered when they saw this.

"Fugui must have been too rough last night," they joked.

Jiazhen laughed, too. She stood up and tried to pick her load back up, but her legs began to tremble. They shook so badly that her pants looked like they were being blown by a strong wind. I thought she was probably just tired.

"Take a rest," I told her.

She immediately sat right back down on the ground. The basket full of manure tipped over, covering her leg. Jiazhen's face suddenly turned red as she said to me, "I don't know what's wrong with me."

I just thought she needed some sleep and she'd have her energy back the next day. Who would have imagined that from then on Jiazhen wouldn't be able to carry loads, that she would only be able to do light work in the field? It was a good thing we had the people's commune; otherwise, I'm not sure how we would have made it through those days. After Jiazhen got sick, she naturally felt bad inside as well. Late at night she'd often whisper to me, "Fugui, I'm sorry for making it more difficult for you."

"Don't worry about that," I'd say. "Everybody gets like that when they get old."

Up until that time I still hadn't really given Jiazhen's illness much consideration; I just thought that ever since Jiazhen married me she had never had a good life. Now that she was getting older, I should give her the opportunity to rest. I was caught off guard a month later when Jiazhen's illness suddenly took a turn for the worse. As Jiazhen and I were watching over the petrol tank and the smelting iron, she collapsed. Only then did I really get scared, and decided to bring her to the town hospital for an examination.

By then we had been smelting iron for over two months and it was still hard as a rock. The team leader felt he couldn't let the strongest workers watch over the tank all day and all night, so he said, "From now on we'll rotate house by house."

When it was our family's turn, the team leader said, "Fugui, tomorrow is National Day. You'll have to make the fire bigger. No matter what, I want to see that iron smelted for tomorrow."

I had Jiazhen and Fengxia go first thing that morning to wait by the dining hall, so they could bring the food back early. This way, after eating, we could go relieve the people at the smelting cauldron. I was afraid that if we showed up late people would talk. But after Jiazhen and Fengxia came back with the food, Youqing was still nowhere to be seen. Jiazhen stood in the doorway calling him until sweat began to drip down her forehead. I knew that Youqing must have been bringing grass over to the animal pen, so I said to Jiazhen, "You go ahead and eat."

Heading off to the village livestock shed, I thought to myself, this kid really doesn't understand how things work in this world. He doesn't help Jiazhen do any work around the house. All he knows how to do is cut grass for his lambs; he spends every spare second he has on those lambs. When I got to the livestock shed I saw Youqing emptying the grass onto the ground. There were only six lambs left in the pen, and they all rushed over to fight for the grass. Carrying his basket, Youqing asked Wang Xi, "Will they kill my lambs?"

"No way," replied Wang Xi. "If we eat all the lambs where will we go for fertilizer? The crops won't grow well without fertilizer."

Wang Xi, seeing me coming over, said to Youqing, "You'd better hurry home. Your dad's here."

As Youqing turned around, I extended my hand and patted him on the head. The sad tone of his voice when he asked Wang Xi about his lambs had quelled my temper. As we walked home, Youqing, seeing I hadn't lost my temper, happily told me, "They're not going to kill my lambs!"

"It would be better if they did kill them," I replied.

That night all four of us watched over the petrol tank and the iron smelting. It was my job to add water to the cauldron. Fengxia used a fan to stoke the flames, and Jiazhen and Youqing collected branches and sticks to feed the fire. We kept working late into the night, beyond when everyone in the village had gone to sleep. After adding water three times, I grabbed a branch and stuck it into the cauldron. The iron was still as hard as a rock. Jiazhen was so exhausted that her face was covered in sweat. When she bent over to throw sticks into the fire, she couldn't support herself and had to kneel on the ground. I put the wooden lid back on and said to her, "I'm afraid you're sick."

"I'm not sick," replied Jiazhen. "I just feel a bit sore."

Youqing was leaning against a tree, looking like he had fallen asleep. Because her arms were sore, Fengxia had to keep switching hands as she fanned the flames. I went over and patted her on the shoulder. Thinking I wanted to take over for her, she turned around and shook her head. I pointed to Youqing; I wanted her to carry him home. She nodded and got up. It was then that a "baa, baa" sound coming from the animal pen made its way to Youqing. Still asleep, he smiled when he heard it. Then as soon as Fengxia picked him up he suddenly opened his eyes and said, "Those are my lambs that are crying!"

I thought he had been asleep. Seeing him open his eyes and start up again about this lamb business, I really got mad. I said to him, "They're the commune's lambs, not yours!"

Youqing was scared out of his wits. Completely awakened from his nap, he glared at me. Jiazhen nudged me.

"Don't scare the kid," she said.

She squatted down beside Youqing and quietly said to him, "Youqing, go to sleep. Sleep."

Looking at Jiazhen, Youqing nodded his head and closed his eyes. Before long he was in a deep sleep. I picked Youqing up and placed him on Fengxia's back. Then I gave Fengxia a hand sign telling her to bring Youqing home to go to sleep, and not to come back.

After Fengxia carried Youqing off, Jiazhen and I sat in front of the fire. It was already quite cool out, so it was nice sitting before the warm fire. Jiazhen was so exhausted that she had not a drop of energy left—even raising her arms took more strength than she had. I let Jiazhen lean up against me.

"Close your eyes and get some sleep," I said.

The moment Jiazhen's head rested against my shoulder, I also slipped into a light slumber. The first time my head started to droop I straightened right up, but in my tired state I came closer and closer to drifting off. I nodded off again after adding wood to the fire—only that time I didn't pick my head back up.

I wasn't sure just how long I'd been asleep when I heard a massive rumbling sound. It scared me so bad that I sprang to my feet. By then it was almost light out, and I saw that the petrol tank had fallen over. The fire spread out like a pool of water, scorching the ground and everything in its path. When I noticed that Jiazhen's jacket was draped over my shoulders, I was struck with fear. I ran around the petrol vat twice but didn't see Jiazhen. I was scared out of my wits. I roared, "Jiazhen, Jiazhen!"

I heard Jiazhen's faint voice coming from the pond. I ran over and saw Jiazhen sitting on the ground, trying with all her might to stand up. As I helped her up, I discovered that her clothes were soaked.

After I had fallen asleep, Jiazhen had woken up and kept herself awake so she could continue throwing branches into the fire. Then, realizing that there was almost no water left in the cauldron, she grabbed a wooden bucket and headed over to the pond to fetch some. Carrying the bucket, she took only five or six steps before collapsing on the ground. She sat there resting for a while before returning to the pond to fill the bucket back up. This time she rested after each step, but as soon as she got to the pond, she fell down again. Altogether, two buckets of water spilled over her. She sat there on the ground beside the pond, lacking the energy to get back up—she remained there, virtually paralyzed, until that thunderous sound woke me.

Seeing that Jiazhen wasn't hurt, my anxious heart relaxed a bit. I helped Jiazhen over to the petrol vat. A few flames were still smoldering, and as soon as I noticed that the bottom of the cauldron had been burned out I knew the situation was bad. Jiazhen, seeing what had happened, was also stupefied. She blamed herself right away. "It's all my fault, it's all my fault."

"No, it was me," I said. "I shouldn't have fallen asleep."

I thought I'd better hurry up and inform the team leader. I helped Jiazhen over to a tree. Leaning her up against the trunk, I ran toward the house that was once mine, later Long Er's and that now belonged to the team leader. When I got to the team leader's house I yelled, "Team leader, team leader!"

The team leader answered from inside, "Who is it?"

"It's me, Fugui," I responded. "The bottom of the cauldron's burned out."

"Did you succeed in smelting the iron?" the team leader asked.

"No," I replied.

The team leader barked back, "Then what the hell are you yelling about?"

I didn't dare open my mouth again. I just stood there, not knowing what to do. By then it was already light outside. After thinking about it, I figured I'd better take Jiazhen to the town hospital. It seemed like her illness was pretty serious. I would have to deal with this cauldron business later when I got back from the hospital. First I went home and woke Fengxia so she could help me. I couldn't move Jiazhen alone; I was getting old and feared I wouldn't be able to carry her the twenty-odd *li* to the hospital. I had no choice but to take turns with Fengxia.

With Jiazhen on my back and Fengxia beside me, I walked toward the city. From behind Jiazhen protested, "I'm not sick, Fugui, I'm not sick."

I knew that she was just saying that because she didn't want to spend the money needed to go to the hospital. I said, "We'll let the hospital decide whether you're sick or not."

Jiazhen didn't want to go to the hospital, and the whole way there she kept complaining. I was out of energy after walking part of the way, so Fengxia, who was stronger than I was, took over. As she trudged on with her mother on her back, her feet made a peculiar sound. As soon as Fengxia picked her up, Jiazhen stopped complaining and suddenly smiled. Comfortingly, she said, "Fengxia has really grown up."

Jiazhen's eyes turned red, and she added, "If only Fengxia hadn't gotten sick that time."

"What are you bringing that up for?" I said. "It's already been god knows how many years."

The town doctor said Jiazhen had "soft bone disease,"° adding that there was no one who could cure this kind of illness. He said we should take Jiazhen home and, if we could manage it, get her some more nutritious food. He warned us of the possibility of Jiazhen's sickness getting worse, and I feared he would be right. Fengxia carried her all the way home; I walked beside them with my thoughts in disarray. Jiazhen had an incurable disease—the more I thought about it, the more terrified I became. How quickly our life was coming to an end. I looked at Jiazhen's thin and bony face and realized that I hadn't brought her a single day of happiness since we'd been married.

Jiazhen, on the other hand, was happy. From atop Fengxia's back she said, "It's a good thing it's not curable. Where would we get the money for medicine if it was?"

° Osteomalacia, or *ruan gu bing* in Chinese. A disease characterized by the softening of the bones. The adult equivalent of rickets.

As we approached the village, Jiazhen said she was feeling better and wanted to get down and walk for herself.

"I don't want to scare Youqing," she said.

She was worried that Youqing would be upset if he saw her like this. Mothers always think about these little things. As she got down from Fengxia's back, we went to support her. She said she could walk by herself.

"Actually, I'm not really sick," she said.

It was then that the sound of bells and gongs made their way over to us. The team leader and a group of people approached us from the edge of the village. After catching sight of us, the team leader gleefully waved his hand, yelling out, "Fugui, your family has done a great deed!"

I had no idea what he was talking about—what kind of great deed had we done? Only after they got close did I see two young villagers carrying a chunk of clumpy iron. The top of this metal clump was shaped like half a pot, and pieces of iron sheets jutted out from the sides. A red cloth was draped over its top. The team leader pointed to this mosh of worthless metal and said, "Your family smelted the iron just in time for National Day. We're heading up to the county seat to bring the good news."

As soon as I heard that, I was shocked. I had been worrying about how I was going to explain to the team leader how the bottom of the cauldron had been burnt out. Who would have guessed that in the meantime the iron had actually smelted? The team leader patted me on the shoulder.

"We'll be able to make three bombs out of this iron, and all of them are going to be dropped on Taiwan," he proudly declared. "We'll drop one on Chiang Kai-shek's bed, one on his kitchen table and one on his goat shed!"

With that the team leader waved his hand, and about a dozen people started banging on their drums and gongs in excitement. As they passed by, the team leader turned around and yelled through the uproar, "Fugui, tonight at the dining hall we'll all eat steamed buns and we'll stuff a whole lamb in each one! It'll be all meat!"

After they got far off I asked Jiazhen, "Was the iron really finished smelting?"

Jiazhen shook her head—she didn't know how it got smelted, either. I figured that it must have happened when the bottom of the cauldron burned out. If Youqing hadn't come up with that stupid idea of his about adding water, the iron would have smelted a long time ago.

When we got home Youqing was inside, weeping so hard his shoulders were shaking.

"They took my lambs and slaughtered them," he whimpered. "They killed both of them."

Youqing was depressed for a good couple of days. He woke up early each morning, but there was no longer any need for him to run to school. I watched him pacing back and forth in front of our hut, not knowing what to do. Normally, basket in hand, he would have been off to cut grass. When it was time to eat, Jiazhen only needed to call him once and he would come right in and sit down at the table. After eating he'd put on his backpack and go out of his way to stop by the lamb pen before listlessly heading toward school.

All of the village lambs were slaughtered and eaten. Only the three oxen's lives were spared because they were needed to plough the fields. Even the grain supply was almost gone. The team leader made several trips to the commune to get some food, each time bringing ten young men with him. The men brought shoulder poles to carry the food back on. Those ten men with their ten poles left ready to carry a mountain of gold back with them, yet each time they returned, all they had in hand were their poles. They hadn't even gotten their hands on a single grain of rice. After the team leader returned for the last time, he announced, "From tomorrow on, the dining hall will be closed. Everybody better hurry up and go into town to buy pots. It'll be just like before: Every family will cook for themselves."

Back when all this had started, all it took was one word from the team leader and we had all smashed our pots, and now with another word from him we all had to go buy new ones. The dining hall divided up the remaining grain according to how many people were in each family. The grain our family got would be enough for only three days. It was a good thing that the rice in the fields would be ready for harvest in a month. No matter what, we should be able to hold out for one month.

When the other villagers went down to the fields to work, they started to keep track of work points.* I was considered a strong worker, so they gave me ten points. If Jiazhen hadn't gotten sick she would have had eight points, but once she got sick she could

---

* A unit indicating the quantity and quality of labor performed and the amount of payment earned in rural communes.

only do light work and so had to settle for four. It was a good thing that Fengxia had grown up. Compared with the other women, Fengxia was considered very strong, so she was allocated seven points a day.

Jiazhen was upset that she only got half as many points as she could have gotten. She couldn't get over it. A couple of times she went to the team leader and told him she knew she was sick but she was still able to do heavy labor. She said, "Wait until I really can't work, and then give me four points."

After giving her request some thought, the team leader agreed and said to her, "Okay, get back to cutting the rice."

Jiazhen grabbed her sickle and went down to the rice field. At first she worked really fast, and as I watched I wondered if the doctor could have been mistaken. But then after a swing of the sickle she began to shake. She took a second swing and her movements grew noticeably slower. I walked over and asked her, "Can you handle it?"

Her face covered in sweat, she straightened herself up and grumbled at me, "You do your own work. What the hell did you come over here for?"

She was afraid that my going over would attract other people's attention.

"You've got to take care not to overexert yourself," I said.

She started to get frustrated and said, "Hurry up and get away from here."

Shaking my head, I had no choice but to walk away. Not long after I left I heard a thump coming from where she was. Thinking it didn't sound good, I raised my head and saw that Jiazhen had fallen down. I walked over to her, and although she had gotten up, her legs continued to tremble. When she had fallen she'd grazed her head on the sickle, cutting open her forehead; blood was seeping out. She gazed at me with a forced smile. I picked her up and piggybacked her home without saying a word. She didn't resist, but after getting part of the way home, Jiazhen began to cry.

"Fugui, will you still be able to take care of yourself?" she asked.

"I will," I said.

Jiazhen gave up after that. Although she was depressed about those four work points, she was able to get some comfort from the fact that she could still support herself.

After Jiazhen got sick, things became even harder for Fengxia. She had to do the same amount of work in the fields as before, but even more at home. It was a good thing that she was still young. By night she'd be exhausted, but after a good night's rest she'd have strength and energy. Youqing began to help out with our small, private plot of land. One day at dusk, as I was coming home from work, Youqing called out to me from our yard. I went over to him and, rubbing the handle of his hoe and lowering his head, he said, "I learned a whole lot of characters."

"Good," I replied.

He raised his head and looked at me for a moment, adding, "I've learned enough to use my whole life."

I thought, this kid's really got a big mouth. Not really paying attention to what he was saying, I told him, "You've got to continue studying hard."

It was only then that he finally said what was really on his mind. "I don't want to study anymore."

As soon as I heard this my face dropped.

"No way," I said.

Actually I had already thought about letting Youqing drop out, but I had given this idea up because of Jiazhen. If Youqing stopped going to school, Jiazhen would think it was because of her sickness. I said to Youqing, "If you don't study hard, I'll kill you!"

I regretted it a bit after I said it. It was only because of his family that he wanted to give up school. This kid was only twelve years old and already so sensitive, it made me both happy and uncomfortable. I realized that I would have to start being more careful about scolding him and hitting him. That day I went into town to sell firewood, and on the way home I bought Youqing five *fen* worth of candy. This was the first time that I had bought anything for my son. I felt I should show Youqing that I loved him.

Carrying a pole on my shoulder, I went into Youqing's school. The school was made up of only two buildings, and the kids were inside muttering and babbling as they studied. As I approached one building I saw Youqing. He was in the classroom all the way at the end, where a woman teacher stood at the blackboard talking about something or other. I stood outside the window and saw Youqing, but the second I laid eyes on him I began to lose my temper. This kid wasn't even studying! He was throwing something at the kid in front of him. We had given Fengxia away so he could have the opportunity to get an education, and even then, with Jiazhen as sick as she was, I still hadn't let him drop out. All the while, here he was jolly and gay, running off to school to screw around. I was so angry that I couldn't even think straight. I threw down my pole, rushed into the classroom and slapped Youqing in the face. Only after I hit him did Youqing see me. He was so scared his face turned white. I said, "You really piss the hell out of me!"

Yelling like that made Youqing tremble, and I slapped him again. Scared completely senseless, Youqing drew his body back. Then the teacher rushed over.

"Who the hell are you?" she demanded. "This is a school, not your home in the countryside."

"I'm his father!" I answered.

I was so mad that my voice was especially loud. The teacher also started to lose her temper.

"What kind of father are you?" she said sharply. "Get out! You're more like a fascist or even the Nationalists!"

I didn't know what a fascist was, but the Nationalists I knew. She was insulting me. No wonder Youqing didn't study hard—he had a teacher who insulted people.

"*You're* like the Nationalists, not me," I said. "I've seen them before and you're just like them!"

The teacher opened her mouth, but instead of yelling back she began to cry. The teachers from the classrooms nearby came over and pulled me out. Once I was outside, the teachers surrounded me and started babbling at me. I couldn't understand a single word out of their mouths. Then another woman teacher came over, whom I had heard them address as the principal. She asked me why I had hit Youqing, so I systematically went through the whole story. I explained how I had given Fengxia away and how even now with Jiazhen ill I still hadn't allowed Youqing to drop out. After listening to me, the female principal said to the other teachers, "Let him go home."

As I picked up my pole to leave, I saw the classroom windows filled with little heads checking out the excitement. This time I had really hurt my son. Youqing wasn't upset because I had hit him, but because I had made a scene in front of so many of his teachers and classmates. By the time I got home, I still hadn't calmed down. I told Jiazhen what had happened, and after listening to me she said it was all my fault.

"Look at you," she said. "How do you expect Youqing to face anyone at school with you barging into his classroom and making a scene like that?"

After hearing her out, I thought about it and realized that I really had gone a bit too far. I had made my son lose face, not to mention having lost my own. That afternoon when Youqing got home from school I called him over, but he flat out ignored me. He simply put down his book bag and headed outside. When Jiazhen called him though, he stopped in his tracks. Youqing walked over to his mom, his shoulders shuddering as he cried in sadness.

For over a month after that, Youqing wouldn't pay any attention to me. If I told him to do something he'd do it right away, but he wouldn't say a word to me. The thing was, the kid didn't do anything wrong, so even if I had wanted to lose my temper, I didn't really have a reason to.

Thinking about it now, I really did go too far—my son was crushed by what I'd done. It was a good thing that Youqing was still little. After a while, he seemed to warm up to me. He still wouldn't answer me when I talked to him, but from the look on his face I could tell he wasn't holding a grudge. Sometimes he'd even steal a glance at me when he thought I wasn't paying attention. I knew that after not speaking to me for so long he was embarrassed to suddenly start talking to me again. As for me, I was in no rush. Sooner or later my son would reach out to me again.

After the dining hall closed, no one in the village had any real resources. Just getting by was becoming more and more difficult. I decided to use the last of our savings to buy a lamb. Lambs are the best animals for people—they fertilize the land and in the spring you can sell their coats for extra money. But more than anything, the lamb was for Youqing. If I brought a lamb home for him, heaven knew how happy he would be.

I talked it over with Jiazhen, and she was also excited about the idea. She told me to hurry up and go buy it. That afternoon, with the money tucked under my shirt, I went into town. I bought a lamb in the western part of town near the Guangfu Bridge. On the way back I went by Youqing's school. At first I wanted to go in and surprise him, but on second thought I decided it was best not to. The last time I'd gone in I'd ended up causing a scene, and I didn't want to upset Youqing again.

After I led the lamb out of town and got within sight of home,

I heard the sound of someone running up behind me. Before I could turn around to see who it was, Youqing called out from behind, "Dad! Dad!"

I stopped and saw Youqing running over, his face bright red. As soon as this kid saw me leading a lamb, he forgot that he wasn't talking to me. Trying to catch his breath, he asked, "Dad, did you buy him for me?"

I smiled and, nodding my head, handed the leash over to him. "Take him," I said.

Youqing, taking hold of the leash, picked up the lamb and walked a couple of steps with it in his arms. He then put the lamb back down and, holding on to its hind leg, squatted down to have a look. When he finished he said, "Dad, it's a female."

I laughed out loud and reached out my hand to squeeze his shoulder. Youqing's shoulder was skinny and slight, and I don't know why, but the moment I touched him a sadness came over me. As we walked home together, I told him, "Youqing, you're slowly growing up. Dad won't hit you anymore, and even if I do happen to hit you, I'll make sure it isn't in front of other people."

Having said that, I looked down at Youqing. He looked away. What I said had actually embarrassed him.

Now that we had a lamb again, Youqing had to get back into the routine of running to school every day. Besides cutting grass for the lamb, he still had to do the work in our private plot. I never imagined that with all that running back and forth, Youqing would actually run himself into a bit of an achievement. The day Youqing's school held an athletic meet I went into town to sell some vegetables. After selling them, I was getting ready to head home when I saw a crowd of people standing beside the street. I asked what was going on and found out that the kids were running a ten-lap race around town.

That year Youqing was in the fourth grade. It was the first time a town-wide athletic meet was held, and the kids from elementary school and junior middle school ran together. I put my pole and empty baskets down beside the road and went to see whether Youqing was running with them. After a while I saw a group of kids about the same height as Youqing run by. There was one kid whose head bobbed up and down as he ran, then there were two others who staggered along with their heads hanging low. It really looked like they weren't going to make it. Only after they passed did I catch sight of Youqing. Holding his shoes in his hands, he went barefoot, huffing and puffing as he ran. He was running all alone. Seeing him dragging behind I thought, this one's really hopeless, he's probably going to end up embarrassing me. But everyone was rooting for him. I was really confused. I watched dumbfounded as a couple more junior middle school students ran by, leaving me even more confused. I wondered what kind of a race they were running here. I asked someone beside me, "How come the older kids can't seem to catch up with the younger ones?"

"Those kids who just ran by have already lapped the others a couple times," replied the man standing next to me.

The second I heard that, I suspected that Youqing was one of the kids he was talking about. The happiness I felt at that moment was indescribable. Even the kids four or five years older than Youqing were a lap behind him. With my own eyes I witnessed my son, in his bare feet, shoes in hand and face red, be the first to run ten laps around the town. After finishing, he didn't even have to struggle to catch his breath. One at a time, he just lifted up the soles of his feet, wiped them on his pants, and put on his cloth shoes as if nothing had happened. After getting his shoes on, he put his hands behind his back and watched, proud as a peacock, as the older kids ran by.

Deep down I was ecstatic. I called out to him, "Youqing!"

Carrying my empty load I proudly went over to him. I wanted everybody around to know I was his father. As soon as Youqing saw me, he started to get uncomfortable and immediately took his hands out from behind his back. I patted him on the head and said loudly, "That's my boy, you made your dad proud."

Hearing how loud my voice was, Youqing hastily looked around to make sure none of his classmates had seen me. It was then that a big fat guy called over to him, "Xu Youqing!"

He quickly turned around and began running toward that guy. Youqing was blowing me off. As he rushed off he turned around to say, "My teacher's calling me."

I knew that he was afraid that I'd get even with him after we got home, so I waved my hand and said, "Get going."

The fat guy was really enormous—when he put his hand on Youqing's head, I couldn't even see my son's face. It looked like a giant hand was growing out of Youqing's shoulders. The two of them affectionately walked over to a little shop, and I saw the fat guy buy Youqing some candy. Youqing held the candies with both hands and stuffed them into his pockets. He let his right hand linger in his pocket so he could hold on to the candy. When he came back over to me, Youqing's face was bright red—that was because he was happy.

That night I asked Youqing who the fat guy was.

"He's my gym teacher," he replied.

"He acts like he's your father," I added.

Youqing took the candy that the fat guy had given him and spread it out on his bed. First he separated his candy into three piles, and after looking at it for a while he took two pieces from two of the piles and put them in the pile closest to himself. Then after looking at the piles again he returned two pieces from his pile back to the other two piles. I knew he was going to give one pile to Fengxia, one to Jiazhen and leave one for himself. He wasn't going to give any to me. I didn't expect that he would then take all three piles and mix them up together, separating them again into four piles. He went back and forth like this, but in the end there were still only three piles.

After a couple of days, Youqing brought his gym teacher home with him. The fat guy couldn't stop praising Youqing, saying that when he grew up he was going to be a great athlete and go abroad to compete against foreigners. Youqing sat on the doorstep, so happy that sweat dripped from his face. I didn't think it was a good idea to say anything in front of the gym teacher, but after he left I called Youqing over. As Youqing looked at me his eyes lit up. He thought I was going to go on boasting about him, but I said to him, "You've made your mother, your sister and me all proud, and for this I'm very happy. But I've never heard of any-one making a living by running. We sent you to school because we wanted you to read and study, not so you could learn how to run. Running isn't something you need to study or learn. Hell, even chickens can run!"

Youqing immediately lowered his head and walked over to the corner to pick up his basket and sickle. I asked him, "Will you remember what I said?"

He walked over to the door and, with his back turned, nodded and then went outside.

That year, before the rice had had a chance to turn yellow, while the stalks were still a green color, a seemingly endless downpour began. It rained for almost an entire month straight. Although it cleared up a couple of times, it was never for longer than two days, and then the sky would once again grow dark and the rain would return. We saw the water in the fields accumulating, and as the level of rainwater increased, the rice started to droop. In the end, patch after patch of rice was completely submerged. The older people in the village cried, and they all said, "How are we supposed to get by?"

The younger generation wasn't as pessimistic. They kept thinking that the government would save us.

"What's there to worry about?" they said. "There's always a way out. The team leader went to the county seat to get some grain."

Three times the team leader went to the commune headquarters and once to the county seat, but each time he came back with nothing but a few words. "Everybody calm down! The county magistrate said that as long as he doesn't starve, he's not going to let anyone else starve."

A heat wave lasting several days followed that month of rain, and all the rice in the fields rotted. When night fell and the wind blew, the stench was unbearable, not unlike that of rotting corpses. At first everyone hoped that we would still be able to use the rice straw, but because we couldn't harvest the rice, the straw also rotted. We were left with nothing. The team leader said the county magistrate would send us grain, but no one ever saw any. No one completely believed what the leader said, but then again no one dared not to believe. How could we get by if everyone lost hope?

It got so bad that people would count the grains of rice as they put them in the pot. There was barely any food left. No one would dare to cook rice; instead we'd all cook rice porridge— and the porridge was getting thinner and thinner. Two or three months later all the food supplies were gone, and nothing new was coming in. Jiazhen and I talked it over and decided to bring the lamb into town to sell her. We figured we'd be able to trade her for about one hundred ten *jin*° of rice. That would get us through the season until the next rice harvest.

It had been a month or two since any of us had eaten our fill, but that lamb was just as fat as before. Every day you could hear her "baa baa" sound loud and clear coming from the lamb pen— Youqing could take the credit for that. He had hardly anything to eat himself—every day he would complain about being dizzy— but not once did he shortchange his lamb when it came to her grass. He loved that lamb in the same way that Jiazhen loved him.

° A Chinese unit of weight equivalent to ½ kilogram or 1⅓ pounds.

After Jiazhen and I discussed selling the lamb, I brought it up with Youqing. He had just dumped a basket of grass in the lamb pen. The rustling sound of the lamb chewing the grass sounded like the falling rain. Youqing stood to one side with his basket in hand, laughing as he watched the lamb eat her grass.

He didn't even notice me walk over. I put my hand on his shoulder, and he twisted his head around to look at me.

"She's famished!" he said.

"Youqing," I said, "Dad has something he wants to talk to you about."

Youqing nodded and turned around to face me. I continued, "Our grain at home is almost gone. I talked it over with your mom, and we've decided to sell the lamb. We can trade her for some rice; otherwise, our whole family will go hungry."

Youqing lowered his head and didn't utter a sound. He was unwilling to part with his lamb. I patted him on the shoulder and said, "Wait until things get better and I'll buy you a new lamb."

Youqing nodded his head. He had grown up. He understood much more than before. If it had been a few years earlier, he would have cried and made a scene. As I walked out of the lamb pen, Youqing pulled my shirt and pleaded pathetically, "Dad, please don't sell her to a slaughterhouse."

I thought, during a time like this, who can afford to raise a lamb? Other than a slaughterhouse, who else would buy her? But looking at Youqing's expression, I could only nod my head.

The next morning, with an empty rice bag slung over my shoulder, I led the lamb out of her pen. As soon as I made it to the edge of the village, I heard Jiazhen calling me from behind.

Turning around I saw Jiazhen and Youqing approaching. Jiazhen said, "Youqing wants to go along."

"There's no school on Sunday," I said. "What does he want to come for?"

"Just let him go," said Jiazhen.

I knew that Youqing wanted to spend some extra time with his lamb. I was afraid if I didn't agree Jiazhen would say something. I thought, what the hell, if he wants to come, let him come. I waved him over, and Youqing ran and took the leash right out of my hand. He lowered his head, and we walked off together.

The whole way there Youqing didn't open his mouth once, but the lamb on the other hand wouldn't shut up with her "baa baa." As Youqing led her, she would from time to time bump her head into Youqing's behind. The lamb was practically human. She knew that it was Youqing who fed her grass every day, so she was affectionate with him. The more affectionate she was, the sadder Youqing became. He bit his lip as he struggled to hold back his tears.

It was difficult to watch Youqing continue with his head lowered the way it was. I tried to find something to say that would cheer him up.

"Selling her is better than having to slaughter her," I told my son. "Let me tell you, lambs, they're animals. From the time they're born, this is their fate."

We got to town, and just as we were turning a corner, Youqing suddenly stopped. Looking at his lamb he said, "Dad, I'll wait here for you."

I knew that he was unwilling to watch me sell the lamb. I took the leash from his hands and led the lamb forward. Before I could walk more than a few steps, Youqing called out from behind, "Dad, don't forget your promise!"

"What promise?" I turned to ask.

Youqing got anxious. He said, "You promised not to sell her to a slaughterhouse."

I had already forgotten what we had talked about the day before. It was a good thing Youqing didn't go with me or he definitely would have cried. I said, "I know."

I led the lamb around the corner and headed off in the direction of the meat shop. When I got there I found that the hanging meats which normally filled the shop were gone. During hard times like these, there wasn't even a rump hanging.

Inside sat a listless-looking man who didn't seem at all excited to see me bring in a lamb. His hands wouldn't stop shaking as he weighed the lamb.

"I haven't got any energy," he said. "I'm starved."

Even the people in town weren't getting enough to eat. He said it had been over ten days since his shop had had any meat. He extended his hand, pointing to an electric pole twenty meters away.

"You just wait. Within an hour they'll be lined up all the way over there to buy meat," he said.

He was right. By the time I left, there were already more than ten people lined up there, and they were lined up outside the rice shop, too. Originally I thought I'd be able to get around a hundred ten *jin* of rice for that lamb, but in the end I only took home forty. As I passed a small store on the way home, I took out two *fen* to buy two pieces of candy for Youqing. He'd been breaking his back for the last year, and I figured he deserved an occasional sweet.

As I walked over carrying the forty *jin* of rice, Youqing was pacing back and forth in that old spot of his, kicking small pebbles out of his way. I handed him the two pieces of candy. He put one into his pocket, peeled the wrapper off the other, and popped it into his mouth. Youqing held the candy wrapper in his hand, folding it carefully as we walked. He then raised his head and asked me, "Dad, do you want one?"

I shook my head. "You go ahead."

I carried the forty *jin* of rice home, and as soon as Jiazhen saw the size of the bag she knew exactly how much rice was in it. She sighed but didn't say a word. Jiazhen was in the most difficult position. How was she supposed to feed four mouths every day? She was so worried that she couldn't even get a good night's sleep. But no matter how bad things got we still had to find a way to pull through. Every day, Jiazhen would go out with a basket to search for wild vegetables. She was already sick, and having to endure daily hunger really took its toll on her. The doctor was right: Jiazhen's illness got increasingly worse. She needed a stick to lean on when she walked, and after taking only a few dozen steps her face would be soaked in sweat. When other people would dig for wild vegetables they would squat down, but Jiazhen would kneel. When she would try to stand up, her body would waver as if she had lost her balance. I couldn't bear the sight and said to her, "Why don't you stay home?"

But she refused. Leaning on her stick, she started heading

back outside. I gave her a light tug on her arm, and she fell down. Jiazhen sat weeping on the floor.

"I'm still alive, but you're treating me like I'm already dead," she cried.

I was at my wit's end. There's nothing women won't say or do once they lose their temper. If I didn't let her work, she would worry that I thought she was useless.

In less than three months the forty *jin* of rice was gone. If it hadn't been for Jiazhen's planning and her collecting pumpkin leaves and tree bark, it wouldn't have lasted even two weeks. By then no one in the village had any grain, and all of the wild vegetables had long been dug up. Some families resorted to digging up roots to eat. There were fewer and fewer people in the village; every day more people grabbed alms bowls and took to the road to beg. The team leader went to the county seat a couple times, but before he could even make it to the edge of the village he'd have to sit down on the ground to catch his breath. The few people scavenging the fields for food would walk over to ask him, "Team leader, when will the county provide us with grain?"

With his head tilted to one side, the team leader would say, "I can't walk."

Seeing those taking to the road to beg, the team leader would say, "Don't go. The people in town don't have anything to eat, either."

Knowing all too well that there were no wild vegetables left, Jiazhen, leaning on her stick, would still spend her days staggering through the fields in hopes of finding something edible.

Youqing would always go with her. At his age Youqing was still growing, but without any grain he was as skinny as a bamboo shoot. Youqing was just a kid, and Jiazhen was so sick she could barely walk, yet she'd still wander all over searching for wild vegetables. Meanwhile Youqing would straggle behind her, complaining, "Mom, I'm so hungry that I can't walk."

But where could Jiazhen have gone to find something for Youqing to eat? She could only say, "Youqing, go and drink some water to fill yourself up."

All Youqing could do was go down to the pond and slurp some water to allay his hunger.

Carrying a hoe, Fengxia would go with me to dig for sweet potatoes. God knows how many times that land had been turned over, but the village's people kept digging with their hoes. Sometimes after digging all day we'd end up with nothing but a rotten melon vine. Fengxia was also starved to the point of exhaustion. Her face was pale, and as she raised her hoe it looked as though her head was about to topple off. She couldn't speak; all she knew was work. No matter where I went, she would follow— which, after thinking about it, didn't seem like such a good idea. Fengxia following me around wasn't going to get us anywhere. It would be better if we split up and dug on our own. I made a hand sign to tell Fengxia to go dig somewhere else. Who could have guessed that as soon as Fengxia left me she would run into trouble?

Fengxia was digging on the same plot of land as another guy from our village, Wang Si. Wang Si wasn't really a bad guy. When

I was in the army, he and his father would often help Jiazhen do some work in the field. But hunger can drive people to do all kinds of wicked and immoral things. Clearly it was Fengxia who dug up that sweet potato, but Wang Si took advantage of the fact that she was mute. While Fengxia was using the edge of her shirt to wipe the mud off the potato, Wang Si snatched it out of her hands. Normally Fengxia was extremely well behaved, but given the circumstances her manners went out the window. Fengxia rushed at him, trying to wrest back her potato. And as she did, Wang Si wailed like a baby, making everyone around think it was Fengxia who was stealing from him. Wang Si yelled to me, "Fugui, doesn't your daughter have a conscience? Even if you're on the verge of starving, that's still no excuse to steal!"

Seeing Fengxia struggling with all her might to remove Wang Si's tightly wrapped fingers from the potato, I rushed over and pulled her away. Fengxia was so upset that tears rolled down her face. She used some hand symbols to tell me it was Wang Si who had stolen her sweet potato. The other people in the village also understood what Fengxia meant.

"Did she steal it from you?" they asked Wang Si. "Or did *you* steal it from her?"

Wang Si had an offended look on his face, as if he had been unjustly accused.

"All of you saw it clearly—she was trying to steal it from me," he declared.

"Everyone in the village knows that Fengxia is not that kind of person," I said. "Wang Si, if this sweet potato is really yours, then take it. But if it's not, I hope you get an upset stomach after eating it."

Wang Si pointed his finger at Fengxia and said, "You let her say for herself whose it is."

How could he say such a thing when he knew damn well that Fengxia couldn't speak? He made me so furious that my body began to tremble. Fengxia stood to one side, and her mouth opened but no sound came out; instead, tears poured down her face. I waved my hand at Wang Si.

"If you're not afraid of the god of thunder striking you down, take it," I said.

Wang Si was guilty but he didn't even blush. Instead, he straightened his neck and said, "It's mine. Of course I'll take it."

Saying that, he turned around to go. No one imagined that Fengxia would pick up her hoe to hit Wang Si. If someone hadn't screamed out in terror, giving Wang Si a chance to duck out of the way, I'm afraid he would have been killed. When Wang Si saw Fengxia trying to hit him, he stretched out his hand and slapped her. Fengxia had nowhere near as much strength as Wang Si did, and that one slap knocked her to the ground. The sound of the slap went straight to my heart; it was like the sound of someone diving into a pond. I rushed forward and hit Wang Si in the face. His head bobbed, and my hand ached. After Wang Si came around he grabbed hold of a hoe and aimed it right at me. After jumping out of the way, I also grabbed hold of a hoe.

If the villagers hadn't restrained us, that day would have marked the end for at least one of us. Then the team leader came. After we finished telling him what had happened, he yelled at us,

"Fuck, if you kill each other what the hell am I supposed to say to the higher-ups?"

After having it out with us, the team leader said, "Fengxia's not the kind of person to do a thing like that. But then again no one saw Wang Si steal it, either. So this is what we'll do: We'll split it, and each of your families will get half."

With that, the team leader held out his hands to Wang Si, expecting him to hand over the potato. But Wang Si held on to it with both hands, unwilling to let go.

"Hand it over," the team leader ordered.

Wang Si had no choice. With a long face he handed the potato over to the team leader. The team leader borrowed a sickle from someone beside him, put the potato down on the ridge and with one swift swipe the sweet potato was split in two. But the team leader's aim was off, leaving one huge piece and one tiny piece. I said, "Team leader, how do we split this up?"

The team leader said, "That's easy."

With another swift swipe, he cut a chunk off the big piece and put it into his pocket—that chunk was his. He handed Wang Si and me the two remaining pieces.

"Are they about the same size?" he asked.

One piece of a sweet potato would never be enough to feed a family, but our way of thinking back then was different. At the time we were in dire straits. It had been a month without grain, and just about everything edible in the fields had long been eaten. Back then, if someone had offered a bowl of rice for your life, he would have had more than a few takers.

The day after we fought over the potato with Wang Si, Jiazhen, leaning on her little stick, made her way to the edge of the village. I was in the fields at the time. When I saw her I asked where she was off to. She said, "I'm going into town to see my dad."

It's natural for a daughter to want to see her father, and even if I had wanted to stop her I wouldn't have been able to. Seeing how much energy it took her to walk, I said, "Let Fengxia go along. She'll be able to take care of you on the way."

When Jiazhen heard this, she answered without even turning her head, "I don't want Fengxia to come."

Jiazhen had a short temper during those difficult days, so I didn't bother trying to argue with her. I watched her walk slowly toward town. She was so skinny it looked like she had no meat on her bones. Her once-stretched clothes had become loose and droopy, blowing back and forth in the wind.

I didn't know that she was going into town to beg. She didn't come back until near dusk, and by the time she got home she couldn't even walk. Fengxia saw her first. Fengxia tugged on my clothes, and I turned around to see Jiazhen standing on the trail. Resting against her stick, she waved to us. As she raised her arm it looked as if her head were about to tumble off her shoulders.

I rushed over, and just as I was about to reach her she fell to the ground on her knees. Clutching her stick with both hands, she cried out in a weak voice, "Fugui, come, come."

As I reached out to help her up, she grabbed hold of my hand and pulled it to her chest.

"Feel," she said, gasping for air.

As I touched her chest I was shocked. Inside her clothes I felt a small bag of rice.

"It's rice," I said.

Tears flowed from Jiazhen's eyes.

"Dad gave it to me," she said.

At the time, a bag of rice was an unheard-of delicacy. It had been at least a month or two since our family had tasted rice. The joy we felt was indescribable. I had Fengxia help Jiazhen to the house while I went to look for Youqing. Youqing was lying beside the pond, where he had just drunk a bellyful of water.

"Youqing! Youqing!" I called.

He answered me wearily and didn't even have the energy to hold his head straight.

"Hurry home for some porridge," I said quietly.

The second Youqing heard there was porridge, he summoned a burst of energy from who knows where. He immediately sat up and called out, "Porridge?"

He nearly scared me to death.

"Not so loud!" I said anxiously.

We couldn't let other people know that Jiazhen had brought home a bag of rice hidden in her clothes. Once everyone got home I shut and locked the door, and only then did Jiazhen take out the little bag of rice. She dumped half the bag into the pot and added some water. Fengxia started a fire, and before long the porridge was cooking. I had Youqing look out through the crack in the door just in case anyone from the village came by. As soon as the water began to boil the fragrance of rice filled the hut. Youqing couldn't stand it any longer. He ran over to the pot and took deep whiff after whiff. "It smells so good!"

I pushed him away, saying, "Go back to the door and keep guard."

Youqing took two more quick whiffs before going back to the door. A smile emerged on Jiazhen's face, and she said, "It looks like I'll finally be able to give you a good meal."

Tears fell from Jiazhen's eyes as she spoke.

"This rice came from between my father's teeth," she sobbed.

It was then that someone started to approach from outside. As he got to the door he yelled, "Fugui!"

We were so scared that we didn't dare breathe. Youqing stood bent over at the door, not moving a muscle. Only Fengxia, who couldn't hear anything, continued happily adding wood to the fire. I patted her to be quieter. Not hearing anyone respond, the person outside said angrily, "There's smoke puffing out your chimney, but nobody inside answers!"

After a while it seemed that the man had left. Youqing peered outside for some time before finally whispering to us, "He's gone."

Jiazhen and I could finally take a deep breath and relax. When the porridge was ready, the four of us sat at the table and ate it. Never in my life have I eaten with more relish than on that day. Just thinking about the taste makes me drool. Youqing was anxious and ate quickly—he was the first to finish. He opened his mouth wide and took big breaths to cool it down. But he still wound up with a bunch of little blisters in his mouth that were sore for a few days. Just as we finished, the team leader showed up, bringing along practically everyone in the village.

It had been almost two months since anyone in the village had eaten rice. When we closed our door and smoke wisped out of our chimney, everybody saw. After we ignored that first guy who showed up, he went and told the others. Now a whole bunch of people were coming, and leading the way was the team leader. They figured we had some goodies, and everybody wanted a taste.

As soon as the team leader walked in, his nose twitched.

"What's that you're cooking?" he asked. "It smells great."

I giggled but didn't say anything. I figured if I didn't answer him, the team leader would probably be too embarrassed to ask again. Jiazhen asked them to have a seat, but a few of them were nosy and went about looking in the pots and under the mattress. It was a good thing that the remaining rice was hidden in Jiazhen's clothes; this way it didn't matter if they turned things upside down looking. After a while, the team leader put a stop to the snooping.

"What the hell are you doing?" he said. "This isn't your house! Leave! Leave! Get the fuck out," he cursed.

After the team leader drove the others out he got up to close the door. Then, without even trying to chum up to us, he turned right around and said, "Fugui, Jiazhen, if you've got something good to eat, let me in on it."

Jiazhen and I looked at each other. The team leader was normally pretty nice to us, and now here he was begging. How could we not help him out? Jiazhen reached into her clothes and took out that little rice bag. She gave the team leader a small handful, saying, "Team leader, that's all I can give. Take it home and cook some rice soup."

"That's enough, that's enough," the team leader repeated.

The team leader had Jiazhen put the handful of rice in his pocket. Then, clasping his pocket with both hands, he laughed out loud and went out the door. As soon as the team leader left, tears fell from Jiazhen's eyes—she was crying for that handful of rice. Seeing Jiazhen weeping, I could only sigh deeply.

The days went on like this all the way up until after the rice harvest. Although it wasn't a very strong harvest, at least we finally had some grain, and things suddenly started to look up. But who could have known that Jiazhen's illness would continue to get worse? By the end, she couldn't walk more than a few steps. It was that terrible year that had ruined her health like this. But Jiazhen still wouldn't resign herself to her condition. Even though she couldn't work in the field, she insisted on doing housework. Leaning against the wall, she'd make her way around the hut to dust and sweep. Then one day she fell down, and no matter how hard she tried, she just couldn't get back up. When Fengxia and I got home from working in the field, she was still lying there with an open scrape on her face. I carried her to bed, and Fengxia got a towel to wipe the blood from her face.

"From now on you'd better stay in bed," I told her.

Jiazhen lowered her head.

"I don't know why I couldn't get up," she whispered.

I guess you could say Jiazhen was tough. Even at a time like that she didn't utter a single complaint or cry out in despair. While she was bedridden, she had me bring every piece of beat-up old clothing over to her.

"I'll feel better if I have some work to do," she said.

She unraveled the fabric and made new clothes for Fengxia and Youqing, and after the kids put them on, they really did look new. It was only later that I discovered she had also unraveled her own clothes. When I discovered what she had done I got mad, but she just smiled and said, "Clothes don't last long if you don't wear them. I'll never wear those clothes, so what's the point of them rotting away with me?"

Jiazhen said she'd make an outfit for me, too, but who'd have known that before she could finish she would be too weak to lift even a needle? At the time Fengxia and Youqing were asleep, but under the light of the kerosene lamp Jiazhen was still sewing my outfit. She was so exhausted that sweat dripped from her face. I kept telling her to get to sleep, but she would only sigh and shake her head, insisting she was almost done. After a while she dropped the needle, and as she reached for it her hand began to tremble. I saw her struggling to pick it up and bent over to get it for her. I handed it to her, but she dropped it again. Teardrops trickled down from Jiazhen's eyes; this was the first time she had cried since getting sick like this. She thought she would never be able to work again.

"I can't even get out of bed. What am I supposed to do with myself?" she asked in despair.

I wiped her tears away with my sleeve. She was so skinny that her bones were protruding from her face. I told her that it was just exhaustion, that even a healthy person wouldn't be able to do the amount of work she'd been doing. I tried comforting her by telling her how Fengxia had already grown up and was earning more work points than even Jiazhen used to. I told her that from now on there would be no reason for us to worry anymore about money.

"But Youqing is still young," said Jiazhen.

Jiazhen's tears didn't stop that whole night. She kept telling me, "When I die, don't wrap me in a gunnysack. You have to use a fast knot to tie gunnysacks, so I won't be able to undo it when I get to the other world. Just use a clean piece of cloth and that'll be fine. And before you bury me, remember to give me a bath."

Jiazhen continued, "Fengxia's already grown up. See if you can find her a husband—that way I'll be able to rest in peace. Youqing's still small. There's a lot of things he doesn't understand, so make sure you don't hit him too much and scare him."

After hearing her go through all this, my heart felt wave after wave of sadness. I said to her, "Actually, I probably should have died long ago. So many people died during the war, but somehow I survived. Every day I told myself that I had to stay alive so I could come home and see you. And now you're just going to abandon us?"

My words must have had some effect on Jiazhen, because the next morning when I woke up I saw her staring at me.

"Fugui," she whispered, "I don't want to die. All I want is to be able to wake up every day and see you and the kids."

After a few days resting in bed, Jiazhen gradually started to get her strength back. Before long she could sit up in bed, and she said she felt much better. She was happy and said she wanted to try going back to the fields, but I wouldn't let her.

"From now on you can't risk wearing yourself out," I said.

"You've got to save your strength—we've still got a long road ahead of us."

That year Youqing was in the fifth grade. There's a common saying that "Calamities never come singly." With Jiazhen as sick as she was, I was hoping that Youqing would grow up quickly. His grades were terrible, and I thought I'd better not force him to go to middle school. After he graduated from elementary school, I'd let him go with me out to the fields to earn work points. How could I have known that just as Jiazhen was starting to feel better, something would happen to Youqing?

That afternoon, Youqing's principal, the wife of the county magistrate, lost a lot of blood giving birth in the city hospital—they said she had one foot in the grave. The teachers from Youqing's school immediately called all fifth graders to the track and sent them to the hospital to donate blood. As soon as the kids heard that the blood was for the principal, they were so happy you would have thought it was a holiday. A few of the boys even rolled up their sleeves right there, ready to donate on the spot. As soon as they left the school gates, Youqing took off his shoes and, clutching them in his hands, started running toward the hospital with four or five other kids. My son was the first one to get there, and was first in the line that formed once the other students arrived.

"I was the first one here!" Youqing proudly told his teacher.

After which his teacher dragged him aside and gave him a lecture about abiding by the rules. Youqing had no choice but to stand off to one side watching as, one by one, the other kids pressed up against one another on their way in to have their blood type checked. More than ten kids were tested, but not one had the same blood type as the principal. Youqing grew increasingly anxious as he watched them. He was afraid he'd be the last one and that by then they wouldn't even need his blood. He walked over to his teacher and said shyly, "Teacher, I realize I made a mistake."

The teacher just grunted but didn't answer him. He waited until two more kids had gone in to have their blood checked. That was when a doctor wearing a gauze mask emerged from the delivery room, shouting over to the man doing the blood tests, "The blood? Where's the blood?"

The man responsible for checking the blood said, "None of them has the right blood type."

"Quick, send the rest of them in!" the doctor yelled. "We barely have a heartbeat on the patient!"

Youqing once again walked over to his teacher and asked him, "Is it my turn?"

The teacher looked at Youqing and waved his hand. "Go in."

Only when they got to Youqing did they find a match. My son's face turned bright red, he was so ecstatic. He ran over to the door and yelled to his friends outside, "They're gonna take my blood!"

If they wanted to take some blood, they should have taken only a little. But to save the magistrate's wife, the people in the hospital wouldn't stop taking Youqing's blood—they just kept extracting more and more. When his face turned white, Youqing didn't say anything. Only after his lips turned white did he finally say, "I'm dizzy."

The guy doing the blood work said, "You always get dizzy when you donate blood."

Youqing had already given more than his body could take, but out came another doctor saying there still wasn't enough blood. The fucking asshole doing the blood work extracted almost every drop of blood from my son's body. Youqing's lips turned blue, but the guy still didn't stop. Only after Youqing's head slumped and fell to one side did he finally begin to panic. He called a doctor over, who squatted down and listened with a stethoscope.

"I can't get a heartbeat," muttered the doctor.

The doctor didn't seem to think it was a big deal. He just scolded the blood technician. "You're really an idiot."

He then went back into the delivery room to save the magistrate's wife.

That evening as dusk fell, when I was just getting ready to pack it in for the day, a kid from one of the neighboring villages, a classmate of Youqing's, came running over. He rushed right over to me and shouted at the top of his voice, "Is Xu Youqing's father here?"

My heart jumped. It was getting late, and I had just begun to worry that something might have happened to Youqing. Before I had a chance to respond, the kid yelled again, "How about his mother?"

I quickly answered, "I'm Youqing's father."

Wiping his nose, the kid looked at me and said, "I was right, it's you. You're the one who came to our classroom."

My heart felt as if it was going to jump out of my chest, and then he finally said, "Xu Youqing's almost dead. He's in the hospital."

My vision instantly went blurry. I asked the kid, "What did you say?"

"Hurry up and get to the hospital," he repeated. "Youqing's dying."

With my thoughts in disarray, I threw down my hoe and ran toward town. It just didn't make sense. Youqing had been fine that morning when he went to school, and now they were saying he was almost dead. My head buzzed wildly as I ran to the town hospital. As soon as I saw a doctor I stopped him and asked, "My son?"

The doctor looked at me and laughed, "How would I know your son?"

As soon as I heard this I was stunned. I thought, perhaps they made a mistake—how wonderful it would be if it was all just a mistake.

"They said my son was dying and that I should go to the hospital," I said.

Just as he was getting ready to walk away, that doctor suddenly stopped and looked at me.

"What's your son's name?" he asked.

"Youqing," I replied.

He extended his arm and pointed toward the room at the end of the hall. "Go ask over there."

I ran down to the room he had pointed toward and saw a doctor sitting there, in the middle of writing something. My heart was pounding as I walked over to ask, "Doctor, is my son still alive?"

The doctor raised his head and looked at me for a long time before asking, "Do you mean Xu Youqing?"

I quickly nodded my head.

"How many sons do you have?" the doctor asked.

Immediately my legs went soft. Standing there trembling, I said, "I only have one son. I beg you, please, save my son."

The doctor nodded his head to let me know that he understood, but then he asked, "How come you only had one son?"

How was I supposed to answer this? I got anxious and asked him, "Is my son still alive?"

He shook his head and said, "He's dead."

Suddenly I could no longer see the doctor—my mind went blank and my head began to spin. All I felt were the tears pouring down my face. Only after what seemed like an eternity did I ask the doctor, "Where's my son?"

Youqing was lying alone in a small room on a bed made of bricks. When I went in, night had not yet fallen, and I could see Youqing's small, frail body lying there. He was wearing the new outfit Jiazhen had made for him. My son's eyes were tightly closed, as was his mouth. "Youqing! Youqing!" I kept calling to him. Only after he didn't move did I know that he was really dead. I went to hug my son, but Youqing's body was stiff and cold. That morning when he had gone to school he was alive and well; by evening he had become stiff and cold. I couldn't understand it—the body before me seemed like a different person from the one I'd seen that morning. I looked at Youqing and caressed his skinny shoulders—it was really my son. I cried and cried, not even noticing the arrival of Youqing's gym teacher.

When he saw Youqing, he cried too, as he kept repeating to me, "How could it be? I can't imagine . . ."

The gym teacher sat down next to me, and we cried together. I caressed Youqing's face; so did he. After a while I suddenly realized that I still didn't even know how my boy had died. I asked the gym teacher, and only then did I learn that he had died from having too much of his blood extracted. At the time I wanted to kill somebody. I put my son down and rushed out. Charging into the patient ward, I grabbed hold of the first doctor I saw—I didn't care who he was—and hit him in the face. That doctor fell to the floor and started screaming for help.

"You killed my son!" I barked at him.

I lifted my leg to kick him, but someone grabbed me from behind. Turning around, I saw Youqing's gym teacher.

"Let me go!" I demanded.

The gym teacher said, "Don't do anything crazy."

"I'm going to kill him," I said.

With the gym teacher restraining me, I couldn't get loose from his grip. Crying, I begged him, "I know you've always been good to Youqing. Please let me go."

But no matter what, the gym teacher wouldn't let go. All I could do was elbow him, but he still wouldn't loosen his grip. He gave the doctor time to get up and run away, and by then a whole crowd had surrounded us. I saw that there were two more doctors in the crowd and said to the gym teacher, "I beg you, please let me go."

The gym teacher was really strong—with him holding me I couldn't move a muscle. I kept trying to elbow him, but he didn't seem at all afraid of getting hurt. He just kept saying, "Don't do anything stupid."

It was then that a man wearing a Sun Yat-sen–style tunic suit walked over and told the gym teacher to let me go. He asked me, "Are you Xu Youqing's father?"

I ignored him, and as soon as the gym teacher let me go I rushed over to pounce on one of the doctors. The doctor immediately turned and ran. I heard someone address the guy wearing the tunic suit as the county magistrate and I thought, oh, so *he's* the county magistrate—it was his wife who took my son away. I raised my leg and kicked the magistrate in the stomach. He let out a groan as he fell to the ground. Youqing's gym teacher grabbed hold of me again and yelled, "That's Magistrate Liu!"

"The magistrate's just the person I want to kill!" I said.

I raised my leg to kick him again when the magistrate suddenly asked me, "Aren't you Fugui?"

"I'm going to kill you!" I screamed.

The magistrate got to his feet and said, "Fugui, it's me, Chunsheng."

As soon as he said that I went numb. I gazed at him for a while, and the longer I looked at him the more he resembled the Chunsheng I once knew. I said, "Chunsheng, is it really you?"

Chunsheng took a step closer and looked me over.

"Fugui, it's you," he said.

Seeing Chunsheng seemed to quell my anger. Through my tears, I told him, "Chunsheng, you've gotten tall and gained weight."

Chunsheng's eyes also turned red.

"Fugui, I thought you were dead," he said.

I shook my head. "I survived."

"And all this time, I thought you'd died the same way as Old Quan," Chunsheng added.

As soon as he mentioned Old Quan the two of us began to cry like children. After crying for a while I asked Chunsheng, "Did you ever get your hands on that flatbread?"

Wiping away his tears, Chunsheng said, "No, you still remember that? Just as I went out to look for some I was taken prisoner."

"Did you get to eat steamed buns?" I asked him.

"I sure did," he smiled.

"I did, too," I said.

Saying that, we both laughed. We laughed and laughed until I remembered my dead son. I wiped my eyes and began to cry again. Chunsheng put his hand on my shoulder.

"Chunsheng," I said, "my only son is dead."

Chunsheng heaved a deep sigh, saying, "How could it have been your son?"

I thought of my son lying all alone in that little room—the pain was unbearable. I said to Chunsheng, "I want to see my son."

No longer did I want to kill anyone. Who could have guessed that Chunsheng would suddenly appear? I took a few steps and turned around to say to him, "Chunsheng, you owe me a life. You'll have to repay me in your next lifetime."

That night I carried Youqing home. I kept stopping from time to time on the way. When my arms got tired from carrying him,

I'd put him on my back for a while. But each time I placed him on my back I'd instantly start to panic, so I'd hold him again in front of me. I couldn't help but look at my son. When I saw I was approaching the village, it got more and more difficult to go on—what was I supposed to say to Jiazhen? Jiazhen was already so sick. I knew that once she found out Youqing had died she wouldn't be able to go on much longer. I sat down on the ridge just outside the village with Youqing resting on my leg. As soon as I looked down at him I couldn't hold back the tears. After crying for a while, I started to think about how to break the news to Jiazhen. After going through everything in my head, I decided I should keep Youqing's death a secret from her for the time being. I put Youqing down on the ridge and snuck home to get my hoe. I then picked Youqing back up, headed over to my parents' gravesite, and started digging a hole.

I had to bury him, but at the same time I couldn't bear to part with him. I sat down before my parents' graves and embraced Youqing, not letting go. I let his face rest up against my neck. Youqing's face felt like it was frozen stiff—it felt like ice pressing on my neck. The night wind whisked against the leaves above our heads, and Youqing's body was dampened by the dew. The image of him going to school that morning wouldn't leave me. I remembered his backpack bouncing up and down as he ran off to school. When I realized that Youqing would never again utter a single word or go off running barefoot, I felt wave after wave of pain—it hurt so much that I couldn't even cry. I kept sitting there until I saw the sky beginning to turn light. I had to bury him. I took off my clothes and, ripping off my sleeves, used them to cover Youqing's eyes. I used the rest of my clothes to wrap his body. I placed his body down in the pit I had dug and told my parents, who were buried beside him, "Youqing's coming. You'll have to take care of him. When he was alive I was never good to him. You'll have to love him for me."

The longer I looked at Youqing lying in that hole, the smaller he looked. He didn't look like someone who had lived thirteen years; he looked more like he must've looked as a newborn, just after Jiazhen had given birth to him. I pushed the dirt into his grave with my hands. I made sure I picked out all the little pebbles and rocks, afraid that the coarse pebbles would press against him and make him uncomfortable. As daylight broke, I finished burying Youqing. I slowly made my way home, but after taking a few steps I turned around to take one last look. As I got to the door of our hut, I realized that I would never see my son again. I couldn't help crying a few more tears, but fearing Jiazhen would hear, I covered my mouth and squatted down. After squatting down for a long time I began to hear the sound of people heading out to the fields to work—only then did I get back up and go inside. Fengxia was standing next to the door, staring at me with her wide-open eyes. She still didn't know that her little brother was dead. When the little kid from the other village had come to give me the news, Fengxia had been right there with me, but she couldn't hear. From her bed, Jiazhen called me. I walked over and told her, "Youqing's had an accident. He's in the hospital."

It looked like Jiazhen believed me.

"What happened?" she asked.

"I can't say for sure," I said. "During class Youqing suddenly fainted and was sent to the hospital. The doctor said that this type of illness might need some time to cure."

A sad expression began to appear on Jiazhen's face, and tears began to trickle from the corners of her eyes.

"It's exhaustion," she said. "He's been working too hard ever since I got sick. It's all my fault."

"It's not that," I said. "Even if he's tired, exhaustion doesn't cause someone to get sick like that."

Jiazhen looked me over.

"Your eyes are all swollen," she said.

I nodded. "Yeah, I didn't sleep all night."

I cut our conversation short and hastily made my way outside. Youqing was dead—I had only just put his body into the cold earth—and there was no way I'd have been able to control my emotions if I'd kept on with Jiazhen like that.

For the next few days I would work the field during the day, and then when night fell I would tell Jiazhen that I was going into town to see if Youqing was doing any better. I would slowly walk toward town, and as it got darker I would turn back around. When I got to the western side of the village, I would sit down in front of Youqing's grave. The night sky was a dense black, and the wind would waft against my face as I spoke to my dead son. My words were carried away by the wind; they didn't even seem to belong to me. I would sit there until the middle of the night before finally going home. The first couple of days Jiazhen would be waiting up for me, and as soon as I stepped through the door she would ask if Youqing was any better. I would be forced to make up some stories to keep the truth from her. But after a few days Jiazhen would already be asleep by the time I came home, lying there with her eyes closed. I knew that going on lying to her wasn't going to solve anything, but that was all I could do—take one day at a time. As long as Jiazhen believed that Youqing was okay, that was all that mattered.

One night, after arriving home from Youqing's grave, I climbed into bed next to Jiazhen. I thought she was asleep, but she suddenly said, "Fugui, I don't have much time left."

My heart sank. As I went to caress her face, I realized that her cheeks were covered with tears. Jiazhen continued, "You've got to take good care of Fengxia. I'm worried most about her."

Jiazhen didn't mention Youqing, and I immediately started to worry. I couldn't even think of anything to say to console her.

The next night, as usual, I told Jiazhen that I was going into town to see Youqing, but Jiazhen told me not to go. Instead, she asked me to carry her around the village for a walk. I had Fengxia pick up her mother and put her on my back. Jiazhen was getting lighter and lighter—she was so skinny it felt like there was nothing but bones left. As soon as we got outside, Jiazhen said, "I want to go to the western part of the village to look around."

That was where Youqing was buried. I said all right, but no matter what, my feet didn't want to go in that direction. After trudging along, we ended up at the eastern end of the village. Jiazhen whispered to me, "Fugui, don't lie to me. I know Youqing's dead."

The moment she uttered those words I stopped walking, and

suddenly my legs began to feel weak. I felt liquid dripping on my neck, and I knew that it was Jiazhen's tears.

"Take me to see Youqing," she said.

I knew I couldn't go on deceiving her. As I carried her to the western side of the village, Jiazhen whispered to me, "Each night I heard you returning from the west, so I knew that Youqing was dead."

When we got to Youqing's grave, Jiazhen wanted me to put her down. With tears streaming down her face, she climbed atop Youqing's burial mound. She placed both her hands upon the earth above his grave as if she wanted to caress Youqing, but she had so little energy that all she could do was move a few fingers. Seeing Jiazhen like this, my heart hurt so much it felt like it was all blocked up. I really shouldn't have buried Youqing—I should have let Jiazhen see him one last time.

Jiazhen stayed there until dark. I was afraid the night dew would make her sick, so I picked her up and put her on my back. Jiazhen had me take her over to the edge of the village. By the time we got there my collar was soaked.

"Youqing won't be able to run down this trail to school any-more," Jiazhen said, crying.

I gazed at that narrow, twisting trail that led to town and heard the sound of my son running barefoot. The moonlight was shin-ing on the trail, giving the illusion that a layer of salt had been sprinkled along it.

I spent that entire afternoon with the old man. Even after he and that old ox of his had gotten enough rest and gone back to plowing the field, I didn't think of leaving. I was like a sentinel watching over them from under the tree.

The farmers' voices from down in the fields carried in all directions. The most enthusiastic of the voices came from a ridge just beyond the adjacent field, where two well-built men guzzled down bucketfuls of water in a drinking contest. The young folks beside them were yelling and screaming—although they wouldn't have been nearly as excited if they'd been the ones drinking. Fugui looked kind of lonely being so far away from all the excitement. Transplanting rice seedlings in the irrigated field next to him were two women wearing scarves. They were talking about someone I didn't know. It seemed the guy they were talking about was strong, and he probably made more money than anyone else in the village. From what they said, I gathered that he often worked in town as a porter. As one of the women stretched her torso and massaged her back, I heard her say, "He spends half his money on his wife and the other half on other men's wives."

It was then that, leaning on his plough, Fugui approached them.

"There are four rules people should remember," announced Fugui as he made his way over to them. "Don't say the wrong thing, don't sleep in the wrong bed, don't enter the wrong house and don't rub the wrong pocket."

Once Fugui got close to them he turned and said, "That guy, he forgot the second rule. He slept in the wrong bed."

The two women giggled, and I saw a proud expression light up

Fugui's face. After calling out to his ox, he saw that I was laughing, too.

"These are the rules of life," he told me.

Later he sat back down with me in the shade, and I asked him to continue his story.

He looked at me with a thankful expression, as if I was doing him some kind of favor. He felt a deep happiness because someone had expressed interest in his life experience.

At first I thought that as soon as Youqing died, Jiazhen wouldn't be able to carry on much longer. And there was a period when it really didn't seem like she'd make it. She'd lie in bed all day gasping for breath, her eyes barely open. She didn't have an appetite, either; at every meal, Fengxia and I would have to lift her up and force porridge and soup down her throat. Jiazhen didn't have any meat left on her bones. Picking her up was like lifting a piece of firewood.

The team leader had come over to the house twice, and each time, after seeing Jiazhen, he would just shake his head. He pulled me aside and whispered, "I'm afraid she's not going to make it."

As soon as I heard this my heart sank. It had been less than two weeks since Youqing had died, and now, right before my eyes, Jiazhen was going to leave, too. How were we supposed to get by if we suddenly lost half our family? It's the same as if you smash a pot in two—it's no longer a pot. Our family would no longer be a family.

The team leader said he'd go to the commune hospital and get a doctor to come look at Jiazhen. He was a man of his word. When he came back from a meeting at the commune headquarters, he really did bring a doctor back with him. That doctor was very slight and wore a pair of glasses. He asked me what kind of sickness Jiazhen had.

"She's got soft bone disease," I said.

The doctor nodded and sat down on the bed to take Jiazhen's pulse. As he took her pulse he talked to her. Hearing someone talking to her, all Jiazhen could do was open her eyes; she couldn't say anything. The doctor didn't know why, but for some reason he couldn't find Jiazhen's pulse. He looked disturbed and extended his arm to lift her eyelid. Then, holding her wrist with one hand and feeling for a pulse with the other, he tilted his head to one side, as if straining to hear. After a while, the doctor stood up and said to me, "Her pulse is so weak I can barely feel it."

After a pause he added, "You'd better make arrangements for her funeral."

The doctor virtually killed me with that one sentence. I almost collapsed on the floor that very moment. I walked the doctor outside and asked him, "How much longer can my wife live?"

"She won't make it another month," the doctor replied. "People who have your wife's illness usually don't last long once the paralysis sets in."

That night, after Jiazhen and Fengxia had gone to sleep, I went outside and sat down by myself until daybreak. At first all I did was cry like a baby, and then I started to think about the past. The more I thought, the more tears fell. Time really flies—it seemed like ever since Jiazhen and I were married we'd been through nothing but hard times. And now, in the blink of an eye, it was time for her to leave me. I decided that just crying and feeling upset was no use. When it came to times like these, a man had to be practical. I decided to make sure Jiazhen would have a decent burial.

The team leader had a good heart. Seeing how depressed I was, he said, "Fugui, don't take it too hard. Everyone's got to go sometime. Right now don't worry about anything, just try to let Jiazhen feel at ease during her last days. You can have any plot of land in the village you want for her burial."

But by then I had already decided. I said to the team leader, "Jiazhen wants to be buried with Youqing. They should be buried together."

Poor Youqing, buried with only a layer of clothes to protect him. I wouldn't let Jiazhen be buried like that. No matter how poor we were, I had to buy her a coffin. Otherwise I wouldn't have been able to live with myself. If Jiazhen had married someone else, she would have never had to suffer with me, and she would never have ended up working herself to the point of illness. I went from house to house around the village borrowing money. I'm not sure what was wrong with me, but as soon as I said the money was to buy Jiazhen a casket, I couldn't help but cry. Everyone in the village was poor, and all the borrowed money put together still wasn't enough to buy a coffin. It was only after the team leader gathered together some public funds that I was finally able to go to the neighboring village to hire a carpenter.

At first Fengxia didn't know her mother was dying, but she noticed that every chance I got I kept running off to the neighboring village's lamb pen, which is where the carpenter worked. Every time I went down there I would stay half the day, even forgetting to come home to eat. Fengxia would come to get me, and after a few trips she saw the coffin gradually starting to take shape. It was only then that she began to realize what was happening. Her eyes opened wide as she made a sign with her hands to ask me. I thought Fengxia should know, so I told her.

Fengxia just kept shaking her head. I knew what she was thinking, so I used my hands to tell her it was for Jiazhen. I told her Jiazhen would use it after she was gone. Fengxia kept shaking her head and pulled me home. Even after we got home Fengxia still wouldn't let go of my sleeve. She nudged Jiazhen, and Jiazhen opened her eyes. Then she forcefully shook my shoulders to show me that Jiazhen was still alive and well. Finally, she extended her right hand and made a downward chopping motion—she wanted me to get rid of the coffin.

Fengxia had never even dreamed her mother would die, and even if I had told her she wouldn't have believed it. Seeing Fengxia like that, I could only lower my head. I didn't even attempt to gesture to her at all.

Once Jiazhen took to her bed, she didn't get up for over twenty days. Sometimes it seemed like she was getting better and she might pull through after all. Then one night as I lay down next to her and was about to turn out the light, Jiazhen suddenly reached out her arm and pulled me toward her—she told me not to turn out the light. Her voice was weaker than the buzz of a mosquito. She had me turn her on her side. That night my wife couldn't stop staring at me. She kept calling out to me, "Fugui."

She smiled at me and closed her eyes. After a while Jiazhen opened her eyes and asked, "Is Fengxia asleep?"

I propped myself up to look at Fengxia and said, "She's asleep."

Although she kept pausing between her words, Jiazhen talked quite a bit that night, and only after she was utterly exhausted did she finally go to sleep. I, on the other hand, was terrified and couldn't get to sleep no matter how hard I tried. Jiazhen seemed so much better, but I was afraid it was that "last radiance of the set-ting sun" that everyone talks about. I caressed Jiazhen's body, and only after I realized she was still warm did I begin to relax a bit.

The next morning when I got up, Jiazhen was still asleep. She had been up late the previous night so I didn't wake her. Fengxia and I had some porridge before heading out to work. We fin-ished early that day, and when Fengxia and I got home I was shocked to find Jiazhen sitting up in bed. She had sat up all by herself. Seeing us come in, she said quietly, "Fugui, I'm hungry. Would you cook me some porridge?"

I just stood there in shock for a long time. I had never imag-ined that Jiazhen would get better. Only after Jiazhen called me a second time did I snap out of my daze. Tears rushed down my face, and forgetting that Fengxia couldn't hear, I said to her, "You did it. It's all because in your heart you wouldn't let your mom die."

As soon as she got her appetite back, I knew that Jiazhen was going to be okay. Before long Jiazhen was well enough to do some needlework from her bed. If she keeps improving at this rate, I thought, she might even be able to get out of bed and walk again. I could finally rest at ease.

The moment I got some peace of mind, however, I myself became ill. I had actually gotten sick a long time before, but after Youqing died and with Jiazhen on the verge of following him, I couldn't worry about my own illness—I just didn't let it get to me. But while Jiazhen had defied her doctor and gradually started getting better, I began to feel increasingly lightheaded and dizzy. This dizziness continued until I passed out one day while transplanting rice seeds. Only after someone carried me home did I realize I was sick.

As soon as I fell ill, things became terrible for Fengxia. With both Jiazhen and me bedridden, Fengxia had both of us to take care of, and at the same time she still had to go out to the fields to earn work points. After a few days I realized that Fengxia was beyond the point of exhaustion. I told Jiazhen I was feeling a lot better and dragged my sick body out to the fields to work. When the other villagers saw me they were taken aback. They said, "Fugui, your hair's all gray."

"It's been gray for a long time," I laughed.

"No, you used to have a lot of black hair left," they said. "How could it all turn gray in just a few days?"

In just a matter of days, I had really grown old. The strength I had had was gone. My shoulders and lower back would get sore when I worked, and if I pushed myself too hard sweat would stream from every pore in my body.

Just over a month after Youqing died, Chunsheng arrived. He was no longer called Chunsheng—he was called Liberation Liu. When other people saw him they'd all address him as Magistrate Liu, but I still called him Chunsheng. He told me that after he was taken prisoner he joined the Liberation Army. He fought all the way down to Fujian and later went to war in Korea. Chunsheng was lucky to have come back in one piece after all those battles he had fought in. After the Korean War he was transferred to civilian work and moved to a nearby county. He didn't come to our county until the year Youqing died.

We were all home when Chunsheng arrived. Before Chunsheng even got to the door the team leader announced him, calling out, "Fugui, Magistrate Liu has come to see you."

The team leader and Chunsheng both came in.

"It's Chunsheng, Chunsheng's here," I told Jiazhen.

Who could have known that as soon as Jiazhen heard it was Chunsheng, tears would trickle from her eyes? She rushed at Chunsheng, screaming, "Get out!"

I was completely caught off guard by Jiazhen's reaction and didn't know what to do. The team leader got anxious.

"How can you talk like that to Magistrate Liu?" he demanded.

But Jiazhen couldn't have cared less about all that. Screaming through her tears, she cried, "You give me back my Youqing!"

Chunsheng shook his head and said to Jiazhen, "This is a little token of my regard."

Chunsheng tried to hand some money to Jiazhen, but she wouldn't even look at it. Lunging at him again, she shouted, "Leave! Get out!"

The team leader rushed over to Jiazhen to keep her from Chunsheng.

"Jiazhen, you've got everything mixed up," the team leader explained. "Youqing was killed in an accident. It wasn't Magistrate Liu's fault."

Seeing that Jiazhen wouldn't take the money, Chunsheng handed it to me.

"Fugui, take it. I beg you," he said.

Seeing Jiazhen like that, how could I take the money? When Chunsheng stuffed the money into the palm of my hand, Jiazhen's anger instantly switched to me. She screamed, "Your son's life is worth only two hundred *yuan*?"

I quickly stuffed the money back into Chunsheng's hand. After Jiazhen threw him out, Chunsheng came back on two other occasions, but no matter what, Jiazhen wouldn't let him in. Women are stubborn—once they get their minds set on something, no one can budge them. As I saw Chunsheng off to the edge of the village I told him, "Chunsheng, from now on it's probably best if you don't come back anymore."

He nodded and left. It would be years before I would see Chunsheng again. I didn't see him until the Cultural Revolution.

When the Cultural Revolution hit, the whole town turned upside down. The streets were crawling with people, and there were fights every day. People were even beaten to death. No one from the countryside dared go into town. Compared with what was happening in town, the countryside was much more peaceful. Everything was just like before, except that you didn't feel as safe when you were asleep at night. That was because Chairman Mao's supreme directives were always issued in the middle of the night. The team leader would stand in the middle of the drying field and blow his whistle with all his might. When we'd hear that whistle we'd all jump out of bed and rush down to the drying field to hear the announcements. The team leader would be standing there yelling, "Everybody to the drying field! The venerable Chairman Mao has some instructions for you!"

We were just your average everyday folk. It wasn't that we didn't care about national issues, it was simply that we didn't understand that kind of stuff. We would listen to the team leader in the same way that the team leader would listen to the higher-ups. All it took was one word from the higher-ups and we'd all think and do whatever they wanted.

Jiazhen and I were worried about Fengxia. She was getting older, and we felt we should really find her a husband. Fengxia looked just like Jiazhen did when she was younger. If it hadn't been for that sickness when she was little, the matchmakers would have already broken down our door. As time went by I had less and less energy, and it seemed like Jiazhen would never fully recover from her illness. We'd been through a lot in this life, and just as a pear falls from a tree when it's ripe, we were also getting to ripe old age. But we couldn't stop worrying about Fengxia. She was different from other people. Who would be there to take care of her when she got old?

Fengxia may have been a deaf-mute, but she was still a woman, and she had to have known that it was only natural for men and women to get married eventually. Every year there were village women marrying out and other new brides who married in. During the excitement of the drums and gongs, Fengxia would always stand there holding on to her hoe as if in a trance. The young people in the village would always point at her and laugh.

When the Wang family's third son married, everyone in the village said that his bride was a real beauty. The day the bride was welcomed into the village, she was wearing a quilted red jacket and couldn't stop her nervous giggling. Watching from the field I could see her—she was red all over. Her apple-red face was especially attractive.

Everyone working in the fields ran over to see. The groom took a pack of Flying Horse cigarettes out of his pocket and passed some out to the more senior men. A few of the younger guys nearby yelled out, "Hey, what about us?"

The groom gave a sinister laugh and stuffed the cigarettes back into his pocket. The young guys rushed over to steal them, yelling, "You've got a woman who's gonna sleep with you tonight and you can't even spare a damn cigarette!"

The groom tried with all his might to hold on to his pack of Flying Horses, but the guys pried his fingers open and snatched his cigarettes away. Once they got them, one of the young men held them up in the air while his buddies rushed up the ridge to get their share.

The young men who were left surrounded the bride, snickering obnoxiously and making lewd comments. The bride just lowered her head and smiled. There isn't much that can spoil a woman's wedding day; new brides are happy regardless of what goes on around them.

Fengxia was in the field, and as soon as she saw the scene she seemed to enter a trance. She didn't even blink; she just stood there motionless, holding her hoe tightly in her hands. Standing off to one side watching her, I felt so sad. Deep down I thought that if she wanted to see the wedding I should let her. Fengxia had a tough life, and the only bit of happiness she had was watching another woman getting married. No one expected that after standing there watching for a while she would actually walk over. Standing next to the bride, she smiled awkwardly and then followed the bride off on her procession. All the young guys started to laugh hysterically. Fengxia was wearing an outfit covered with patches, while the bride was wearing an immaculate and brightly colored dress—she was pretty, too. Seeing them walk together, there was no comparison. It was sad to see Fengxia ridiculed like that. She wasn't wearing any makeup, but her face was just as red as the bride's. She kept turning around, unable to keep her eyes off the new bride.

The young guys from the village continued to laugh and holler. "Fengxia wants a man!" they taunted.

That comment wasn't so bad, but who could have guessed that before long they would start in with their nasty jokes?

"Fengxia's got her eye on your bed!" someone said to the bride.

As soon as Fengxia started walking beside her, the bride stopped smiling. It was obvious that she looked down on Fengxia. It was then that somebody said to the groom, "You little bastard, you really got a good deal. You get to marry two for the price of one. Tonight you'll have one on top and one on the bottom!"

After hearing that the groom laughed slyly. But the bride couldn't take it. She didn't care if new brides were supposed to be shy or not. She straightened her neck and yelled at her husband-to-be, "What the hell's so funny?"

I couldn't stand it anymore. Walking up the ridge I said to them, "How can you act like that? If you want to pick on somebody, pick on me, but don't you bully Fengxia."

I pulled Fengxia away and headed home. Fengxia was smart—as soon as she saw the look on my face she knew what had happened. She lowered her head and followed me home. When we got to our door, teardrops were dripping from her eyes.

After that, Jiazhen and I decided that no matter what, we had to find a man for Fengxia. We were bound to die before she did, and after we were gone Fengxia would bury us. If things continued like this for Fengxia, there wouldn't be anyone to bury her when she died. But who would be willing to marry Fengxia?

Jiazhen said we should ask the team leader for help. The team leader knew a lot of people. He could ask around and, who knew, maybe someone would want Fengxia after all. I went to talk to the team leader, and after hearing me out he said, "You're right, Fengxia should really get married. It's just hard to find a good match."

"We don't mind if the guy's missing an arm or has got a broken leg," I said. "As long as he's willing to marry Fengxia, we'll approve."

After saying that I started to feel bad. Fengxia was really no different from other people; she just couldn't speak. When I got home I told Jiazhen. Upon hearing what I had said she also felt bad. Without a word, she sat down on the edge of the bed. After a long pause she sighed and said, "There's really nothing else we can do at this point."

But before long the team leader found a man for Fengxia. I was fertilizing our private plot when the team leader came by and said, "Fugui, I found a husband for Fengxia. He's from town and works as a porter. He makes a lot of money."

As soon as I heard that, it sounded too good to be true. I thought the team leader was playing with me. "Team leader, don't joke around," I said.

"I'm not joking," the team leader replied. "His name's Wan Erxi. He's got a crooked head. His head rests against his shoulder—no matter what, it won't stand up straight."

It wasn't until the team leader told me this that I believed the match was for real.

"Hurry up and arrange for him to come and check out Fengxia," I hastened to say.

The moment the team leader left, I threw down the manure ladle and ran toward our hut, yelling, "Jiazhen! Jiazhen!"

Sitting in bed, Jiazhen thought I'd had an accident. Her eyes widened as she saw me come in.

"Fengxia's got a man!" I said.

Only then did Jiazhen breathe easy and say, "You really scared me."

"He's not missing a leg, and his arms are okay, too," I said. "Plus he lives in town."

I began to cry. At first Jiazhen smiled, but seeing me cry, tears also streamed from her eyes. We were happy for a while, and then Jiazhen asked, "It sounds so good, are you sure he would want Fengxia?"

"He's got a crooked head," I said.

Only after hearing that did Jiazhen relax a bit. That night Jiazhen had me take out some of her old clothes so she could make a new outfit for Fengxia. Jiazhen said, "Fengxia will finally have a reason to get dressed up. Everyone's going to come for the wedding."

Wan Erxi showed up just a few days later. His head really was crooked; when he saw me he raised his left shoulder. When he saw Fengxia and Jiazhen he did the same thing. Fengxia started to giggle the moment she laid eyes on him.

Wan Erxi was wearing a neat and clean tunic suit. If it hadn't been for his crooked head he would have looked just like one of those big city cadres. He came in accompanied by the team leader and carrying a bottle of wine and a calico cloth. Jiazhen was sitting on the bed. Her hair was neatly combed, and although her clothes were a bit tattered, they were very clean. I had also put a new pair of cloth shoes under the bed especially for Jiazhen. Wearing a red outfit, Fengxia sat next to her mother with her head lowered. Jiazhen giggled as she looked at her unofficial son-in-law. Deep down she was filled with happiness.

Wan Erxi put the wine and the cloth down on the table and then, raising his shoulder, he walked around our hut. He was checking out our home.

"Team leader, Erxi, have a seat," I said.

Erxi grunted and sat down on a stool. The team leader waved his hand and said, "I can't stay, but let me introduce you. Erxi, this is Fengxia, and these are her parents."

Fengxia's hands were resting on her legs. When she saw the team leader point to her, she smiled at him. When the team leader pointed to Jiazhen, Fengxia turned to her mother and continued smiling.

"Team leader, please have a seat," insisted Jiazhen.

The team leader replied, "No, I've really got to go. But why don't you all go ahead and chat."

The team leader turned around to leave. I knew there was no way to convince the team leader to stay, so I saw him out. When I came back in I pointed to the wine on the table and said to Erxi, "You must have gone broke buying this. To tell you the truth, I haven't had a drink in decades!"

Erxi didn't say anything. He just grunted and lifted his shoulder, all the while looking the house up and down. The way he kept looking over our hut made me begin to feel anxious. Jiazhen forced a smile as she explained, "Our family's a bit poor."

Erxi grunted again and raised his shoulder to look at Jiazhen. Jiazhen continued, "It's a good thing we've been raising a lamb and a couple of chickens. Fugui and I have decided that when Fengxia gets married we'll sell them for her dowry."

After hearing this, all he did was grunt again. I had no idea what he was thinking. We sat for a while before Erxi got up and said he had to go. The moment he got up I figured the match was a failure. He hadn't even taken a good look at Fengxia. All he had done was stare at our beat-up old hut. I looked at Jiazhen. Forcing a smile, she said to Erxi, "My legs are no good anymore, so I can't see you off."

Erxi nodded. As he walked outside, I asked him, "You're not taking those gifts?"

Grunting, he raised his shoulder to look at the straw roof. After nodding once more, he left.

I went back inside and sat down on a stool. Thinking about what had happened made me a little mad.

"What right does he have to be so picky?" I said. "The guy can't even hold his head straight."

Jiazhen sighed as she said, "You can't blame him."

Fengxia wasn't stupid. As soon as she saw us like that she knew that he didn't like her. She stood up and went into the other room. She changed into some old clothes, grabbed her hoe and headed out to the field.

That night the team leader came to ask me, "Did it work out?"

I shook my head and said, "Too poor, our family's too poor."

The next afternoon I was out plowing the field when someone called me. "Fugui, look over there. It looks like that crooked-headed son-in-law of yours is coming."

I looked up to see five or six guys pulling a cart down the trail from town. Except for the one in front with the crooked head, they all walked with a sway. With just one glance from far away I knew it was Erxi—I never imagined he would come back.

When Erxi saw me, he said, "It's about time you had the straw on your roof replaced. I also brought a cart of lime to whitewash the walls."

I looked in the cart and saw the lime along with two brushes to paint the walls with. On top of the cart was a small table, and on top of the table was a pig's head. Erxi was carrying two bottles of white sorghum wine.

It was only then I realized that when Erxi was staring at our house, it wasn't because he looked down on our poverty. He had noticed everything, even the pile of straw outside our door. I'd been planning to change the straw on our roof for a long time, but I'd wanted to wait until the slow season when some of the other villagers would have time to give me a hand.

Erxi not only brought five people with him, but he brought meat and spirits—he had really thought of everything. When they got to the door they put down the cart, and Erxi walked right in as if he were walking into his own home. Carrying the pig's head in one hand and the small table in the other, he went in and put them down in front of Jiazhen. Erxi said, "This way you won't have to worry about cooking."

Jiazhen was so moved that tears came to her eyes. She hadn't thought that Erxi would come back either, and never in a thousand years had we imagined that he would bring with him a bunch of guys to replace our roof and prepare a small meal all in the same day.

"Erxi, you're so considerate," said Jiazhen.

Erxi and his friends moved our table and stools outside and covered the ground around the tree out front with rice straw.

Then Erxi went over to the bed to carry Jiazhen outside. Jiazhen laughed and waved her hands, calling out to me, "Fugui, don't just stand there and watch."

I rushed over and let Jiazhen climb onto my back. I smiled at Erxi and told him, "She's my wife, I'll carry her. One day you'll have to carry Fengxia."

Jiazhen nudged me after hearing that, but Erxi couldn't stop laughing. I carried Jiazhen over to the tree and sat her on the straw-covered ground with her back against the trunk. I watched Erxi and his friends separate the pile of straw into a number of small bundles. Erxi and one of his friends got up on the roof and started to replace the straw while the other four guys stayed on the ground. As soon as I saw them get to work I knew that the guys Erxi had brought had a lot of experience doing this kind of work—they were both quick and neat. The four men on the ground used bamboo poles to pass the straw up while Erxi and his friend spread it out. The fact that his head rested on his shoulder didn't affect his work one bit. When the straw was tossed up he would first kick it up with his foot and then grab hold of it with his hand. There wasn't a single person in the whole village who had that kind of skill.

By noon the roof was already finished. I boiled a bucket of tea, and Fengxia poured it for everyone. Fengxia was really busy running back and forth, but she was happy. She couldn't stop smiling after seeing so many people suddenly coming to help out.

A whole bunch of people from the village came to look.

"You're so lucky," one woman told Jiazhen. "Your son-in-law hasn't even got to the altar yet and already he's helping out."

"It's Fengxia who's lucky," Jiazhen replied.

When Erxi came down from the roof I said to him, "Erxi, take a rest."

Wiping the sweat from his face with his sleeve, he said, "It's okay, I'm not tired."

He raised his shoulder so he could look around, and when he saw a patch of vegetables he asked me, "Is that part of our land?"

"It sure is," I said.

He went inside to get a vegetable knife, then went down to the field to cut some fresh vegetables and brought them back inside. After a while he started to slice the pig's head. I went over to stop him—he should have left it for Fengxia to do—but he just wiped the sweat from his face and continued.

"I'm not tired," he insisted.

I had no choice but to go outside and get Fengxia. Fengxia was standing next to Jiazhen, and as I pushed her inside she kept turning around in embarrassment to look at her mother. Only after Jiazhen laughed and waved for her to go in did she finally go inside.

Jiazhen and I kept Erxi's friends company, chatting and drinking tea. At one point I popped in for a moment to see Fengxia and Erxi together. One of them was tending the fire while the other was cooking—they looked like a little family. The two of them kept sneaking glances at each other; neither one of them could stop giggling.

I went out to tell Jiazhen, and she laughed. After a while I couldn't stand it anymore and had to go in for another peek. But just as I stood up Jiazhen stopped me by whispering, "Don't go in."

After we ate, Erxi and the others used the lime to whitewash our walls. As soon as the lime dried the following day, our walls were a brilliant white, just like those brick houses in town. It was still early when they finished the whitewashing, so I said to Erxi, "Why don't you stay for a while and leave after dinner?"

"No, thanks," he said.

He proceeded to lift his shoulder in the direction of Fengxia— I knew he was looking at her. Then, lowering his voice, Erxi asked Jiazhen and me, "Mom, Dad, when can I marry Fengxia?"

As soon as I heard this, as soon as I heard him call Jiazhen and me Mom and Dad, I was so ecstatic that you couldn't have wiped the smile off my face if you'd tried. After looking to Jiazhen, I said, "Whenever you want. You set the date."

After that I added quietly, "Erxi, it's not that I want you to go bankrupt or anything. It's just that Fengxia's had a hard life. Let's make the wedding day special for her. Invite some extra people to make it a real event. It would be good if you called some of the people from the village over, too."

Erxi said, "Dad, I'll take care of it."

That night, Fengxia caressed the cotton print Erxi had brought. She would gaze at it and smile, and after smiling she'd go back to gazing at it. Every once in a while she'd look over at Jiazhen and me. Seeing that we were smiling, too, she'd instantly get nervous and blush. Jiazhen and I were pleased. It looked like Fengxia really liked Erxi.

"Erxi is an honest and trustworthy fellow," Jiazhen said. "With him caring for Fengxia, I can rest easy."

We sold the chickens and lamb and brought Fengxia into town to buy her two new outfits plus some household items like a blanket and washbasin. We made sure that Fengxia got whatever the other girls in the village had gotten when they married. As Jiazhen put it, "We can't let Fengxia feel like she's different from the other girls."

The day Erxi came to marry Fengxia, you could hear the crashing of the bells and gongs from far away. All the farmers rushed over to the village entrance to watch. Erxi brought more than twenty people with him, and everyone wore Sun Yat-sen–style tunic jackets. If it hadn't been for the red flower pinned to Erxi's jacket, it would have looked just like some big cadre was coming to town. The sound of more than ten gongs beating at the same time along with the thunderous "bong" sound of two drums made all the country folks' ears ring. But by far the show-iest part of the procession was an emerald green cart draped with red sashes, on top of which sat a chair that was painted a matching red and green.

As soon as everyone got to the village, Erxi opened up two car-tons of Front Gate cigarettes and stuffed packs into the hands of all the men he saw. He kept repeating, "Thanks for coming, thank you."

When other families in the village got married, the best ciga-rettes they would give out would be Flying Horse, if that. But Erxi gave out pack after pack of Front Gates—nobody could compete with that. As soon as someone got his hands on a pack, he would stick it right into his pocket, afraid that someone else would try to snatch it away. Those lucky enough to get their hands on a pack would stick their fingers deep into their pockets, fishing around for a cigarette. When they would finally manage to pull one out, they'd swiftly stick it between their lips.

The twenty-odd guys who came with Erxi were working hard. Not only were they shaking the heavens with their gongs and drums, but they were screaming with all their might. Their pockets were bulging, and when they saw the village women and children they'd throw them pieces of candy. I was stunned by the extravagance and kept thinking about how much money they were throwing away.

When they got to my house, they all went in to see Fengxia. They left their instruments outside so the young guys from the village could keep the music going. Wearing her new clothes, Fengxia looked really stunning. Even I, as her father, had never imagined she could look so beautiful. She was sitting by Jiazhen's bed, checking each man who came in to see if he was Erxi. When she finally saw him she lowered her head. When Erxi's friends from town saw Fengxia, they all said, "Wow, this crooked-head of ours really lucked out."

For years after that, whenever other girls in the village were married off, it would be said that none of their weddings compared to Fengxia's. That day, when Fengxia was called out of the house, her face was as red as a tomato. Never before had so many people looked at her at the same time, and aside from burying her head in her chest, she didn't know what to do. Erxi took her by the hand and led her over to the cart. Even after seeing the chair, Fengxia still didn't quite know what to do. A roar of laughter erupted from the people watching when Erxi, who was a full head shorter than Fengxia, picked her up and placed her in the chair. Fengxia laughed, too.

"Mom, Dad, I'm taking Fengxia away," Erxi told Jiazhen and me.

With that, Erxi started pulling the cart away. The moment the cart began to move, Fengxia abruptly raised her head and turned around, anxiously looking back. I knew that she was looking for Jiazhen and me. But I was standing right beside her, with Jiazhen on my back. As soon as she caught sight of us, she started to cry. She twisted her body around to look at us through her tears. Suddenly I thought back to when Fengxia was thirteen and that guy had taken her away—she had that same tearful look in her eyes as she had back then. As soon as I thought of that, tears began streaming down my face, and at the same moment I felt moisture on my neck and knew that Jiazhen was crying, too. But this time it's different, I thought. This time Fengxia's getting married. I smiled and said, "Jiazhen, today's a happy occasion. You should be smiling."

Erxi had a good heart. While he was pulling the cart he kept looking back at his bride. When he noticed a teary-eyed Fengxia turning back to look at us, Erxi stopped and turned to look at us as well. The more Fengxia cried, the sadder she seemed to get, and her shoulders began to tremble. I could feel my heart tightening up. I yelled to Erxi, "Erxi, what are you waiting for? Fengxia's your wife now."

When Fengxia moved to town it felt like our spirits had gone with her—no matter what Jiazhen and I did, we couldn't help but feel empty inside. We didn't use to notice Fengxia coming and going all the time, but the moment she left it became so quiet. Jiazhen and I were the only ones left. We just kept looking around the house as if, after decades of living there, we hadn't already seen enough. For me it was okay; working in the field, I could get my mind off Fengxia. But it was really hard on Jiazhen. Sitting in bed all day with nothing to do, how could she not feel the loss with her Fengxia gone? She used to stay in bed all day without saying anything, but after Fengxia left she started to feel really terrible. Her lower back was tender and her shoulders were sore. It seemed like no matter what she did she couldn't get comfortable. I could completely sympathize with her—staying in bed all day is even more exhausting than working in the field. Her body couldn't even move. At dusk I would carry her piggyback around the village, and when the other villagers saw Jiazhen they would affectionately ask her all about how she'd been doing. Jiazhen would feel much more at ease and, leaning close to my ear, she'd whisper, "They won't laugh at us, will they?"

"Why would they laugh at us? What's so funny about me carrying my own wife?" I'd reply.

Jiazhen began to like reminiscing about the past. When we'd get to a certain spot she'd want to tell stories about back when Fengxia and Youqing were children. After going on and on about them, she'd laugh. When we got to the edge of the village, Jiazhen brought up the day I came home. She had been working in the field that day when she heard someone call out to Fengxia and Youqing in a loud voice. She looked up and saw me immediately, but at first she didn't believe her eyes. When Jiazhen got to this point her laughter mixed with tears. Teardrops ran down my neck as she said, "Once you came home, everything was great."

According to custom, Fengxia was supposed to come back to visit in a month—we were also supposed to wait at least a month before we went to visit her. So you can imagine our surprise when she came home in less than ten days. One evening, just after we had eaten, someone called from outside, "Fugui, you'd better head down to the village entrance. It looks like that crooked-headed son-in-law of yours is coming."

At first I didn't believe him. Everyone in the village knew how much Jiazhen and I missed Fengxia, so I figured they were just playing a joke on us. I remember telling Jiazhen, "It can't be them, it's been only ten days."

But Jiazhen started to get anxious and said, "Hurry up and go take a look."

I ran down to take a look, and what do you know, it really was Erxi. Lifting his left shoulder, he was carrying a cake; Fengxia was walking beside him. Hand in hand, they were all smiles as they approached me. When the people from the village saw them they all laughed—in those days you'd never see couples holding hands. I told them, "Erxi's a city boy. Those people in town have got a bit of that foreign flavor."

Jiazhen was ecstatic when Fengxia and Erxi came home. As soon as Fengxia sat down on the corner of the bed, Jiazhen couldn't stop caressing her hand. She kept saying that Fengxia had gained weight, but how much weight could someone really gain in ten days?

"We had no idea you were coming," I told Erxi. "We didn't even prepare anything."

Erxi giggled. He said he hadn't known he was coming, either. Fengxia had taken him by the hand, and he'd just blindly followed her all the way.

After Fengxia came home that day, I also said to hell with the old custom and started going into town just about every other day. Now that I mention it, it was really Jiazhen who wanted me to go, but I'd be lying if I didn't admit that I enjoyed visiting them, too. When I'd go into town it would be with the same fervor and enthusiasm I had going into town when I was young, only this time I was going for a different reason.

Before I left, I went down to our private plot to cut some fresh vegetables and put them in a basket. I was wearing the new cloth shoes Jiazhen had made for me. When I cut the vegetables I got my shoes dirty, and when Jiazhen saw she stopped me and told me to wipe off the mud before I left.

"An old man like me couldn't care less about some mud on my shoes," I told her.

"You can't say that," Jiazhen retorted. "Even though you're old you're still a person. And as long as you're a person you should try to keep clean."

She was right. Even after being sick in bed for so many years, unable even to go down to the fields, she still made sure her hair was neat and combed every day. So I put on some clean clothes and walked to the edge of the village. When the other villagers saw me carrying the basket of fresh vegetables they asked, "Off to see Fengxia again?"

I nodded, "Yep."

"You keep going back there. Doesn't that crooked-headed son-in-law of yours get sick of you?" they asked.

"Erxi isn't like that," I answered.

Erxi's neighbors took a real fancy to Fengxia. As soon as I'd get there they'd all compliment her by saying how hardworking and intelligent she was. Once she started sweeping she'd sweep the ground in front of her neighbors' houses—hell, once she got going, she'd sweep half the street. Seeing Fengxia beginning to break a sweat, the neighbors would go over and pat her on the back to tell her to stop. Only then would she go back inside with a bright smile on her face.

Since our family was poor and never had the luxury of wearing sweaters, Fengxia had never learned how to knit. When Fengxia saw one of the neighbors knitting a sweater, her hands weaving back and forth, Fengxia was so excited she pulled a stool over to watch. Once she sat down she ended up staying there half the day—she was spellbound. Seeing how much Fengxia seemed to like it, the neighbor decided to teach her step by step. As soon as she began to teach her, the neighbor was shocked by how quickly Fengxia picked it up. Within three or four days Fengxia could knit just as fast as the rest of them. When they saw me they would comment, "How great it would be if Fengxia wasn't deaf and mute."

Deep down they felt sorry for Fengxia. From then on, whenever she finished with her housework, she'd sit with the neighbors and knit for them. All the women on the block thought that Fengxia did the neatest and tightest knitting job, so they'd all send their wool to Fengxia to have her knit for them. Naturally, Fengxia was a bit more tired than before, but she was happy. When the sweaters were finished she'd give them back. The neighbors would give her the thumbs-up sign, and Fengxia's broad smile would beam for what seemed like an eternity.

When I'd arrive in town, the neighbors would come over one by one to tell me how great Fengxia was. I heard nothing but compliments from them and started to blush.

"You people here in town are really nice," I said. "It's rare that anyone in the country says anything nice about Fengxia."

I was really pleased to see how much Erxi loved her and how all the neighbors liked her. Every time I went home, Jiazhen would complain that I had stayed too long. She was right. All alone at home, staring at the door with her neck outstretched, she would wait for me to come home so she could hear all the latest news about Fengxia. After waiting all day and still not seeing any sign of me, it was only natural for her to start getting anxious.

"Sorry, as soon as I see Fengxia I forget the time," I'd say.

Whenever I returned home I'd spend a long time sitting on the edge of the bed telling Jiazhen everything that was going on in and around Fengxia's house. I'd even have to tell her what color clothes Fengxia was wearing and whether the shoes she had made for Fengxia were holding up. Jiazhen had to know everything—there was no end to her questions, just as there was no end to my answers. I talked so much that my throat would get dry, but even then Jiazhen wouldn't let me go. She'd ask, "Is there anything you forgot to tell me?"

Once we started talking we wouldn't stop until after dark. Just about everyone in the village had already turned in, but we still hadn't even eaten.

"I'll go fix something to eat," I'd say.

But Jiazhen would pull me, practically begging. "Tell me some more about Fengxia."

I was always willing to go on about Fengxia. Even after telling Jiazhen everything, I still couldn't say enough. When I went to work down in the field, I'd tell the other villagers about her. I'd tell them how well she was doing in town, how everyone there complimented her for being hardworking and intelligent and how she knitted faster than anyone else. A few of the villagers were upset after hearing this.

"Fugui, how could you be so muddleheaded?" they'd say. "Those city people are always up to no good. How's Fengxia to cope with all this work they're giving her? They'll work her to death!"

"Now, I wouldn't say that," I said.

"If Fengxia knits sweaters for them it's only right that they give her some kind of present," they'd say. "Do they give her anything?"

Country people are really narrow-minded—all they do is nitpick over these little things. The women in town aren't as bad as country people make them out to be. Twice I heard them say to Erxi, "Erxi, go buy a few *jin* of wool thread. Fengxia should have a sweater, too."

Erxi laughed after hearing this but didn't say a word. He was an honest guy. When he married Fengxia he listened to me and spent a lot of money, and now he still had a debt to pay off. When we were alone he whispered to me, "Dad, as soon as I pay off the debt I'll buy Fengxia a wool sweater."

Meanwhile, the Cultural Revolution was raging more and more intensely in town. All the streets were filled with big character posters.* The people who hung them up were a bunch of lazy bums. When they hung new posters up, they didn't even bother to tear the old ones down. The layers of posters just got thicker and thicker, making the walls stick out as if they had a whole bunch of pockets. There were even posters hanging over Fengxia and Erxi's front door. Inside they had good ol' Chairman Mao's words written on their washbasin, and printed on Fengxia's pillowcase was "Never Forget Class Struggle." The characters on their quilt read "March Forward Through the Great Storms." Every night Erxi and Fengxia literally slept on the words of Chairman Mao.

When I went into the city I'd try to avoid crowded areas. There were always people getting into fights in town, and on a few occasions I saw people beaten so badly they couldn't get up off the ground. No wonder the team leader stopped going into town for meetings. The commune headquarters sent someone to

---

* Big character posters, or *da zi bao*, are large posters featuring handwritten slogans, announcements or protests, and are one of the key forms of political expression, and often political dissent, in modern China. They played an important role during the Cultural Revolution and the Democracy Wall Movement (1978–79).

notify him that he was to take part in the county's third-level cadre meeting, but the team leader wouldn't go. In private the team leader told me, "I'm scared to death. There are people getting killed there every day. Going into town for a meeting at a time like this is like digging your own grave."

The team leader hid out in the village and wouldn't go anywhere, but in the end he only had a few months of peace and quiet. If he wouldn't go, they would come and get him. One day we were all in the fields working when we saw a flapping red flag approaching from far away. A group of Red Guards from the city were coming. The team leader was also in the field. When he saw them coming his neck tightened and, with his heart in his mouth, he asked me, "They can't be coming for me, can they?"

Leading the Red Guards was a young woman. They made their way over, and the woman looked at us and yelled, "Why aren't there any slogans here? Where are the big character posters? The team leader—who's the team leader?"

The team leader quickly threw down his hoe and ran over, bowing and nodding.

"Comrade Red Guard Leader," he addressed her.

The girl waved her arms as she asked, "How come there are no slogans or big character posters?"

"There are slogans. We've got two painted behind that building over there," answered the team leader.

At most, the girl couldn't have been more than sixteen or seventeen, yet she acted so cocky in front of our team leader, her eyes casting sidelong glances at him. A few of the Red Guards were carrying paint buckets, and she ordered them, "Go paint some slogans."

The Red Guards ran right down to the village houses to paint slogans. The girl in charge of the Red Guards ordered our team leader, "Assemble everyone in the village together!"

The team leader quickly fumbled for his whistle. He blew it with all his might, and everyone working in the fields ran over. The girl waited until just about everyone showed up, then yelled at us, "Who's the landlord here?"

As soon as everyone heard this, they turned to look at me; their collective gaze made my legs quiver. Thank god the team leader said, "The local landlord was executed just after Liberation."

"Are there any rich peasants?" she asked.

The team leader humbly responded, "There was one, but he passed away two years ago."

Keeping an eye on the team leader, the girl yelled at us, "Then are there any capitalist roaders?"

Maintaining his smiling face, the team leader said, "How could there be capitalist roaders in a little village like this?"

She suddenly shot out her hand, almost hitting the team leader in the nose, and asked, "Who are you?"

The team leader was so scared that he stuttered, "I'm the team leader, the team leader."

Who could have known she would scream, "You're the capitalist roader! Abusing your power to walk the road to capitalism!"

The team leader, overcome with fear, kept waving his hands and saying, "No, no, I never took that road."

The girl ignored him and turned to us.

"He's been making you live through a white terror, oppressing and belittling you!" she shouted. "You must stand up and rebel! Break his fucking legs!"

Everyone in the village was stupefied. Normally the team leader had a certain air of authority about him. We listened to whatever he said, and no one ever really thought he said or did anything wrong. And now here was the team leader suffering so badly at the hands of these city kids that he couldn't even stand up straight. He kept begging for mercy, saying all the things we didn't dare say. After begging for a while, the team leader turned to us and yelled, "C'mon, tell them I've never bullied or oppressed you!"

Everyone looked at the team leader and then at those Red Guards. Finally, in twos and threes, we uttered, "The team leader's a good man. He's never bullied or oppressed us."

The girl frowned as she looked at us.

"You're hopeless," she said.

With that, she turned to her fellow Red Guards and waved her hand. "Take him away."

Two of the Red Guards walked over to the team leader and grabbed hold of his arms. The team leader stretched out his neck, screaming, "I'm not going! Help me, I can't go into town! Going into town is like going to the grave!"

But no matter how much the team leader screamed and yelled, it was useless. They twisted his arms behind his back so that he had to stoop over, and they took him away. Everybody watched as the Red Guards shouted slogans and marched off with a look of murder in their eyes. Not a single person went up to try to stop them. No one had that kind of courage.

As soon as the team leader was carried off like that, everyone was struck by the grim possibilities. The entire town was in a state of pure chaos. Even if the team leader was able to hold on to his life, he'd probably end up losing an arm or a leg. But who could have known that he would come back in less than three days? He stumbled down the road toward home with a blackened nose and swollen eyes. When the people working in the fields saw him they rushed over and called out, "Team leader!"

The team leader raised his eyebrows and looked at everybody but didn't utter a word. He kept walking until he got to his house, where he lay down and slept for two whole days. On the third day he picked up his hoe and went back to the fields. By then the swelling on his face was not nearly as bad. When he came out everyone surrounded him, asking all sorts of questions. When they asked him if he was still sore, he shook his head and said, "The pain wasn't so bad. The worst part was they didn't let me get any fucking sleep—it was like torture."

As the team leader continued, tears came to his eyes. "I guess I've finally seen it all. I've always taken care of everyone as if you were my own children, but now that I'm in trouble I just have to live with my bad luck, huh? Not a single one of you came to help me."

After the team leader said that, none of us had the nerve to look him in the eye. The team leader was dragged into town and had to withstand three days of beating, but in the end he came out all right. Chunsheng, on the other hand, lived in town, and he wasn't as lucky. I wasn't aware that Chunsheng had run into trouble until I went into town to visit Fengxia one day. On my way there I saw a group of people being paraded around the street wearing signs around their necks and all different kinds of paper dunce hats. At first I didn't pay much attention to them, but as soon as they passed by me I was taken aback. The one in front was Chunsheng. Chunsheng had his head lowered, so he didn't notice me. As soon as he passed by, he picked up his head and chanted, "Long live Chairman Mao!"

A couple of kids wearing red armbands rushed over to him. Kicking and hitting him, they cursed, "Was that you who yelled? You fucking capitalist roader!"

Chunsheng was knocked partly to the ground, his body resting on the wooden sign that hung from his neck. One of the kids kicked his head, making a "bong" sound; it sounded like a hole had been knocked in his head. His whole body collapsed to the ground. Chunsheng was beaten until he couldn't make a sound—never in my whole life had I seen a person beaten like that. Lying on the ground, enduring relentless kicking, Chunsheng looked like a dead carcass. If they kept on like that, Chunsheng would be beaten to death. I went over and pulled two of them by the sleeve, saying, "I beg you, don't beat him."

They pushed me away with so much force I nearly fell to the ground.

"Who the hell are you?" they demanded.

"Please, stop hitting him," I repeated.

One of them pointed to Chunsheng and said, "Do you know who he is? He's the old magistrate, a capitalist roader!"

"I don't know anything about that," I said. "All I know is that he's Chunsheng."

Once they started talking, they stopped beating Chunsheng and ordered him to get up. After being beaten like that, how was Chunsheng supposed to get up? Just as I approached to help him up, Chunsheng recognized me. He said, "Fugui, get out of here."

That day when I got home I sat on the edge of the bed and told Jiazhen what I had seen. After hearing what had happened, Jiazhen lowered her head and said, "I shouldn't have kept Chunsheng from coming in that time."

Although Jiazhen didn't say anything else, I knew that we were thinking the same thing.

Over a month later, Chunsheng made a secret visit to our house. It was the middle of the night, and Jiazhen and I were both asleep when we were awakened by a knock at the door. I opened the door and by the light of the moon saw that it was Chunsheng, his face so swollen that it was round and inflamed.

"Chunsheng, hurry up and come in," I said.

Chunsheng stood at the door, unwilling to come inside.

"Is it okay with your wife?" he asked.

"Jiazhen, it's Chunsheng," I called over to her in a hushed tone.

Jiazhen sat up in bed without answering. I asked Chunsheng in again, but without Jiazhen's invitation Chunsheng wouldn't budge.

"Fugui, can you come out for a second?" he asked.

I turned to Jiazhen and repeated, "Jiazhen, Chunsheng's here."

Jiazhen still didn't answer, leaving me no choice but to drape a jacket over my shoulders and go out. Chunsheng walked over by the tree in front of our house and said to me, "Fugui, I came to say good-bye."

"Where are you going?" I asked.

He bit his teeth trying to hold back his emotions as he uttered, "I don't want to live anymore."

His words shocked me. I quickly grabbed hold of his arms and said, "Chunsheng, don't be ridiculous. You've got a wife and son."

As soon as he heard this, Chunsheng started to cry.

"Fugui, every day they tie me up and beat me," he said. As he spoke he stretched out his hands. "Feel my hands."

The second I touched them I realized his hands felt as if they had been boiled. They were so hot it scared the hell out of me. I asked him, "Does it hurt?"

He shook his head. "I can't feel them anymore."

I gently pushed his shoulders and said, "Chunsheng, sit down.

"No matter what, you have got to think straight," I told him. "The dead all want to keep on living. Here you are alive and kicking; you can't die."

I went on, "Your life is given to you by your parents. If you don't want to live, you have to ask them first."

Wiping his tears, Chunsheng said, "My parents passed away a long time ago."

"Then that's all the more reason to keep on living," I said. "Think about it: from north to south you were in so many battles during the war. Staying alive wasn't easy, was it?"

That night Chunsheng and I talked endlessly. Sitting inside in bed, Jiazhen heard everything. By the time dawn was approaching it seemed like Chunsheng had come around. When he stood up to leave, Jiazhen called from inside, "Chunsheng!"

For a moment the two of us were caught off guard. Only after Jiazhen called a second time did Chunsheng answer. We walked over to the door, and Jiazhen called out from bed, "Chunsheng, you've got to hang in there. You've got to keep on living."

Chunsheng nodded his head, and Jiazhen began to cry.

"You still owe us a life," she told him. "Hold on to your life to repay us."

Chunsheng stood there for a moment.

"I know," he finally said.

I saw Chunsheng off. But when we got to the edge of the village, Chunsheng made me stop; he wouldn't let me see him off any farther. I stood at the edge of the village, watching Chunsheng hobble off toward town. He had been beaten so badly that he walked with a limp. He lowered his head, and it looked like those steps were consuming his last bit of energy. I felt uneasy.

"Chunsheng," I called out to him. "Promise me you'll keep on living!"

Chunsheng took a few more steps and turned around to say, "I promise you."

But in the end Chunsheng didn't keep his promise. Just over

one month later I heard the news that Magistrate Liu had hung himself. No matter how lucky a person is, the moment he decides he wants to die, there's nothing that will keep him alive. I told Jiazhen what had happened, and she was depressed for the whole day. That night she said to me, "We shouldn't have blamed Chunsheng for Youqing's death."

When work in the fields started to pick up, I wasn't able to go into town to visit Fengxia as often as I would have liked. It was a good thing there was the people's commune at the time so I could work with the other villagers—that way I didn't have to worry about not carrying my weight. But Jiazhen still couldn't get out of bed. I had to work from dawn till dusk, rushing home several times during the day to make sure Jiazhen wasn't hungry. I was really exhausted. I was getting older, too. If it had been twenty years earlier, it would have been a different story. Back then I would have been okay with just a bit of sleep, but once I got older, sleep didn't seem to do much to replenish my strength. While I was working, I barely had the energy to raise my arms. Every day I'd hide among the other villagers, pretending to be working. They understood that I was in a difficult situation, and not one of them said anything bad about me.

During the busy season, Fengxia came back to stay a few days with us. She boiled water, cooked and took care of Jiazhen, making things a lot easier for me. But when I thought about it, I knew that a daughter married off was just like a pail of water that had been dumped out. Fengxia already belonged to Erxi, and I knew she wouldn't be able to stay too long. Jiazhen and I discussed it and decided that, no matter what, we couldn't let her stay, so we sent Fengxia away. I literally had to push her all the way to the edge of the village. The villagers laughed when they saw us, saying they'd never seen a father like me. When I heard that, I also giggled—I figured that there probably wasn't a single daughter in the entire village who was as good to her father as my Fengxia.

"Fengxia's only one person. If she spends all her time taking care of Jiazhen and me, who's gonna take care of my crooked-headed son-in-law?" I said.

Not long after I forced Fengxia to leave she came back, only this time my crooked-headed son-in-law came with her. From far away I saw a couple holding hands, and I knew it was them. I didn't even need to see Erxi's crooked head; the second I saw them walking hand in hand I knew it was them. Erxi was carrying a bottle of yellow rice wine and couldn't stop smiling. Fengxia had a basket under her arm and was smiling in the same way as Erxi. I wondered what had happened for them to be so happy.

When they got to the house, Erxi closed the door and said, "Mom, Dad, Fengxia's pregnant."

As soon as Jiazhen and I heard this, our faces lit up with happiness. Only after the four of us had smiled for what seemed like an eternity did Erxi remember the bottle of wine in his hand. He went over to the bed and put the bottle down on a small table while Fengxia took a bowl of peas out of her basket.

"Let's all go over to the bed," I suggested.

Fengxia sat down beside Jiazhen, while I brought back four bowls and sat down next to Erxi at the other end of the bed. Erxi poured me a full glass of wine, gave Jiazhen one, too, and then he went to pour some for Fengxia. Fengxia grabbed hold of the bottle and kept shaking her head.

"Today you get to drink, too," Erxi told her.

It seemed that Fengxia understood what he had said because she stopped shaking her head. We raised our bowls to drink, and after taking a sip Fengxia looked at her mother with furrowed brows. Jiazhen was also frowning, but then she smiled through her closed lips. Erxi and I both finished off our bowls with one chug, sending a whole bowl of wine right into our stomachs. Tears came to Erxi's eyes as he said, "Dad, Mom, I never dreamed that a day like this would come."

As soon as she heard this Jiazhen became teary. Seeing Jiazhen like that, tears also fell from my eyes.

"I also never thought things would turn out like this," I said. "Our biggest worry used to be what Fengxia would do after Jiazhen and I passed away. Once you married Fengxia we could finally rest at ease. Now that you're going to have a child, that's even better. Fengxia will have someone to bury her after she dies."

Seeing us in tears, Fengxia also began to weep. Through her tears Jiazhen said, "If only Youqing were still alive. Fengxia practically raised him; they were so close. But he can't be here to share today with us."

Erxi started to wail, his crying even more violent than before. He said, "If only my parents were still alive. When my mom died she was squeezing my hand and wouldn't let go."

The more the four of us cried, the more depressed we

became. After crying for a while, Erxi smiled and pointed to the bowl of peas, saying, "Mom, Dad, try some. Fengxia made them herself."

"Okay, I'll have some," I said. "Jiazhen, you try some, too."

Jiazhen and I looked at each other and laughed—we were about to become grandparents. That day the four of us laughed and cried until dusk, when Erxi and Fengxia left.

Once Fengxia was pregnant, Erxi seemed to love her even more. When summer came, their house was filled with mosquitoes, and they didn't have a mosquito net. As soon as it got dark, Erxi would have Fengxia sit outside in the cool night air while he lay down in bed to let the mosquitoes feed on him. Only after all the mosquitoes had had their fill would he let Fengxia come in to sleep. A couple of times Fengxia went in to check on him, and he'd get all anxious and carry her back out. Erxi's neighbors told me all this. They'd say to Erxi, "You should buy a mosquito net."

Erxi laughed but didn't say anything. Only later did he tell me, "It wouldn't be right, considering I still haven't finished paying off the debt."

I felt bad seeing Erxi covered from head to toe with little red spots where he'd been bitten. I told him, "Don't be like that."

Erxi said, "I'm just one person—it doesn't matter if they take a few extra bites. But Fengxia's different—she counts for two people now."

Fengxia gave birth on a winter day. The snow was falling so heavily that we couldn't even see out our window. Fengxia went into the delivery room and didn't come out all night. Waiting outside, Erxi and I became increasingly anxious and worried. Each time a doctor came out we'd rush up to ask how Fengxia was doing. We'd relax as soon as we found out she was still in labor. As dawn neared Erxi said, "Dad, why don't you get some rest."

I shook my head, saying, "I'm too anxious to sleep."

Erxi urged me, "The two of us can't both stay up like this. After Fengxia gives birth, someone is going to have to take care of her and the baby."

I realized that what Erxi said made sense, so I told him, "Erxi, you get some sleep first."

The two of us kept going back and forth, and in the end neither one of us got any sleep. By the time the sun had come out there was still no sign of Fengxia, and we began to get scared again. All the women who had come in after Fengxia had given birth and gone home already. How were Erxi and I supposed to sit still? We pressed up against the door to listen to what was going on inside. Only after I heard a woman's voice screaming did I relax.

"Poor Fengxia," said Erxi.

But after a while I realized something was wrong: Fengxia was mute—she couldn't scream. I mentioned this to Erxi, and his face instantly turned pale. He ran up to the delivery room door, yelling, "Fengxia, Fengxia!"

Two doctors came out and, glaring angrily at Erxi, yelled, "What the hell are you screaming about? Get out!"

Erxi was wailing like a baby.

"How come my wife still hasn't come out?" he asked.

Someone else in the waiting room told us, "Some deliveries are fast, and some are slow."

Erxi and I looked at each other, thinking maybe this guy was right. We sat back down, but my heart was still pounding. Before long a doctor came out to ask us, "Do you want the big one or the little one?"

Her question left us both utterly stupefied.

"Hello, I'm talking to you," she said.

Erxi fell at her feet. Kneeling before her, he pleaded through his tears, "Doctor, please save Fengxia. I want Fengxia."

Erxi was on the ground crying uncontrollably. I helped him up and tried to get him to calm down, telling him to take it easy or he was going to hurt himself.

"Just as long as Fengxia pulls through everything will be okay," I told him. "You know there's a saying: 'As long as the green mountain remains, there's no reason to worry about firewood.'"

Erxi was still crying as he said, "My son's gone."

So was my grandson. I lowered my head and began crying uncontrollably. But around noon a doctor came out and said, "She delivered. It's a boy!"

The second Erxi heard this he got anxious. Leaping forward he yelled, "I said I didn't want the little one!"

The doctor said, "The big one's okay, too."

Fengxia was okay. I suddenly began to feel dizzy—I was getting older, and my body couldn't take this kind of stress anymore. Erxi was as happy as could be. He sat down beside me with his body shaking. He was shaking because he was laughing too hard.

I said to Erxi, "Now we can finally relax. I'm going to get some sleep. I'll be back in a while to take your place."

But who could have guessed that the moment I left, something would happen to Fengxia? Just a few minutes after I went out the door, a whole army of doctors ran into the delivery room, some of them even carrying oxygen tanks. After Fengxia gave birth she started hemorrhaging and lost a lot of blood—before dusk she was gone. My two children both died during childbirth—Youqing during someone else's delivery, Fengxia during her own.

The snow was especially heavy that day. After Fengxia died her body lay in that tiny room. I went to see her, and as soon as I saw the room I couldn't bring myself to go in. Ten years earlier, Youqing had died in that same room. I stood in the heavy snow, listening to the echoes of Erxi's voice calling Fengxia. The pain in my heart was so great I had to squat down on the ground. I could barely see the entrance to the room with the heavy snowflakes falling. All I could hear was the wrenching sound of Erxi's cries. Only after I called Erxi a few times did he finally respond. He came to the door and said to me, "I wanted the big one, and they gave me the little one."

"Let's go home," I said. "This hospital and my family have a score left over from another life. Youqing died here, and now so did Fengxia. Erxi, let's go home."

Erxi lifted Fengxia onto his back, and the three of us headed home. By then it was completely dark out. The road was covered in a thick blanket of snow, and there was not a soul in sight. When the western wind blew, snowflakes beat against our faces like pellets of sand. After getting part of the way home, Erxi raised his voice, which had grown hoarse from his constant crying.

"Dad, I can't go on," he said.

I told him to give Fengxia to me, but he wouldn't let me take her. Then after walking a few more steps he squatted down, saying, "Dad, my back's so sore I can barely take it."

That was because of his crying. He had cried so hard that he had hurt his back. When we got to Erxi's place, he put Fengxia down on the bed and sat on the edge of it gazing at her. Sitting there, Erxi's body looked like it had shriveled into a little ball. I couldn't look at them; just seeing their shadows on the wall was unbearable. Their looming shadows were dark and large. One was lying while the other looked like it was kneeling. Neither moved. The only things moving were Erxi's tears—I kept seeing those large black drops falling from one shadow to the other. I went into the kitchen to boil some water to warm up Erxi. By the time the water had boiled and I'd brought it out, Erxi had dozed off—now they were both asleep.

That night I sat in Erxi's kitchen until dawn. The wind outside howled, and for a time sleet pattered wildly against the doors and windows, but there wasn't a sound from Erxi and Fengxia sleeping in the other room. The cold winter wind snuck in through the crack in the door, bringing a draft that made my knees feel cold and sore. There was a numbness inside of me like ice. Just like that, my two children had left me. I wanted to cry, but there were no tears left. I thought of Jiazhen, who was at home, probably with her eyes glued to the door waiting for me to bring the news. When I left she kept reminding me over and over to hurry home as soon as Fengxia gave birth to tell her if it was a boy or a girl. But how was I to tell her that Fengxia was dead?

When Youqing died, Jiazhen almost went with him. Now that Fengxia was gone, how would she be able to bear it? The next day, carrying Fengxia on his back, Erxi went home with me. It was still snowing, and Fengxia's body was almost completely shrouded in white, as if it were covered in a blanket of cotton. When we got home I saw Jiazhen sitting in bed, her head leaning against the wall and her hair a mess. The moment I saw her like that I knew she understood that something bad had happened to Fengxia. It had already been two days and two nights since I'd left home. My tears came down in waves, and Erxi, who had already stopped crying once, couldn't hold himself together either. The moment he saw Jiazhen's baby-like tears, he called out, "Mom, Mom . . ."

Jiazhen's head was no longer resting against the wall, but it didn't move. Her eyes remained fixed on Fengxia draped over Erxi's back. I helped Erxi put Fengxia down on the bed, and Jiazhen lowered her head to look at her. Jiazhen's gaze was so intense, it was as if her eyes were going to pop out of their sockets. I never imagined Jiazhen would have that kind of reaction. She stopped crying and just stared at Fengxia, caressing her face and hair. Erxi was crying so hard that he had to stoop down and rest against the side of the bed. I stood to one side looking at Jiazhen, not knowing what she would do next. That day Jiazhen didn't cry or scream; from time to time she'd just shake her head. The snow on Fengxia's body slowly melted, soaking the whole bed.

Fengxia was buried alongside Youqing. The snow stopped falling, the sun beamed down from the heavens and the western wind grew even fiercer, its whistling roar almost completely drowning out the sound of the rustling leaves. The wind was blowing so hard that after we buried Fengxia, Erxi and I had to hold on to our hoe and shovel to keep our balance. The ground was covered with snow, and under the sun the white radiance was almost blinding. The plot of land where Fengxia was buried was the only area in sight free of snow. Staring at that patch of damp earth, neither Erxi nor I was willing to walk away. Erxi pointed to an empty plot of land beside Fengxia's grave and said, "Dad, when I die, bury me there."

I sighed as I told Erxi, "This spot is for me. Besides, no matter what happens, I'll die long before you."

After we buried Fengxia we went back to the hospital to bring the baby home. Erxi carried his son over twenty *li* to our hut. When he arrived he put the baby down on the bed. The boy opened his eyes, looking all around, and frowned. I wondered just what he was looking at. Seeing the kid like that, both Erxi and I laughed. Jiazhen was the only one who didn't smile—her eyes remained fixed on the child, with her hand resting beside his face. She looked at the child with the same expression she had when she looked at her dead Fengxia. At the time I was really worried. The look on Jiazhen's face was scaring me; I didn't know what was wrong with her. Erxi looked up, and the second he saw Jiazhen, he, too, stopped laughing. With his arms lowered, he stood there not knowing what to do. After a while he quietly said to me, "Dad, you give the kid a name."

It was only then that Jiazhen opened her mouth. When she spoke her voice was hoarse and rough.

"This child has been without a mother from the moment he entered this world. Let's call him Kugen, 'Bitter Root,'" she said.

Less than three months after Fengxia died, Jiazhen also passed away. In the days just before she died, Jiazhen would often say to me, "Fugui, you buried both Youqing and Fengxia. Thinking that it'll also be you who buries me, I can rest at ease."

She knew that she was going to die soon, but she was very much at ease. By then she didn't even have the energy to sit up in bed; she'd just lie down and close her eyes. But her hearing was still keen—as soon as I'd come through the door after work she'd open her eye and begin to move her mouth, and I'd know that she wanted to talk to me. During those last days she especially loved to talk. I'd sit on the bed and lean over to listen to her— Jiazhen's voice was as faint as a heartbeat. No matter how many hardships and difficulties people face in life, they always find a way to console themselves when they get close to death. Jiazhen also found a way; she kept telling me, "This life's almost over for me. Knowing how good you've been to me, I'm content. I bore you a pair of children, which I guess you could say was my way of repaying you. I hope that I'll be able to spend my next life together with you again."

The moment Jiazhen said she was willing to be my wife again in the next life, my tears trickled down onto her face. After blinking her eyes twice she smiled and said, "Even though Fengxia and Youqing both died before I did, I can still rest easy. I don't need to worry about them anymore. No matter what, I'm still a mother. Our kids were good to me when they were alive, and just for that I should know contentment.

"You've got to keep on living," she told me. "There's still Erxi and Kugen to take care of. Actually, Erxi is also our child, and when Kugen grows up he'll listen and be just as good to you as Youqing was."

Jiazhen died in the afternoon. After I got back from working I saw her eyes opened wide, but as I passed by her on my way to the kitchen to make her some porridge I didn't hear her say anything. When I sat down next to her with the porridge, Jiazhen, with her eyes closed, suddenly grabbed hold of my hand. I was shocked. I never imagined she had so much strength. I couldn't pull my hand away. I quickly put the bowl of porridge down and used my other hand to feel her forehead. Only when I realized she was still warm did I relax a bit. Jiazhen's face looked peaceful, as if she were asleep; it didn't look like she was in any kind of pain. But who could have known that before long the same hand that had just grabbed me would begin to grow cold? I felt Jiazhen's arms, and one at a time they too became cold; by then her legs went cold, too. Her whole body was cold; only a small area around her chest remained warm. I kept my hands on Jiazhen's chest, where I could feel the warmth from her heart escaping through the cracks between my fingers. Finally her grip loosened, and her hand, which had been holding mine, fell lifeless against my arm.

"It was really nice the way Jiazhen died," Fugui said. It was late afternoon, and the people working in the fields began heading up to the ridge in small groups. The sun, hanging in the west, wasn't as hard on the eyes. It now looked more like a red wheel in the sky, spreading out amid the layers of glowing crimson clouds.

Fugui looked at me with a smile. The light from the setting sun made his face look especially spirited.

"It was really nice the way Jiazhen died," he said again. "When she died it was all so simple, so peaceful. There wasn't anything left up in the air, unlike with some of the other women in our village, whom people would go on gossiping about long after they'd died."

Hearing this old man sitting across from me talk like this about his wife, who had passed away over ten years ago, created an almost indescribable feeling of warmth deep within me. Like a blade of grass swaying in the wind, I caught a glimpse of the movement of a distant tranquillity.

After everyone around us left the fields, an atmosphere of unfolding emerged, which seemed so broad, so vast, so boundless. The setting sun was like a pool of water giving off ray after ray of light. Fugui's hands were resting on his legs, and his eyes squinted as he looked at me. He didn't look like he was ready to get up, so I knew he still hadn't finished his story. I thought I'd encourage him to finish his story while he was still resting. And so I asked him, "How old is Kugen now?"

A strange look appeared in Fugui's eyes—I couldn't tell if it was sadness or a kind of joyful gratification. His eyes drifted over *my head into the distance, and then he said, "If you're going according to years, he should be seventeen."*

⌐⌐

After Jiazhen died, all I had was Erxi and Kugen. Erxi hired someone to make a backpack that would allow Kugen to spend the whole day on his dad's back. But this made work even more exhausting for Erxi. As a porter, he had to pull a cart filled with supplies and carry Kugen at the same time. Erxi would always be huffing and puffing, completely out of breath. He'd have to carry another bag with him, too—Kugen's diaper bag. Sometimes when the weather was overcast the diaper wouldn't dry, and because Erxi only had one diaper for his son he had no choice but to tie three bamboo sticks to his cart, two horizontal and one upright, and hang the diaper on top to dry. The city people would all laugh when they saw this. But Erxi's coworkers knew how difficult things were for him, and as soon as they saw people laughing they'd yell, "What the fuck's so funny? You keep at it and I'll really give you something to laugh about!"

Kugen would be in his backpack, and the moment he'd cry Erxi would know whether he was hungry or had dirtied his diaper.

"If he cries for a long time, then he's hungry," Erxi told me. "If it's just for a short time, then he's uncomfortable down there around his butt."

It was true: if Kugen peed or messed his pants he'd go "uh,

uh"—when I first heard it I thought he was laughing. A little guy
like that and he already knew how to cry in different ways. That
was because he loved his dad—he could make things easier on
Erxi by letting his dad know right away what to do.

When Kugen was hungry, Erxi would put down his cart and
look for a woman breast-feeding her child. When he found one
he'd hand her one *mao* and gently ask, "Please, could you give
him some?"

Erxi wasn't like other fathers who simply watched their children grow up. Carrying him on his back, he would feel Kugen
getting heavier, and that way he knew that Kugen was getting
bigger. As a father he was naturally ecstatic.

"Kugen's getting heavier," he would boast to me.

When I went into town to visit them I'd often see Erxi, covered in sweat, pulling his cart down the street. Kugen would be
in his backpack with just his little head sticking out, bopping
from side to side as Erxi walked. Erxi appeared beyond the point
of exhaustion. I tried to convince him to let me bring Kugen
to the country and take care of him for a few days, but Erxi
wouldn't let me.

"Dad, I can't bear to be apart from Kugen," he said.

It was a good thing that Kugen grew fast. Before we knew it he
was walking, and that made things much easier for Erxi. While
Erxi was loading and unloading he'd let Kugen play off to one
side, and when it was time to go he'd pick Kugen up and put him
in the cart. When Kugen got a little bigger he figured out who I
was. After hearing Erxi call me Dad enough times, it stuck with

him. Every time I'd go into town to visit them, little Kugen, sitting in his dad's cart, would immediately look up at Erxi and scream in that sharp voice of his, "Dad, your dad's coming!"

While he was still on his dad's back, Kugen had learned how to curse. When he was angry, his face would turn bright red, and his little mouth would make all kinds of strange sounds, "pssh, pssh, paaa, paaa." No one could understand what he was trying to say. Only when bubbles of saliva flew out of his mouth would Erxi realize what was going on.

"He's cursing somebody," Erxi explained to me.

Once Kugen could walk and had learned a few words, it got even better. As soon as he saw the other kids playing with something that looked fun, he'd giggle and wave them over with his hand. "Come, come, come!" he'd repeat, all the while frantically waving his hand.

When the other children came over he'd reach out and try to steal their toys. If they refused to hand them over, Kugen would lose his temper and push the other children away, saying, "Go, go, go!"

Erxi never got over the loss of Fengxia. He was never a man of many words, but as soon as Fengxia died he spoke even less. Other people would say things to him, but he'd just grunt and that would be it; only when he saw me would he open up a bit. Kugen became the core of our lives. But the bigger he got the more he resembled Fengxia and the more he resembled Fengxia, the harder it was for us to look at him. Sometimes after Erxi looked at Kugen for a while, tears would begin to trickle down Erxi's face. As his father-in-law, I would try to console him: "It's been a while since Fengxia died. You should try to forget her if you can."

By then Kugen was three. He sat in his stool rocking back and forth. His eyes were wide open as he tried as hard as he could to understand what we were saying. Erxi tilted his head to the side in thought. After a while he finally said, "My memories of Fengxia are my only happiness."

Later, I had to get back to the village and Erxi had to get back to work, so we left together. Keeping to the wall, Erxi bolted off the moment we got outside. With his head tilted, he moved like lightning, as if he were afraid someone was going to see him. He pulled Kugen by the hand, practically dragging him. Kugen tripped and stumbled, his whole body aslant. It was not my place to say anything to Erxi—I knew that he had become like that only after Fengxia had died. But as soon as the neighbors saw him they yelled, "Erxi, you'd better slow down! Kugen's going to fall."

Erxi acknowledged them with a grunt, but he continued walking just as fast as before. Being pulled by his dad, Kugen's body would twist about, his eyes rolled around to take everything in. When they got to the corner I told Erxi, "I'm heading back."

Only then did Erxi stop and raise his shoulder to look at me. I said to Kugen, "I'm going."

Kugen looked at me and, waving his hands, said in a sharp voice, "Get going."

Whenever I had some free time I'd head into town. With both Erxi and Kugen there, I couldn't stand staying at home—I felt that my true home was in town. When I returned all alone to the village, I couldn't relax. A few times I brought Kugen back with me. Kugen loved it; he'd happily run all over the fields. Once he wanted me to help him catch a sparrow. I asked him how I was supposed to catch one, and he pointed up at a tree and said, "You climb up."

"I'll break my neck!" I protested. "Are you trying to kill me?"

"No, I'm not trying to kill you. I'm trying to catch a sparrow!" he replied.

Kugen seemed to be very much at home in the country, but it was hard for Erxi to be away from his son. Going one day without seeing Kugen was unbearable for him. Every day after work he'd be so exhausted he could barely move, yet he'd still walk over ten *li* to come see Kugen. And then he'd have to get up the next morning and walk back into town to work. I realized that continuing like this was no solution to anything, so from then on I'd see Kugen home before it got dark.

After Jiazhen died I didn't have any other attachments, so when I got to town Erxi would say, "Dad, why don't you stay over?"

And so I'd stay in town a few days. If I had wanted to move in with them, Erxi would have happily obliged. He kept saying that having three generations under one roof was better than two. But I wasn't willing to rely on Erxi to take care of me. I was still good with my hands and quick on my feet, still able to make a living. Having the two of us working and making money, Kugen would have an even better future.

Things went on like this until Kugen was four. That's when Erxi died. Erxi was crushed between two slabs of cement. As a porter it's common to get bumped or scraped up a bit, but to lose one's life—Erxi was the first. It seems like everyone in the Xu family had a tough fate. The day of the accident, Erxi and the rest of them were moving cement slabs into carts. Erxi was standing in the cart in front of a pile of cement slabs while the crane was lifting four more of them. I don't know what went wrong, but suddenly they all fell on him. No one had even noticed Erxi standing there; they suddenly just heard a loud scream: "Kugen!"

Erxi's buddies told me the sound of that final shriek had scared the hell out of them. They had never imagined Erxi could have such a powerful voice—it was as if his chest had exploded. By the time they got to Erxi, my crooked-headed son-in-law was already dead. He was lodged between the pile of cement slabs, and except for his head and feet his whole body was crushed flat. They couldn't find a single unbroken bone, and the blood and flesh were spread like a thick paste over the cement slabs. They said that when Erxi died his neck suddenly stuck out straight and his mouth opened wide—that was the moment he called out to his son.

Kugen was beside the nearby pond throwing pebbles into the water when he heard his father's last scream. He turned around and said, "What does he want?"

He paused for a while, and since he didn't hear his dad call him again, he went back to tossing pebbles into the water. Only after Erxi's coworkers brought his remains to the hospital and he was officially declared dead did someone go tell Kugen, "Kugen, Kugen, your father's dead."

Kugen still didn't quite know what death was. He turned around to answer, "I know."

After that he just ignored the guy and went on throwing stones.

I was in the field working when one of Erxi's coworkers ran down to tell me, "Erxi's dying! He's in the hospital. Hurry!"

As soon as I heard something had happened to Erxi and that he was in the hospital, I immediately began to cry. I yelled over to Erxi's coworker, "Hurry up and get him out of that hospital. You can't leave him in that hospital."

The guy stared at me in confusion—he must have thought I was crazy. I told him, "Once Erxi enters that hospital, there's no telling if he'll come out alive."

Both Youqing and Fengxia had died in that hospital, but I had never imagined that Erxi would end up there, too. Can you imagine, three times in my life I had to go to that small room where the dead lay, and all three times it was my own relatives I saw lying there? By then I was old, and I couldn't deal with it anymore. I went to get Erxi to bring him home, but the moment I saw that little room I collapsed on the floor. Just like Erxi, I had to be carried out of that hospital.

After Erxi died I brought Kugen to the country to live with me. The day we left town I gave Erxi's furniture and things to his neighbors; I picked out only a few of the lighter things to take with me. By the time I left with Kugen it was almost dark. All the neighbors came out to see us off. They walked us to the end of the street and said, "Be sure to come back and visit."

A few of the women even cried and caressed Kugen.

"Poor child's really got it tough," they said.

Kugen didn't like their tears falling on his face. Pulling me by the hand he tried to get me to leave. "Come on, let's go! Hurry!"

As I walked down the street holding Kugen's hand, the icy wind whisked down my neck. The farther I walked, the more empty I felt inside. I thought about how we'd had a big, happy family and how now all that was left was an old man and a little boy. I was in so much pain that I didn't even have the strength to sigh. But just looking at Kugen brought me comfort. Having him was better than anything. There was hope for the Xu family after all. I had to keep on living.

As we approached a noodle shop, Kugen suddenly yelled out, "I don't want any noodles!"

I had other things on my mind and didn't really pay attention to what he'd said. But when we got to the shop entrance, Kugen called out again, "I don't want any noodles!"

After yelling he pulled my hand and wouldn't let me go any farther, and only then did I realize that he really did want some noodles. This kid didn't have a mother or father—if he wanted a bowl of noodles I figured that buying the kid a bowl of noodles was the least I could do. I brought him in and paid nine *fen* for a small bowl. I sat there and watched him slurp down his noodles. He ate so quickly his face became covered in sweat. When we left he was still licking his lips.

"Can we come back tomorrow to have some more?" he asked.

I nodded, "Okay."

Before we got too far we came to a candy store, and once again Kugen pulled my hand. Looking up, he said in a serious voice, "At first I wanted to have some candy, but since I already had noodles, it's okay."

I knew that he was trying a new tactic, this time to get me to buy him some candy. I reached my hand into my pocket and felt two *fen*, and after thinking for a second I pulled out five *fen*. I gave the money to Kugen so he could buy five pieces of candy.

When we got home, Kugen said his feet were aching really badly and were tired from walking all that way. I let him lie down in bed while I went to heat some water for him to soak his feet in. By the time the water was heated, Kugen was already asleep. He had propped his two feet up on the wall and conked right out. Seeing him like that, I couldn't help laughing. Sore feet always feel better propped up. Kugen was so little, yet already he had learned how to take care of himself. But right after that, a sadness came over me. Kugen still didn't know that he'd never see his father again.

After I went to sleep that night, I kept feeling a kind of pressure, a weight around my heart. Only once I sat up did I realize that Kugen's little butt had been pressing against my stomach. I pushed his rump away, but just as I was about to fall back asleep his little bottom slowly made its way back over. I reached out my hand and realized that he had wet his side of the bed. No wonder his little ass kept coming over to press against me. So I just let it.

The next day Kugen started to miss his dad. He was playing on the ridge while I was working out in the field. After playing all day Kugen came over to ask me, "Are you taking me home? Or is Dad coming to pick me up?"

When the villagers saw Kugen like this, they shook their heads and remarked on what an unfortunate kid he was. But then one of the farmers told him, "You're not going home."

He shook his little head and said seriously, "Oh yes I am."

That evening Kugen started to get anxious when he saw his father still hadn't come. His little mouth chirped along, saying all kinds of things, but I couldn't understand a word of it. I thought that maybe he was cursing someone. Finally, he looked up at me and said, "Forget it. If he's not coming, he's not coming. I'm just a little kid. I don't know the way home. You'll have to take me."

"Your dad's not coming to get you, and I'm not taking you home," I told him. "Your dad is dead."

"I know he's dead," Kugen replied. "It's already dark and he still hasn't come to get me."

That night, lying under the covers, I told Kugen what death was. I told him that after people die they are buried, and that people still living won't be able to see them anymore. At first he was so scared that he trembled all over. Afterward, when he realized that he wouldn't see Erxi again, he began to cry. His little face pressed against my neck, and warm tears dripped on my chest. He sobbed and wailed until finally crying himself to sleep.

After a couple of days I thought I ought to let Kugen see where Erxi was buried. I brought him to the western part of the village and told him which grave was his grandma's, which was his mom's and which was his uncle's. Before I pointed out Erxi's grave, Kugen pointed to it. In tears he said, "This one's Dad's."

Kugen and I were together only six months when the village fixed the output quotas for each family. That's when it started to become even more difficult to get by. Our family got only one and a half *mu*. From that point on I couldn't hide among the others while working or drag my feet when I was tired. The fields never stopped calling me. If I didn't do the work, there was no one who was going to do it for me.

Once I got old I began to fall apart. Every day my back was sore and my vision blurry. I used to be able to carry a load of vegetables into town all in one breath, but by this time I had to take periodic rests as I went. Unless I set out a full two hours before dawn there wouldn't be any buyers by the time I got to the market. I'd finally become that "slow bird who starts early." Now Kugen was the one who had it the hardest. I'd pull him out of bed when he was fast asleep. Then, with his eyes half-closed, he would grab hold of the bamboo basket and follow me into town. Kugen was a good kid. Noticing that I kept taking breaks because the load was too heavy, he would take a few handfuls of vegetables out of each of my baskets. Carrying them in his arms, he'd walk in front of me, and every so often he would turn around to ask, "Is it any lighter?"

Deep down I was so happy I said, "Oh, it's much lighter."

By then Kugen was five years old, and he had already become my good little helper. Wherever I went he'd follow and help me work; he could even cut the rice stalks. I had the town blacksmith make Kugen a little sickle, and when he got it Kugen was happy as could be. Normally when I brought him into town he'd go looking for his friends as soon as we passed the alley that led to Erxi's old house. No matter how many times I called him he wouldn't answer. But the day I told him we were going to get him a sickle, he grabbed hold of my clothes and wouldn't let go, following me all the way to the blacksmith's shop. When we got there, the two of us waited outside for a while. Someone walked past us to go into the shop, and Kugen couldn't resist pointing to the sickle inside and telling the man, "That's Kugen's sickle."

Now when his friends came to play with him, he just turned his head and said proudly, "I don't have time to talk to you now."

After the sickle was finished, Kugen insisted on sleeping with it. I wouldn't let him, so he had to settle for keeping it under his bed. The first thing he'd do every morning was reach under the bed to caress his sickle. I told him that he'd get quicker with it the more he used it, and that the harder he worked the stronger he'd get. Kugen blinked his eyes and stared at me for a long time before saying, "The quicker I get with the sickle the more stronger I'll get."

Kugen was still little, so naturally he was slower at cutting the rice than I was. He'd get upset as soon as he saw that I was quicker. Staring at me, he'd yell, "Fugui, slow down!"

All the people in the village called me Fugui, so Kugen also grew accustomed to calling me Fugui. He also called me Grandpa. I'd point to the pile of rice I had cut and say, "Look at all that Kugen cut."

He'd be so happy he'd start to giggle. Then he'd point to the pile of rice he had cut and say, "Look at all the rice that Fugui cut."

Kugen was little and got tired easily. He'd always be running up to the ridge to take naps. He'd say, "Fugui, the sickle's slowing down."

What he meant was that he was tired. After lying down on the ridge for a while he would get up and watch me cutting the rice shoots. From time to time he'd yell, "Fugui, don't step on my rice shoots!"

Everyone around would laugh when they heard that—even the team leader. He was just as old as I was, and yet he was still the team leader. There were a lot of people in his family, so they got the five *mu* of land that were right next to mine. The team leader said, "Little bastard's really got a mouth on him, doesn't he?"

"It's to make up for Fengxia's inability to speak," I said.

Those days may have been difficult and exhausting, but at least deep down I was happy. With Kugen around I had a new zest for life. Seeing Kugen getting bigger and bigger by the day, this grandpa of his could rest easier. At dusk the two of us would sit on the doorstep and watch the sun go down. We'd see the fields turn a deep glowing red and hear the sound of the other villagers calling in the distance. The pair of chickens we were raising would totter back and forth in front of us. Kugen and I were really close. When we were together we'd never run out of things to say. Seeing those two chickens made me think back to what my father had said just before he died. I would always repeat those words to Kugen. "When these chickens grow up

they'll become geese, and when the geese grow up they'll become lambs. When the lambs grow up they'll turn into oxen.
And us, we'll get richer and richer!"

Kugen couldn't stop laughing at this. He remembered every
word of what I said. Many times, when he came out of the
chicken coop with the newly laid eggs, he would sing those lines
to himself.

When there were enough eggs we'd take them into town to be
sold. I told Kugen, "When we've saved up enough money we'll
buy an ox, and then you'll be able to go off to play, riding on the
ox's back."

As soon as Kugen heard this, his eyes lit up.

"And the chicken will really turn into an ox!" he exclaimed.

From then on, Kugen was constantly waiting for the day when
we would be able to buy an ox. Every morning after he opened
his eyes he'd ask me, "Fugui, are we going to buy the ox today?"

Sometimes when we'd go into town to sell the eggs I'd feel
sorry for Kugen and want to buy some candy for him. Kugen
would say, "Just one piece is enough. We still haven't saved up
enough for the ox."

In the blink of an eye, Kugen was already seven. He had gotten much stronger, too. One day, just when it was almost time to
harvest the cotton, the village radio broadcast announced heavy
rains. What was I supposed to do? The one and a half *mu* of cotton I had planted was already ripe. If it rained, my whole crop
would be ruined. Early that morning I pulled Kugen out to the
cotton field and told him that we had to strip all the cotton that
day. Kugen looked up at me and said, "Fugui, I feel dizzy."

"Hurry up and start picking," I prodded him. "After you finish you can go off to play."

So Kugen started picking the cotton. After working for a while he went up to the ridge to lie down. I yelled at him, telling him to get up, but Kugen just repeated, "I feel dizzy."

I figured I'd let him rest awhile longer, but once he lay down he didn't get back up. I started to lose my temper a bit. "Kugen, if we don't strip all the cotton today, we're never going to buy that ox," I warned him.

Only after hearing that did Kugen get up. He told me, "I'm really dizzy. My head hurts."

I kept working right up until noon. Only when I saw that more than half the cotton was already stripped did I start to relax a bit. I went up the ridge to get Kugen so we could go home for lunch, but the second I grabbed his hand I knew something was wrong. I quickly felt his forehead—he was burning up. Only then did I realize he was sick. I was really an idiot: there he was, sick, and I was forcing him to work. When we got home I had Kugen lie down. Everyone in the village used to say that ginger is a cure for all kinds of illnesses, so I decided to cook him a bowl of ginger soup. The only problem was, I didn't have any sugar in the house. I thought of just throwing in a little salt, but I couldn't do that to Kugen. So I went to one of the villagers' houses to borrow some sugar.

"I'll repay you in a couple of days when I sell the cotton," I promised.

"Don't worry about it, Fugui," he said.

In addition to the ginger soup, I also cooked Kugen a bowl of porridge. Only after I watched him finish did I eat. As soon as I finished I went right back out to the fields. On my way out I said to Kugen, "You'll feel better after you get some sleep."

But as I went out the door, I still couldn't get Kugen out of my mind. I decided to pick half a pot of fresh beans for him. When I went back inside to cook them, I made sure to add some salt. I moved the stool over next to the bed, putting the half-filled pot of beans on top of the stool. I told Kugen to eat, and seeing that they were beans, he smiled. As I went back outside I heard him say, "How come you're not having any?"

I didn't go back into the house until dusk. By the time all the cotton was reaped I felt like all my joints were out of place. It was only a short walk from the field to my hut, but by the time I got to the door my legs were trembling. As I walked in I called out, "Kugen, Kugen."

Kugen didn't answer; I assumed he was asleep. As soon as I went over to the bed I saw his twisted body. His mouth was half-open, and I could see two unchewed beans inside. The second I saw his mouth like that I began to feel lightheaded, and my ears rang wildly—Kugen's lips were blue. I shook him with all my might and screamed his name. His body swayed back and forth in my arms but he didn't answer. I was flustered, so I sat down on the bed to figure out what to do. I wondered if Kugen could be dead—the second the thought crossed my mind I couldn't keep from crying. I shook him again, but still he had no reaction. I realized he might be dead. I went outside and saw one of the young guys from our village.

"I beg you, please come take a look at Kugen. I think he might be dead," I pleaded.

The young man stared at me for a while before picking up his feet and running over. He shook Kugen back and forth and pressed his ear up to Kugen's chest. Only after listening for a long time did he finally say, "I can't hear a heartbeat."

A whole crowd of people from the village came. I begged them to look at Kugen. After shaking him and listening to his chest they told me, "He's dead."

Kugen had choked to death on the beans. It wasn't that he was greedy and wanted to stuff himself, it was just that we were too poor. Every kid in the village had it better than Kugen. Things were so bad for us that Kugen hardly ever had the chance to eat beans. And just like always I was my old muddleheaded self, giving Kugen too many beans at once, never stopping for a second to think about what might happen. In the end it was my clumsiness and stupidity that killed Kugen.

From then on I had to get by alone. I thought I wouldn't have many days left, either. Who could have known that I'd make it this long? I'm still the same as before. My back's sore and my vision is blurry, but my hearing is still keen. When the villagers are talking, I can tell who's speaking without even looking. Sometimes when I think back I feel sad, and sometimes I feel a kind of peace. I took care of the funerals for everyone in my family. I buried them all with my own hands. When the day comes that my body goes stiff, there will be no one left to worry about. I've also made up my mind that when it's my turn to die, I'll go peacefully and quietly. There's no need for me to worry about not having anyone to bury me—I'm sure the people in the village will take care of it. The moment my body starts to stink, I'm sure the smell will be unbearable and they'll get rid of me in a hurry. I won't let them bury me for nothing; there's ten *yuan* under my pillow, and even if I have to starve to death there's no way I'm touching that ten *yuan*. Everyone in the village knows that money is for whoever buries me. They also know that after I die I want to be buried with Jiazhen and the others.

It seems this life of mine will be over soon. It's been an ordinary life. My dad thought I would bring honor to our ancestors. He thought wrong. As for me, this is my fate. When I was young I used the money my ancestors left me to screw around for a while, but as time went on I became worse and worse off. In the end, though, things worked out for the best. Look at the people around me, like Long Er and Chunsheng. They each had their day in the sun, but in the end they lost their lives. It's better to live an ordinary life. If you go on striving for this and that, you'll end up paying with your life. Take me, for instance: The longer I've managed to squeeze by, the more useless I've become, but in the end I've lived a long time. One by one, everyone I knew died, but I'm still living.

Two years after Kugen died, I had finally saved up enough money for an ox. Seeing that I still had a few years left in me, I decided I should go ahead and get one. An ox is like half a person. He can help me work, and when there's free time he can keep me company, and when I'm bored I can talk to him. Taking him by the reins is just like taking a child by the hand.

The day I went to buy the ox I tucked my money away in my

shirt and headed out to Xinfeng, where there's a big animal market. On the way there I passed through one of the neighboring villages and saw a crowd of people gathered around the drying field. When I went over to have a look I saw this here ox. He was lying on the ground with his head tilted to one side, and tears were streaming from his eyes. Next to him was a bare-chested guy squatting on the ground and sharpening a butcher's knife. The people crowding around were trying to determine the best spot to make the first incision. Seeing this ox weeping so intensely, I couldn't help but feel bad for him. I thought it must be really terrible to be an ox. All their lives they're driven to the point of exhaustion for the work of man, and as soon as they get old and their energy starts to go they get sent off to be slaughtered and eaten.

I couldn't stand to watch this ox get slaughtered, so I quickly left the drying field and went on my way to Xinfeng. But after walking for a while I still couldn't get him out of my mind. He knew he was going to die. Under his head there had been a pool of tears.

The farther I walked the more agitated I became, and then I thought, why don't I just buy him? I quickly turned around and headed back toward the drying field. When I got there they had already tied up the ox's feet. I squeezed my way through the crowd and said to the guy sharpening the knife, "Okay, that's enough. What do you say you sell me this ox?"

The bare-chested man was testing the blade with his finger. He looked me over for a while before asking, "What did you say?"

"I want to buy this ox," I repeated.

He cracked his lips and began to giggle. Everyone around was roaring with laughter. I knew that they were laughing at me. I took my money out from under my shirt and put it in his hand, saying, "Go ahead and count it." The bare-chested guy was stumped. He looked me over and scratched his head.

"Are you for real?" he asked.

I didn't say a word. I just stooped down and undid the rope binding the ox's legs. I patted him on the head and stood up. The ox was really smart; knowing he wasn't going to die, he immediately stopped crying and stood up. As I pulled the ox's leash I told the guy again, "Go ahead and count it."

He held the money in front of his eyes as if checking its thickness. "That's okay, take him away," he said, once he was sure there was enough money.

As I led the ox away, the crowd was laughing at me behind my back. I heard the guy who sold me the ox say, "I really made out today! Not bad at all."

Oxen have feelings just like people do. As I pulled on this one's leash to guide him home, he knew that I had saved him. He rubbed his body up against me to show his affection. I said to him, "Look at you, what's there to be so happy about? I'm taking you home to work, not to be pampered."

When I brought him back to the village, everyone gathered around to see the excitement. They all said I was a fool for buying such an old ox. One guy even said, "Fugui, he looks like he's older than your father!"

Another guy who knew a lot about oxen told me that at most

this one would live only two or three years. I figured two or three should be enough. I was afraid that even I wouldn't live that long. Who could have guessed that the two of us would still be alive and kicking today? Everyone in the village is shocked. Even just the other day someone said we were "a couple of old bastards that just won't die."

Once the ox was home he became a member of my family, so I thought it only right that I give him a name. I thought about it and decided to go with Fugui. After settling on his name, I was really pleased with myself. He really does resemble me. Later, people in the village also started to say that we looked alike. I just giggled—I'd known that for a long time.

Fugui is a good ox. Of course he gets lazy sometimes, but even people drag their feet from time to time—how can you expect an animal not to? I know when to make him work and when to let him rest. If I'm tired then I know he must be tired, too. When my energy returns, then it's time for him to get back to work.

⊔

As he finished, the old man stood up, patted the dust off his bottom and called out to the old ox beside the pond. The ox came right over, walking up beside him and lowering his head. The old man put the plow harness over the ox's shoulders and grabbed the halter, slowly leading him away.

The two Fuguis swayed slightly as they walked off, leaving a trail of footprints in the mud. I heard the old man say to the ox, "Today both Youqing and Erxi planted a whole mu, and Jiazhen and Fengxia each planted almost 80 percent of a mu, and even little Kugen planted half a mu all by himself. How much you planted, I won't even say—if I did you'd think I was trying to embarrass you. But then again you're not a young fellow anymore. Planting this bit of land must have taken everything you had."

The old man and his ox gradually got farther away, but from far off I could still hear the echo of the old man's hoarse and moving voice. It floated through the open night like the wind. The old man sang:

In my younger days I wandered amuck,
At middle age I wanted to stash everything in a trunk,
And now that I'm old I've become a monk.

Chimney smoke swirled upward, dancing in the sky above the roof of a small farmhouse as the last rays of evening sunlight broke up and disappeared.

The sound of mothers calling their children home began to subside as a man carrying a load of manure walked past me. The bamboo pole he used to support the load squeaked as he went by. Gradually, the fields surrendered to silence. All around there appeared a kind of haze as the glow of dusk slowly dissolved.

As the black night descended from the heavens, I knew that in the blink of an eye I would witness the death of the sunset. I saw the exposed and firm chest of the vast earth; its pose was one of calling, of beckoning. And just as a mother beckons her children, so the earth beckoned the coming of night.

I understand now better than ever why I write—
all of my effort is directed at getting as close as possible to reality.[i]

— YU HUA

In 1906, while studying at Sendai University in Japan, a young Chinese medical student named Zhou Shuren saw a news slide from the Russo-Japanese War that changed his life. Depicting a Chinese prisoner being executed by Japanese soldiers, it prompted him to abandon medicine in favor of literature. For Zhou, who would adopt the pen name Lu Xun[ii] and come to be regarded as the father of modern Chinese literature, this indelible image of decapitation and the indifferent expressions of the Chinese onlookers would fuel his literary imagination and drive him to "save the children" suffering from what he perceived to be a long tradition of Chinese cultural "cannibalism."

In 1960, twenty-four years after Lu Xun's death and just miles

[i] Yu Hua, "A Work of Hypocrisy" (Xuwei de zuopin) p. 277 in *The Collected Works of Yu Hua Volume II* (*Yu Hua zuopin ji 2*) Zhongguo shehui kexue chubanshe, Beijing 1994.
[ii] Lu Xun (1881–1936) became an influential intellectual and translator and the author of poetry, fiction and essays. He is best known for his two volumes of short stories, *A Call to Arms* (*Na han*) and *Wandering* (*Panghuang*), which were revolutionary for their modern vernacular form and radical critique of Chinese culture and society.

away from his hometown of Shaoxing in Hangzhou, Yu Hua was born. His parents were doctors, and pursuing a career in medicine seemed a natural course for him. After attending a one-year course at a school for public health, he began to practice dentistry in his home province of Zhejiang. But he disliked the regimented lifestyle of a dentist and resented the limitations it placed on his creativity. As he would recall in an autobiographical essay, "My earliest motivation for writing professionally grew out of a desire to cast off the environment I was ensnared in. At the time my greatest wish was to join the cultural center. I saw that most of the people there were carefree, which made me think that what they did would be the perfect job for me. So I began writing."[iii] Where Lu Xun's decision to become a writer had been driven by his realization that it was the Chinese spirit rather than the Chinese body that needed to be saved, Yu Hua—and others writing in the wake of the Cultural Revolution and the death of Mao—felt that the role of the writer could no longer be that of cultural savior.

In 1984 Yu Hua published his first work of fiction, a short story entitled "Star" ("Xingxing") about a child violinist. It was a promising debut from a young literary talent. That promise would be fulfilled in 1987 with "On the Road at Eighteen" ("Shiba sui chumen yuanxing"), the first in a string of powerful and provocative works of short fiction that shook China's literary scene in the years leading up to the 1989 crisis in Tiananmen Square. Yu

[iii] Yu Hua, "Autobiography" ("Zizhuan") pp. 385–386 in *Collected Works of Yu Hua Volume III* (*Yu Hua zuopin ji 3*) Zhongguo shehui kexue chubanshe, Beijing 1994.

Hua's stories from this period, including "1986" ("Yijiubaliu nian"), "One Kind of Reality" (Xianshi yizhong), "Mistake at River's Edge" (Hebian de cuowu) and "Classical Love" (Gudian aiqing), stood out for their brutal, matter-of-fact depictions of violence, prompting Mo Yan, the author of *Red Sorghum,* to remark, "I've heard that [Yu Hua] was a dentist for five years. I can't imagine what kind of brutal tortures patients endured under his cruel steel pliers."[iv] This reputation, in combination with his daring linguistic experimentation, earned Yu Hua a place among China's foremost avant-garde writers.

The award-winning volume *The Past and the Punishments,* wonderfully translated by Andrew F. Jones, collects eight of the best stories from Yu Hua's early experimental period.[v] Avant-garde fiction, however, is but one facet of Yu Hua's literary imagination. In the early 1990s he took a major turn from short fiction to the novel and adopted a more traditional narrative style that seemed to betray the brutal and uncompromisingly experimental nature of his early work. To date, his career can be divided into three creative periods, each one marked by very different aesthetic concerns and literary forms: the short story, the novel and the essay.

[iv] Mo Yan, "The Awakened Dream Teller: Random Thoughts on Yu Hua and His Fiction" ("Qingxing de shuomeng zhe: Guanyu Yu Hua ji qi xiaoshuo de zagan") p. 1 in *Yu Hua 2000 Collection: Contemporary China Literature Reader (Yu Hua 2000 nian wenku: dangdai zhongguo wenku jingdu)* Ming Pao, Hong Kong 1999.
[v] Yu Hua's stories of this period have been widely anthologized and are also available in Jing Wang (editor), *China's Avant-garde Fiction: An Anthology* (Durham, N.C.: Duke University Press, 1998) and David Der-wei Wang (editor), *Running Wild: New Chinese Writers* (New York: Columbia University Press, 1994).

Published in 1992, *To Live (Huozhe)* was Yu Hua's second novel, following the previous year's *Screaming in the Drizzle (Zai xiyu zhong huhan)*[vi], the first-person story of Sun Guanglin, a child growing up in a cold, desolate world of neglect and loneliness.[vii] *To Live* stood out from Yu Hua's earlier work for its deceptively simple language as well as its sweeping historical vision, spanning over four decades of modern Chinese history, an era marred by war, internal strife, natural disasters and political turmoil. Beginning around the time of the Second Sino-Japanese War (1937–45), *To Live* traces the struggle of Fugui and his family to survive the civil war between the Nationalists and the Communists (1945–49), the founding of the People's Republic (1949), the land reform era (1949–52), the Great Leap Forward (1958–62), the Great Proletarian Cultural Revolution (1966–76) and into the reform era (1978–). Against this vast historical backdrop, Yu Hua's sensitivity to the details of everyday life has left the deepest impression on his readers.

To Live, the first installment of a projected trilogy, proved to be one of Yu Hua's most beloved works. It has been a bestseller in China for a decade and received several major international literary awards, including Italy's Premio Grinzane Cavour in 1998. Even before its publication in book form, *To Live*— initially published in serial form in a literary journal—had

[vi] *Screaming in the Drizzle* was published in Taiwan under the alternate title *Screams and Drizzle (Huhuan yu xiyu).*
[vii] Both novels were published in book form in 1993. The current translation of *To Live* is based on the revised edition that appeared in Yu Hua's 1994 *Collected Works of Yu Hua Volume III.*

attracted the attention of China's premier film director, Zhang Yimou (b. 1951):

> I had originally planned to make another one of Yu Hua's works into a film—a short suspense thriller entitled "Mistake at River's Edge." In order for me to get a better understanding of his work, Yu Hua gave me a complete set of what he had published up to that time. *To Live,* which was originally serialized in the Shanghai literary journal *Harvest,* was his most recent novel. I started reading it that very night and couldn't put it down. I ended up staying awake until four o'clock in the morning and finished the book in one sitting. I met with Yu Hua the following day to discuss the script, but no matter where our conversation went we couldn't seem to get away from *To Live.* Finally we just looked at each other, and I said, "Okay, let's just do *To Live!*" It was really love at first sight.[viii]

The script was adapted by the author in collaboration with Zhang Yimou and the screenwriter Lu Wei, and when it premiered in 1994, *To Live* (titled *Lifetimes* in some English-language markets) proved to be a major critical success. Among the numerous honors and awards it won were the Grand Jury prize and the Best Actor award (for Ge You's portrayal of Fugui) at the 1994 Cannes Film Festival. The international success of the film and the controversy that surrounded it in China—it was

---

[viii] Zeng Jingchao (interview), "Explaining *To Live:* Zhang Yimou on *To Live*" (Gei huozhe yige shuofa: Zhang Yimou tan *Huozhe*), p. 2 in *Lifetimes: The Film Novel* (*Huozhe: Dianying xiaoshuo*) by Sun Hua, Hanguang Publishing, Taipei 1994.

banned there—made the novel an instant bestseller and cata-
pulted Yu Hua into celebrity in his homeland.

There are several key differences between the film and the
novel. In the film the locale has been changed from China's rural
south to a small city in the north; the shadow puppetry has been
added; and Fugui's final companion, the ox, is absent, as is the
second narrator, who mediates Fugui's narration in the novel.
The recurring parable about the Xu family's transformation from
a chicken to an ox illustrates some of the differences between the
film and the novel. In the film, when the parable is told to
Youqing, it is given a playful political dimension:

Fugui: Our family is like a little chicken.
           When it grows up it becomes a goose.
           And that'll turn into a sheep.
           And the sheep will turn into an ox.
Youqing: And after the ox?
Fugui: After the ox is Communism!
           And there'll be dumplings and meat every day.

Fugui says this with an honest smile and a hopeful off-camera
gaze. His faith in Communism represents a political idealism that
is all but absent in the novel. Later in the film the parable is told
to Kugen (who is renamed Mantou, or "Little Bun"):

Mantou: When will the chickens grow up?
Fugui: Very soon.
Mantou: And then?

Fugui: And then the chickens will turn into geese.
         And the geese will turn into sheep.
         And the sheep will turn into oxen.
Mantou: And after the oxen?
Jiazhen: After oxen, Little Bun will grow up!
Mantou: I want to ride on an ox's back!
Jiazhen: Little Bun will ride on an ox's back.
Fugui: Little Bun won't ride on an ox,
         He'll ride trains and planes.
         And life will get better all the time.

Where Fugui had earlier named Communism as the ultimate evolutionary and revolutionary destination, here he is at a loss for words. It is left to Jiazhen to interject, "Little Bun will grow up!" and, by avoiding reference to Communism, suggest the failure of Maoist ideals. Fugui pushes this suggestion further by pointing to the promise of China's new capitalist future of trains and planes.

After tracing much of twentieth-century China's tumultuous history, the film ends with Fugui, Erxi and Kugen gathered around Jiazhen in bed, an image that suggests the possibility of a post-Communist utopia. The novel, by contrast, closes with Fugui prodding his ox, showing Yu Hua's version to be darker and more existential, with survival an end in itself. Compared to the novel, Zhang Yimou's film also allows more room for the hand of fate to hold sway; here Youqing's death is attributed purely to accident, while in the novel it occurs after his blood is literally sucked dry to save the life of an important cadre. Yu Hua's reality is much more brutal, as is his social critique. In

1918 Lu Xun raised his plea to "save the children"; Yu Hua's belated response was to give us blood.

Yu Hua followed *To Live* with his brilliant 1995 novel, *Chronicle of a Blood Merchant,* which in some sense revisits Youqing's death by tracing the life of Xu Sanguan, who literally sells his blood to survive. Although there are striking stylistic similarities between *To Live* and *Chronicle,* according to Yu Hua his two protagonists have very different life philosophies:

> After going through much pain and hardship, Fugui is inextricably tied to the experience of suffering. So there is really no place for ideas like "resistance" in Fugui's mind—he lives simply to live. In this world I have never met anyone who has as much respect for life as Fugui. Although he has more reason to die than most people, he keeps on living. Xu Sanguan is another close friend of mine. He is the kind of person who is always struggling against fate—but in the end he always loses. However, Xu Sanguan doesn't recognize defeat, and this is his most outstanding characterist.[ix]

Beyond the violence and blood that seem to haunt Fugui, Xu Sanguan and so many other inhabitants of Yu Hua's fictional universe, there lies a sensitivity and humanity that speaks to us all.

After *Chronicle of a Blood Merchant,* Yu Hua entered his third creative phase, which he has devoted largely to the essay.

[ix] "To Live Is the Sole Requirement of Life: In Dialogue with *Book Review Weekly* Reporter Wang Wei," p. 219 in *Can I Believe in Myself? Selection of Random Essays* (*Wo nengfou xiangxin ziji: Yu Hua suibi xuan*) by Yu, Renmin Ribao Chuban She, Beijing 1998.

Lu Xun had also turned to the essay during the latter phase of his writing career, but unlike Lu Xun's essays, which exposed the social and political ills of his day, Yu Hua's have been mainly biographical portraits, childhood reminiscences, theoretical discussions on writing and homages to his literary heroes, including Yasunari Kawabata, Franz Kafka, Gabriel García Márquez, William Faulkner and, of course, Lu Xun. In 1994 Yu Hua began cultivating an interest in Western classical music, and in 2000 several of his essays on music were collected in *Climax* (*Gaochao*). Yu Hua's output during this period also includes a short collection of stories, *The Boy at Sunset* (*Huanghun li de nanhai*), and a screenplay (cowritten with Ning Dai and Zhu Wen) for director Zhang Yuan's 1999 award-winning film *Seventeen Years* (*Guonian huijia*). One can only hope that in the new millennium Yu Hua will continue adding shades to his already colorful literary palette.

Having grown up near hospitals and operating rooms during modern China's most vicious and chaotic period, Yu Hua has created a fictional reflection of this reality, a world imbued with violence, death and unspeakable cruelty. At the same time, his world is touched by moments of poetic brilliance, a passion for life and sublime beauty—a world where moonlight on a dirt path creates "the illusion that a layer of salt had been sprinkled along it." Writing is Yu Hua's reality, and now readers of English will finally be able to enter that reality, in all its beauty and brutality.

There are a number of individuals who have contributed their time and hard work to help make this project a reality. Thanks to my family and friends for all of their support over the years, to Yu Hua for allowing me to translate his novel and to Xudong Zhang, not only for his early encouragement, but also for initially putting me in touch with the author. Howard Goldblatt, Peter Li and Joshua Tanzer all read various versions of the manuscript and offered thoughtful comments and suggestions. I was grateful to work with John Siciliano and Katherine Bidwell during the final stages of editing. It was their literary sensitivity and editorial sensibilities that helped shape the final text. Thanks also go to Ha Jin, Perry Link, Tomi Suzuki, LuAnn Walther, the Department of Asian Languages and Cultures at Rutgers University, the Department of East Asian Languages and Cultures at Columbia University and especially David Der-wei Wang for his many years of unfailing support. I would like to dedicate this translation to the memory of Cao Jun, a great friend who taught me what it means to live.

In the introduction to the 1993 Chinese edition of *To Live* I wrote, "I once heard an American folk song entitled 'Old Black Joe.' The song was about an elderly black slave who experienced a life's worth of hardships, including the passing of his entire family—yet he still looked upon the world with eyes of kindness, offering not the slightest complaint. After being so deeply moved by this song I decided to write my next novel—that novel was *To Live*."

For an author, the act of writing always begins with a smile, a gesture, a memory on the verge of being forgotten, a casual conversation or a bit of information hidden in the newspaper—it is these tiny pearl-like details that sometimes transform one's fate and spread like waves into magnificent vistas and scenes. The writing of *To Live* was no exception. An American slave song with only the simplest lyrics grew into Fugui's life—a life imbued with upheavals and suffering, but also tranquility and happiness.

Old Joe and Fugui are two men who could not be more different. They live in different countries and different eras; they are of different nationalities and cultural backgrounds; even their fundamental likes and dislikes are different, as is the color of their skin—yet sometimes they seem to be the same person. They are both so very human. Human experience, combined with the power of the imagination and understanding, can break down all barriers, enabling a person truly to understand that thing called fate at work in his life—not unlike the experience of simultaneously seeing one's reflection in two different mirrors. Perhaps this is what makes literature magical; it is precisely this magic that enabled me—a reader on the other side of the world in China—to read the novels of Nathaniel Hawthorne, William Faulkner and Toni Morrison, and through them, to discover myself.

I would like to thank Ha Jin for recommending *To Live* for publication, my friend Michael Berry for translating it, my agent Joanne Wang for her diligence in placing it and my editors at Anchor Books for publishing, at long last, this English language edition.